D0189224

Praise for the Kitty Norville Series

"With the Kitty series, Vaughn has demonstrated a knack for believable characters (even if they are werewolves) and mile-a-minute plotting."
—*Sunday Camera* (Boulder, CO)

"A great series for fans of the recent werewolf-vampire craze who want to move beyond Stephenie Meyer or Charlaine Harris."
—*The Daily News* (Galveston County, TX)

"Enough excitement, astonishment, pathos, and victory to satisfy any reader."   —Charlaine Harris
on *Kitty and the Midnight Hour*

"Perennial favorite Vaughn is kicking up the conflict and laying out more clues in her overarching Long Game storyline. Go, Kitty, go!"
—*RT Book Reviews* on *Kitty Steals the Show*

"Entertaining and fast-paced, it nicely advances the overall series narrative, particularly as it pertains to Kitty's relationships with Cormac and Ben. . . . The Kitty books continue to be a natural choice for older YA readers."   —*VOYA* on *Kitty Takes a Holiday*

"What makes Vaughn's terrific stories really pop is how she manages to combine outright thrills with an offbeat sense of humor and then mesh it with Kitty's dogged determination. The result—entertainment exemplified!"   —*RT Book Reviews* (4½ stars)
on *Kitty's Big Trouble*

"Suspenseful and interesting."
—*The Denver Post* on *Kitty's House of Horrors*

"Vaughn's deft touch at characterization and plot development has made this series hugely entertaining and not to be missed!"
—*RT Book Reviews* on *Kitty Goes to War*

"Carrie Vaughn is like Laurell K. Hamilton, only better."
—*The Accidental Bard* on *Kitty Raises Hell*

"Convincing and imaginative."
—*Publishers Weekly* on *Kitty Takes a Holiday*

"Vaughn delivers an effortless, fast-paced narrative, with just enough emotional depth to satisfy."
—*VOYA* on *Kitty Goes to Washington*

"A fun, fast-paced adventure for fans of supernatural mysteries."
—*Locus* on *Kitty and The Midnight Hour*

"Do you like werewolves? Vampires? Talk radio? Reading? Sex? If the answer to any of those is yes, you're in for a wonderful ride."
—Gene Wolfe on *Kitty and The Midnight Hour*

Kitty
in the Underworld

CARRIE VAUGHN

TOR®

A TOM DOHERTY ASSOCIATES BOOK
NEW YORK

This is a work of fiction. All of the characters, organizations, and events portrayed in this novel are either products of the author's imagination or are used fictitiously.

KITTY IN THE UNDERWORLD

Copyright © 2013 by Carrie Vaughn, LLC

A Tor Book
Published by Tom Doherty Associates, LLC
175 Fifth Avenue
New York, NY 10010

www.tor-forge.com

Tor® is a registered trademark of Tom Doherty Associates, LLC.

ISBN 978-0-7653-6868-3

Tor books may be purchased for educational, business, or promotional use. For information on bulk purchases, please contact Macmillan Corporate and Premium Sales Department at 1-800-221-7945 extension 5442 or write specialmarkets@macmillan.com.

First Edition: August 2013

Printed in the United States of America

0 9 8 7 6 5 4 3 2 1

For my family

The Playlist

Talking Heads, "And She Was"

Cyndi Lauper, "Romance in the Dark"

Shonen Knife, "Burning Farm"

Will Bradley and His Orchestra, "In the Hall of the Mountain King"

Abby Travis, "Chase Me"

Johnny Cash, "Cry! Cry! Cry!"

Big Mama Thornton, "Hound Dog"

Ruthie Foster, "Lord Remember Me"

Roxy Music, "Out of the Blue"

Pet Shop Boys, "I'm Not Scared"

Björk, "Hunter"

R.E.M., "Try Not to Breathe"

David Bowie, "Oh! You Pretty Things"

Kitty
in the Underworld

Chapter 1

ONLINE RESEARCH was a mixed bag. I found the most insane conspiracy theories, essays, and propositions, which I could then use to incite heated debate on my radio show. Not just flat earth but *cubed* earth, or strawberry-ice-cream-eating aliens living at Wright Patterson Air Force Base, or a pseudoscientific study claiming that vampire strippers make more in tips than mortal strippers because of their hypnotic powers. (Vampire strippers? Really? And could I get one on the show for an interview?) Or I could click through useless links for hours and feel like I've wasted a day.

Sometimes, I typed in my search request and found treasure.

The image currently on my screen was a photograph of a statue called the *Capitoline Wolf*. The sculpture showed a rather primitive-looking wolf with stylized, patterned fur; a glaring, snarling expression; and a couple of human babies suckling at rows of impressively bulging nipples. Housed in a museum in Rome, the age of the wolf portion of the statue was under some debate. Historically, it had been assumed that it was old—pre-Roman, Etruscan even, because of its stocky shape and decidedly nonclassical features. Roman writers even made reference to a famous statue of a wolf that symbolized the founding of Rome. But modern dating techniques established the statue's origin in the late medieval period. The babies—fat and cherubic, in Renaissance detail—had obviously been added later, in the fifteenth century. Wherever it came from, whenever it was made, the statue depicted the legend of the founding of Rome: the she-wolf who discovered the abandoned brothers, Romulus and Remus, and saved their lives. They went on to found the great city of Rome. The statue was so iconic that copies of it could be found all over the world.

That was the official, published, accepted story of the *Capitoline Wolf.* However, I had my own ideas. Other details about the statue intrigued me. For example, the wolf wasn't life size, but it was a bit larger than a female wolf living in that part of the world would be. An average female wolf would weigh about seventy-five pounds, give or take ten pounds. A wolf the size of this statue might weigh, oh, a hundred-ten pounds or so. The weight of a small woman.

Shape-shifters obeyed the law of conservation of mass. A two-hundred-pound man becomes a two-hundred-pound wolf. Hundred-and-thirty-pound me becomes a hundred-thirty-pound wolf. A two-hundred-pound were-bear becomes—a really small bear. I'd never actually seen a were-bear in bear form, so I didn't know what that looked like. Whether I *wanted* to see what that looked like depended on the temperament of the bear. When I read about the *Capitoline Wolf,* learned about the dimensions of the statue, made a mental comparison to the werewolves I'd met in both human and wolf form, my heart beat a little quicker. My journalistic instincts for a good story sang out. Because I wondered then if the story of Romulus and Remus had some basis in reality, and I wondered about the werewolf who'd rescued them.

This was all the fruit of a pointed line of research that steered me in the direction of the *Capitoline Wolf.* I'd heard a phrase: Regina Luporum. Queen of the wolves. According to an ancient vampire I'd met, the story of Romulus and Remus was real—the mother werewolf was real. The Capitoline Wolf, the foster mother of the founders of Rome, had been the original queen of the wolves. I'd been told this label was used to describe werewolves who defended their kind when few others did. Who spoke out and stood up for what was right. A couple of times lately, *I'd* been called Regina Luporum. It wasn't a title I claimed for myself or thought I deserved. I was half of the alpha pair of the Denver werewolf pack, which was small, unassuming, and generally sedate as werewolf packs went, because my husband, Ben, and I worked hard to keep it that way.

On the other hand, publicly and professionally, I had a big mouth. I talked too much. That didn't make me queen of anything.

The statue might have been made in the thirteenth century, belying the tradition and ancient references that said it had stood watch in Rome from the beginning. But that didn't mean it might not be a copy of an earlier piece that had been destroyed. Maybe copies of the statue had been made over and over to ensure that some memory of the events it memorialized lived on. To provide continuity, to create a tradition that might become muddled over time, but would still exist in one form or another.

Stories faded. The existence of werewolves was not openly acknowledged, so she became a wolf rather than a wolf-woman, because then the tale was just another animal fable harkening back to Aesop, or Ovid's *Metamorphoses,* and that somehow seemed safer, more legendary. Time changes stories, no matter how carefully they're written down. Maybe the *Capitoline*

Wolf existed in one form or another two thousand years ago, maybe it didn't. Maybe the legend was true, or maybe it was a metaphor for something else entirely. Mostly, I looked at the alert and glaring expression of the statue, and saw the face of someone who must have been a hero.

Another thing I saw when I looked at the statue: the babies weren't hers—they'd been added later. She'd found them and claimed them. Adopted them. This gave me hope. Women werewolves couldn't bear children because embryos didn't survive the trauma of shape-shifting. I couldn't have children of my own— or maybe I could.

I printed out the image in full color. I wanted to be able to study the *Capitoline Wolf* whether my computer was on or off, by sunlight or by candlelight, not glowing in pixels on a screen. Kind of crazy, kind of romantic, but the picture in printed form seemed to have more dignity, more permanence. When the page emerged from the printer, I tacked it onto the corkboard on my office wall, right next to the full-page picture of another one of my heroes, General William T. Sherman. A couple of years ago, I followed up some *other* stories, some hunches, and determined that Sherman also had been a werewolf. Another one who stood up for what he believed. I wondered if history was in fact littered with werewolves.

I leaned back in my chair in my cramped and cozy

office at KNOB, my desk filled with mail and news-paper clippings, internal memos, and a million notes on scratch paper, a radio in the corner humming softly with the station's daytime alternative music format, and studied the pictures, my two werewolf heroes. They were smart, tough, savvy, and they'd made a difference in the world. They'd had battles to fight and had fought them, and lived on in song and story.

If they could do it, maybe I could do it, too.

MY EXCUSE for all this research: I was supposed to be writing my second book.

My first book had been a memoir—the life and times of America's first celebrity werewolf. This one wasn't going to be about me. It was going to be about history, stories, and the different ways of interpreting them, because they look different when you know that vampires and lycanthropes are real. I wasn't the first person to suggest that Norse berserkers might have been werewolves, but I was going to take the idea and run with it. I was going to talk about the *Capitoline Wolf,* and those Greek myths about people turning into something else. From the beginning, people told stories about the ways humans and animals interacted with each other—and the roles of each weren't always clearly defined. Animals talked, people went mad and ran off to the woods, and maybe it wasn't always a metaphor. Maybe Daniel survived the lion's den because he knew how to talk to the lions.

I'd learned this once, but now I was being reminded in agonizing detail: announcing that you were writing a book was easy. Signing the contract and depositing the check were *very* easy. Actually doing it? Not as easy. Research, online or otherwise, was lots of fun and often yielded treasure, but it was also a deep, endless tunnel one could enter and never return from. I had stacks of notes that I needed to turn into text. Just wishing it would happen wasn't working.

When writing at my office at KNOB didn't work anymore, I rotated back home, to the office in the spare bedroom. I'd pinned up a photo of the *Capitoline Wolf* there as well and sometimes caught myself staring at it, my mind wandering.

Since Ben and I moved out of the condo and bought an honest-to-God house, we now had a home office, half mine and half his. Pretty swank. He was a lawyer with his own practice, mostly criminal defense, a job that involved a lot more paperwork and phone calls than the TV shows let on. I tried not to sprawl out of my half of the room, but with the piles of books and articles I'd collected for research, this was getting difficult. Not to mention outlines, abandoned outlines, rough drafts, and notes from editorial phone calls. If the amount of information I'd collected was any sign, I ought to have more than enough for a book, assuming

I could put it all together. I felt good, looking at my masses of notes. Productive. I could finish and actually make those shiny new house payments.

The room wasn't that big to begin with—ten feet or so on a side, with two desks and a couple of bookshelves shoehorned in. Ben and I could wheel our chairs back and run into each other if we aimed right. Fortunately, he spent as much time out of the office as in it, meeting with clients or appearing in court, so I could do what I wanted. Hence, the sprawl. It was so nice having the *space*.

After dark, I heard a familiar sedan engine hum from down the street, grow close, then stop. Ben's car, parking in the driveway. A moment later, the front door opened and closed, and his scent touched the air. My nose flared, taking in the smell of my mate— male, paperwork, and coffee, the wolfish fur-and-skin of lycanthropy. I smiled. The house was nice, but it didn't feel like home until Ben was here.

His footsteps approached, and I turned to greet him just as he appeared in the doorway.

"Hey," I said, grinning.

He glanced at me, but spent more time looking around at the rest of the office. "I take it you've been busy."

The sprawl had gotten particularly bad this afternoon. I was sitting on the floor, books open around me, manuscript pages marked up with color-coded sticky notes tucked into them, pictures tacked to the wall or lying piled on the desk. If he was careful, he might be able to pick a path through the mess to his desk.

"There's a method to all this. I actually know where everything is." I was a little scared to start straightening up and moving things around—I might never find anything again. "I'm fact-checking, making sure all the references match up. It means I'm almost done. It's a good thing." I tried to sound confident, but ended up sounding defensive.

He pursed his lips, like he was trying to stop himself from saying something. He finally let out a sigh. "Then maybe it's a good thing I'm going away for a couple of days. You'll have a chance to work in peace."

I shoved books and papers away so I could scramble to my feet. "What? No! Terrible things happen when you go away."

"No," he said. "Terrible things happen when *you* go away. I'm just a normal guy who has to take a business trip."

I could have argued with the normal. Once I was standing in front of him, I couldn't resist—I pressed myself to him, wrapped my arms around him, and leaned in for a kiss, which he was all too happy to give me. I didn't even let him put his briefcase down first so he could hug me back properly. He just dropped it.

Yeah, I could have stayed like that for a good long while. "Business trip where?"

"Cheyenne. Friend of the family got in some trouble over illegally grazing his cattle on federal land. I'm going to go help clear it up."

"That sounds . . . arcane."

"It'll be fun. This is the kind of thing that got me into law in the first place. The initial hearing's in a couple of days, and depending how that goes, I may not have to go back." Unless something went wrong, in which case he could be making this trip back and forth for months.

"Better you than me. Do you really have to stay there overnight?"

"I'd spend more time driving back and forth than I would on the case. Unless you really have a problem with it." He said it hopefully, like he wanted me not to be able to live without him for even a day.

We were pack, and this was our territory. He was my mate, and we belonged together. That was what Wolf said, wanting to cling to him at the mere suggestion of a separation. The world always felt off-kilter when we were apart. We'd barely been apart in years. But we were also human, with careers and responsibilities. A normal human couple coped fine with the occasional business trip. We ought to be able to as well. *Or not,* Wolf grumbled.

Theoretically, I could go to Wyoming with him while he worked. But he was right—having the house to myself might help me get work done.

"Only a couple of days?" I said. "Promise?"

"Absolutely."

"Then I suppose I should take advantage of you while I have the chance," I said, hooking my hands over the waistband of his trousers, pulling even closer to him, pressing as much of myself to his body as I could, feeling gratified when his skin flushed and he responded, his hands crawling to my backside.

"Yes, please," he said, bringing his lips to mine for some very enthusiastic encouragement as I wrapped my arms around his neck.

My phone rang. Generic cell phone ring tone, so no clue who it might be. Nose to nose, Ben and I regarded each other.

"It could be important," he said.

"It could be telemarketers," I replied.

If nothing else, the electronic ringing was annoying enough that I wanted to go shut it off before it drove me batty.

"It'll probably just take a second," I said.

"I'm not going anywhere," he said with a suggestive lilt to his brow that made my scalp tingle. Yup, he's a keeper.

After digging my phone out from under the mess of papers on my desk, I checked the caller ID, which stated that the incoming number was in Washington, D.C. Which meant the call could still be important or telemarketers.

Keeping an eye on Ben's cute smirk, I clicked the button and answered. "Hello?"

"Kitty, it's Alette."

I frowned. This was important. Alette was the Mistress of Washington, D.C., quite possibly the most powerful vampire in the U.S., and she sounded somber, no brightness at all to her voice. She appeared to be a dignified woman in her thirties, but near as I could tell was several centuries old. She spoke with a commanding English accent. Now, she sounded tired.

"Alette, hi, what's wrong?" Ben's amusement fell away, his brow furrowing. Before she spoke, a thousand terrible scenarios passed through my mind. This was about Rick, wasn't it? Something had happened to Rick—

"We've lost Barcelona."

The statement made no sense. I had to parse it, then catch up with the pronouncement. Barcelona was one of the cities we counted as an ally in our underground war against Roman and the Long Game—or maybe not, anymore. "What do you mean, we've lost Barcelona? What about Antony—"

"Antony is gone."

I slumped against the desk. Again, the statement made no sense. My heart heard it, but my brain had to catch up. I'd met Antony, Master of Barcelona. He was brash, chatty, and seemed young for a vampire, however many centuries old he actually was. He was astute without taking himself too seriously. I liked him. Ben had been very impressed with his fancy sports car. He couldn't be gone—he was a vampire. Immortal. But not indestructible.

"What happened?" I asked, the only thing I could think to say, my voice catching. Ben came to my side and held my hand, listening in while Alette explained.

"I got the call from Ned as soon as the sun set." Ned, Master vampire of London. Something big had happened, probably this afternoon local time, while I'd been sprawled out on the floor thinking my book deadline was my biggest problem. "Antony got word that Dux Bellorum was in Split."

Dux Bellorum, another name that Roman called himself. It didn't matter how much I thought about the vampire who was essentially my arch nemesis—and how weird was it that I had an arch nemesis?—when I finally learned something about him, an electric shiver traveled down my back, and I resisted an urge to look over my shoulder. Roman, in Split, fighting Antony, and what was he doing there—

"Split?" I asked. "Where's that?"

"Croatia," Alette said patiently, the same time Ben whispered that maybe I should save my questions. "He had a location, he had a plan to find Roman, and he thought he and his people could end him once and for all."

And he'd failed. Alette didn't even have to say it.

"Why? Why'd he do that? We were trying to *avoid* a direct confrontation."

"I think he wanted to be a hero." The weird thing was, I kind of understood that. If he thought he could stop Roman, of course he would have taken the chance. "But he left Barcelona undefended. The city is in the hands of Roman's followers now."

It was a battle lost, not the war, I told myself. But my stomach turned in on itself. This was a person, Antony, and his whole Family. If we'd only been able to stop Roman sooner—there had to have been a way. Ben moved his arm around my shoulder and pulled me close.

"There's more, Kitty. Antony learned some information that he was able to pass on to Ned. I'm passing it on to you. Antony discovered that Roman was in Split to retrieve an artifact he'd hidden there many centuries ago. Something called the Manus Herculei."

"Hand of Hercules," Ben murmured helpfully. The lawyer was pretty good with Latin, it turned out.

"Indeed," Alette said, and might have sounded impressed.

"And what's that? Is it magical? What's he want it for?"

"I can't say. But if I wanted a weapon to use in my quest for power, I might very well want to acquire something called the Hand of Hercules."

Oh, God, it was probably some magical atom bomb

or something. Next thing on Roman's "take over the world" to-do list: acquire weapon referencing invincible Greek demigod. My stomach couldn't feel any sicker. "That sounds really bad," I said.

"It does, rather," she said with icy calm.

"Does he have it? Did Roman find it?"

"We don't know. But we don't think he's left Split, so perhaps not."

"So what do we do?" I asked. Pleaded.

"We wait, I think," she said with a sigh.

That wasn't what I wanted to hear. We had to *do* something, didn't we? "Should we go to Croatia? Send someone? Find out what's really going on there? *Stop* him?"

"Just as Antony did? Split is an ancient Roman city. Dux Bellorum's home territory for some two thousand years. He's most likely very well protected there, and you think we should send someone to confront him directly?" I let out the tiniest of growls. Antony hadn't been part of our pack, but he was *ours*. This felt like an invasion. Alette made a comforting *tsk*. "We hold our own, Kitty. We watch for an opportunity. We find out what this artifact is, and we learn how to oppose it before Dux Bellorum can use it. We hold the line. Do you agree?"

I tilted the phone away, looked at Ben. I imagined my own expression was as somber as his. He pressed his lips into a thin smile that seemed more fatalistic than comforting, and I snuggled closer to his warmth and embrace.

"I—I'm sorry about Antony. I don't know who else to tell."

"I'll pass along your sentiments to Ned. Antony should be commended for contacting Ned and passing along what he could, before the end. He must have felt the information was worth giving up his own safety."

Yeah, that was a nice way of looking at it, drawing some kind of meaning—*any* meaning—from Antony's death, to make ourselves feel better. Only time would tell if we could make Antony's sacrifice worth it.

Chapter 2

I CALLED ANGELO, the Master of Denver, and Ben's cousin Cormac and asked them to meet us at New Moon.

New Moon was the downtown bar and restaurant Ben and I owned. I'd wanted a public place where the wolves of our pack could gather safely; that it had become a financially solvent business on its own was a bonus. One of our wolves—Shaun, our lieutenant—managed it for us, and seemed to have a talent for it. He followed his own taste rather than current trends, which meant the place had a funky vibe—the old brick building had been refurbished with exposed duct-work and an open interior, no TVs, lots of good food at the bar, and tables where groups could gather and talk. Shaun was at the bar now, serving drinks, mar-shaling the troops. Usually the place was a haven, a comforting den to unwind in after doing my show. Tonight we were turning it into a war room.

Cormac arrived before us and occupied a quiet table in the back. Ben and I found him leaning back in his chair and reading a book on police forensics. This seemed very odd to me, not just because he didn't look like the kind of guy who normally sat in a bar reading a book. He had a rugged cowboy look to him, worn jeans and biker boots, a gray T-shirt under a leather jacket. Rough sandy hair, a permanent frown under a trimmed mustache. Cormac was usually the one causing police crime scenes, not investigating them. He'd picked up the reading habit in prison, and part of the reason for *that* was Amelia. As I understood the story, Amelia had been executed for a murder she didn't commit at the very same prison, over a hundred years ago. She didn't *quite* die, though. Instead, her spirit, soul, ghost, something, haunted the place, until Cormac came along. They were partners now. They shared a body, was the way I thought of it. Which meant that was *her* reading about forensics and chewing on his lip.

The pronouns got complicated. I would never be entirely used to it, but I could usually tell which one of them was speaking. Amelia had been upper-class British, and her diction and accent changed Cormac's voice as well as his manner, when she was at the fore.

I gave Shaun a halfhearted wave as we passed the bar. "Want me to bring over the usual?" he asked. He was in his early thirties, well built, dark-skinned with short-cropped hair, wearing jeans and a polo shirt with New Moon's crescent logo on it.

The usual was beer, and I had to think about it a moment. My stomach was still turning; I didn't feel much like drinking anything. "Yes," Ben said for me. "Thanks."

Shaun frowned, but nodded. Our somber manners must have washed through the whole place.

"What is it?" Cormac asked as we sat across from him. Shaun brought our beers, and I took a long drink, just to be doing something.

"Roman's been busy in Europe," Ben said, and summarized what Alette had told us. Cormac listened thoughtfully, his expression still.

"She's right," he said when Ben had finished. "Not much we can do without knowing where he'll turn up next."

"The coins," I said, because I was grasping at straws and this was about the only concrete lead we had. "Have you found out anything at all about the magic in Roman's coins?" We'd collected several of the artifacts, ancient bronze coins the size of a nickel that somehow bound Roman and his followers. Striking out the image on them nullified the magic. I kept hoping we could find a way to use the things against him. No luck there. Yet. Such a thing might not be possible, but I had to stay optimistic.

Before he could answer, Shaun waved from the bar to get my attention. He pointed at the door. Angelo had arrived.

Angelo was what I called an old-school vampire. Haughty and aristocratic, watching the world down his nose and lecturing lesser beings like me on my, and his, rightful place in the world. He'd done better with that when he had Master vampires to stand behind—Arturo, then Rick. He was an excellent henchvampire and gatekeeper. He wasn't particularly happy being in charge himself, as the new acting Master of Denver. The "acting" was an odd designation, one that Angelo insisted on but I wasn't sure if anyone really believed it. For all intents and purposes, he was the Master of Denver. We all hoped Rick would return from his religious pilgrimage someday. We couldn't be sure it would ever happen. So I had to deal with Angelo.

As a commercial place of business, vampires should have been able to move freely in and out of New Moon. However, because it belonged to me and the pack, because we considered it something of our home and den, vampires couldn't enter without permission. I'd had a wonderful couple of moments, standing on one side of the door, grinning out at entirely baffled vampires wondering why they couldn't cross the threshold. But I had to talk to Angelo on a regular basis, so he'd been invited. To his credit, he hadn't given me a reason to regret that.

He strode across the dining room and deposited himself on the chair opposite me. Cormac straightened, backing his chair up an inch or two from the table. His hands weren't visible, which meant they were reaching into his pockets for a stake or vial of holy water. In his preprison life, Cormac had been a bounty hunter specializing in supernatural beings. He didn't much like vampires.

We looked at Angelo, who looked back at us. I didn't meet his gaze—the hypnotic effects of vampires' gazes were one of the powers from the stories that turned out to be true. He could lock eyes with us, draw us in, tell us calmly and serenely to walk off the nearest cliff, and we'd do it.

Taking a seat, Angelo pointed at Cormac and looked sidelong at me. "Isn't he that bounty hunter Arturo hired to kill you years ago?"

I'd forgotten, Angelo and Cormac hadn't met before. Cormac smirked at the reminder of our shared history.

"Cormac isn't really a bounty hunter anymore," I said.

"And I'm sure that makes everything all right." Angelo continued eyeing Cormac suspiciously.

"Angelo, shut up. This is important. Antony, Master of Barcelona, is gone," I said.

The man actually paled. Whatever blood he'd imbibed recently washed straight out of his face. "Then it's started. Dux Bellorum has begun his war."

"I don't think so. Antony went after him first," I said, and repeated the story.

"So it's not a total disaster," he said. "Dux Bellorum isn't coming after us next, is he?"

"Not until he gets this thing he's looking for," Ben muttered.

"And what have we got?" he huffed. "The four of us sitting around a table in a bar, looking morose?"

"We have the coins," Cormac said. He let that hang during a long, dramatic pause. I was about to jump over the table and hang off his jacket collar until he explained, but I didn't have to go that far. "As I was about to say, I think they're dog tags, sort of. We knew that—that they're identifiers Roman uses to tag his allies. But we have to consider—if what the demon said was true, and Roman isn't really the guy in charge, then he's a recruiter. He's tagging his followers so the *real* guy in charge knows who they are."

Roman was Dux Bellorum, the leader of war, the general. We'd come to believe there was a Caesar out there. The king. Roman might have been controlling the Long Game—but someone else was controlling Roman.

"Could we . . . Then maybe we could use them to follow the thread back? To find the guy in charge?"

He gave a shrug. "I don't know yet."

We all sighed, even Angelo, who technically didn't need to breathe. We were still stuck at the same wall we'd been stuck at. Roman was on the move and we couldn't do anything about it.

"At least the bastard isn't here," Angelo said finally. As if saying the man's name would summon him. "He isn't, is he? Coming here."

I didn't know. That was the problem. Roman, aka Dux Bellorum, aka Gaius Albinus, was a two-thousand-year-old vampire with aspirations of world domination. That might have been an exaggeration, but not much of one. He was the central figure in what vampires called the Long Game: rivals collecting allies and power in attempt to be the Master of them all. In a sentence, the one who dies with the most toys wins. Trouble was, vampires were undead . . .

The anxiety Angelo had been masking with his suave indifference broke through in the tightening of his jaw, the stiffening of his spine. "What about any more sign of vampire-killing demons arriving in Denver? Any of those, by chance?"

"We put up those protection spells. It should at least warn us if the demon comes back," Cormac said. He and Amelia had cast the spells—and suggested that they weren't entirely sure the spells would work. The

demon we'd battled last year knew we were looking
for her now. Next time—if there was a next time—her
approach would be different.

"So what do we do now?" I asked, sounding plain-
tive.

"We do what Alette says," Ben answered. "We hold
tight. Nothing much we can do but keep on until we
get more information. I'll go to Wyoming, you'll write
your book and do your show—"

"You can't possibly go to Wyoming, not after all
this."

He pursed his lips, gave me a *look*. "Until we know
for sure that the world is ending, I'm going to work.
You should, too. You can't sit around stewing all day,
every day. At least, you shouldn't." He furrowed his
brow, probably realizing that yes, I was totally capable of stewing all day, every day, if I let myself.

But it seemed weird to just keep on the same after
what had happened.

"Right, that's the plan. We go on with our lives.
Such as they are." Angelo leaned forward. "If you see
anything, hear of anything, you will let me know?"

"You ask that every time you see me. Yes. I told you
about all this, didn't I?" I hoped my thin smile was
comforting. Angelo seemed unconvinced.

"Well, then. Until next time, Regina Luporum."

"I wish people would stop calling me that," I muttered. The title didn't actually mean anything. I'd

earned it for having a big mouth, not for having any real power. Mostly, people teased me with it. The more I complained, the more they teased. I should know better.

"If the European vampires are calling you Regina Luporum, who am I to argue?"

"They're just teasing." Sure enough, Cormac had his lips pressed tight together to keep from smiling, but his eyes shone with amusement.

"Whatever you say. Until next time, then. May our immediate futures be woefully quiet and uneventful." He gave a little bow as he stood, sweeping his arm in a parody of courtliness, and walked away.

So that was the plan. Keep living our lives. Ben goes to work, I go to work . . .

I called out, "Hey, wait a minute—" Angelo turned, scowling, and I asked, "Do you happen to know any vampire strippers? You know, strippers who are vampires?" I winced hopefully.

He rolled his eyes and marched out. Ah, well.

I didn't know anything about Angelo: how old he was, how he'd become a vampire, where he came from, anything. It had taken me years to learn what I knew about Rick, and now I was back at square one. I'd have to start with the needling questions all over again—if I thought Angelo would actually answer them. He wasn't a bad guy, I didn't think. Rick had trusted him—to a point, at least. But he didn't choose the situation he found himself in now, and that made him surly. I could understand that. His prayer for future boredom was heartfelt.

Cormac watched him leave, swinging open the door like it personally offended him and stalking out into the night.

"I never thought I'd say this, but I think I miss Rick," he said.

On the other hand, I knew I'd miss Rick the minute he left.

Chapter 3

BACK TO work, then. It wasn't the end of the world—not yet, anyway—so we had to keep on with our lives. This was better, I knew. The alternative was freezing in place and never moving again.

Angelo came through on finding me a vampire stripper to interview on the show. Or stripper vampire. I still wasn't sure which way to go on that one. Her name was Colette, and when I asked if that was her real name or her stripper name, she just arced a neatly plucked brow at me and smiled.

I had to admit, I hadn't ever known any for-real strippers, and I didn't know what to expect. No expectation at all was better than defaulting to TV stereotypes. She arrived at the studio before the start of the show, and when I met her in the lobby, my first impression was to think, yup, she's a vampire. She had mahogany hair, light brown skin, wore a real rabbit fur stole over a stylish black silk dress and knee-high leather boots, and held herself with a poise that made me swoon a bit. She'd walk into a nightclub and turn heads, and I tried to remember if I'd ever seen her at Psalm 23, the club the Denver vampire Family ran and used as hunting grounds. I didn't think so.

In the studio, I offered her a chair and showed her how the headset worked. She was polite, smiling wryly when I avoided looking directly into her hypnotic gaze.

I watched the clock; we were seconds from go, and through the booth window I saw Matt staring, frozen. I'd warned him that she was coming, and that he shouldn't look directly into her eyes. But it was pretty hard not to, I supposed, when somebody like that walked into the room. The vampire gave him a smile that made him blush. Wrapped him around her finger with nothing more than a glance, and the thing was, that was her vampire nature, and had nothing to do with her profession.

But I could totally believe that she made *really good* tips.

I found a stray pen resting on my table and threw it at the booth window. Matt started at the *thunk* it made, shook his head clear, and got to work, or acted like he was working, flipping switches and cuing up the show's opening.

He counted down, the on-air sign lit, and CCR's "Bad Moon Rising" started playing through my headset. Show time. "Greetings! You've tuned into *The Midnight Hour,* the show that's not afraid of the dark or the creatures who live there. I'm your host, Kitty Norville, and I hope you're ready for another evening of spooky delights and tales of the uncanny. I have a special guest with me tonight. Colette is a vampire with a job you might not expect to find a vampire doing. Then again, I've been meeting vampires for years, and they're always surprising me, which is why I keep talking about them. Colette, welcome to *The Midnight Hour,* thank you for agreeing to this interview. And can you please tell our audience what you do for a living?"

"I'm an exotic dancer. That is, I strip," she said straight-up, with a knowing smile.

"Is this something you did before becoming a vampire, or did you take it up after?"

"Before, which is part of why I keep doing it—it's something I know, and I'm pretty good at it if I do say so myself. It's a lot more fun knowing I won't ever have to worry about competing with the younger girls, as far as looks go."

"That's a perk I certainly hadn't thought of. And dare I ask how long you've been at it?"

"You mean, how long have I been a vampire? Angelo warned me you'd ask me that."

"It's standard," I agreed. "So, how about it? How old are you?"

"Oh, not that old, not compared to someone like Angelo or Rick. I'm just a baby, really."

I raised an eyebrow. "Yeah. Right. Moving on, I've encountered anecdotal evidence that stripping as a vampire is more lucrative than stripping as a mortal human. Can you confirm or deny this?"

"I can understand why someone might think that's the case. But really, there are so many factors involved, as anyone in the business can tell you. The time of day, location, the joint's policies, local ordinances. Being a vampire turns out to be the least of it. In fact, I try not to use my . . . influence too often. It starts to look suspicious, you know what I mean? I may be one of the immortal undead, but the girls in the dressing room can use a bottle of holy water just as well as anyone if I start poaching."

That made a frightening amount of good sense. "Did I promise a peek into a hidden world, or what? So Colette, are you up front with your status as a vampire, or do you keep it secret? Is it a marketing point for you? 'Come see the vampire stripper'?"

"It would be, if I actually advertised it, but I don't. Some of my friends know, and that's it, really. I don't want to turn this into more of a freak show than it already is by advertising I'm a vampire. I mean, look what happened to you when you came out."

"Freak show?" I asked, grinning. "It's worked out pretty well for me."

"I suppose, if you *like* being a target."

Ouch. I kind of did feel like I'd painted one on myself some days. Well, I'd held on this long, hadn't I? Without the benefit of vampire immortality, even.

Moving on, then. "So it's safe to say that becoming a vampire didn't change your ability or desire to be a stripper?"

"Like I said, I do this because it's what I know, it's a way I know I can make some money, and I like to have my own money rather than depending totally on the Family. The Family knows what I do, they're okay with it. It's good to have diverse resources, don't you think?" She purred on this last.

"Remember folks, you heard it here first: vampires have their sticky little fingers in everything, don't they?" I'd probably hear about this from Angelo later. Really, though, if he hadn't wanted Colette to talk, he wouldn't have introduced her to me. "Colette, how do you feel about taking a few calls?"

"Wouldn't miss it," she said. "I know how this works."

"All right, I'm opening the line for calls." I checked the monitor very, very carefully and picked what sounded like a reasonably intelligent question, hoping against hope that however likely this episode was to end up in the gutter, we wouldn't actually start there. "Nancy from Hartford, you're on the air."

"Hi, Kitty, thanks for taking my call."

"You're very welcome, Nancy. Do you have a question for Colette?"

"Omigosh, yes, what an opportunity to talk to a real, live vampire." I could have quibbled with the terminology there, but I didn't. Nancy continued, "I know you can't say exactly how long you've been a stripper, but you must have an interesting perspective, and I wondered if you could talk a little bit about how the field has changed over the course of your career?"

Intelligent and academic, even. For my first question of the night, I chose wisely. Even better, Colette was happy to talk about changes in work environments, music, and traditions. "But in the end, it's always been about watching women take their tops off, and that'll never change," she concluded. "Actually, you know what's changed the most? Male strippers. Equal-opportunity stripping. Maybe a little more high end than what most of us do, but I'm not going to knock it."

I switched lines. "On to the next call, now. Jen, you're on the air."

"Um, gosh, wow. Okay. My question, yeah. If

becoming a vampire didn't change anything about how much you made stripping, why do it at all?"

Colette sat back in her chair, legs crossed. "Why strip, or why be a vampire?"

"Well, yeah," Jen said.

"Really, becoming a vampire had nothing to do with whether or not I was stripping. But what would you say if I told you I've found wonderful pickings at my places of employment."

"You mean . . . oh," Jen said. The phone clicked off.

"And I think we've lost Jen," I said, suppressing an urge to chortle. "Next caller, you're on the air."

The caller was male, brash, and I'd lay money that he'd been drinking. "Yeah, Colette, great talking to you. Do you do private parties?"

"You couldn't afford me."

"But what if—"

"Really," she said. That purr again.

I cut the caller off before he could embarrass himself further. "And how about we break for station ID? This is *The Midnight Hour,* and we'll be back in a sec." I waved at Matt thought the window, but he was a step ahead of me, cuing up the PSAs. The on-air sign dimmed—a reprieve.

I sat back and regarded my guest. "What do you think?" I asked.

"Angelo said this would be fun, and he was right. Certainly shakes things up."

"You're a natural at this," I said. "I have to prod some people to get them to talk.

"Show business is show business."

I could argue about that, but I'd lose. "Maybe you could convince Angelo to come on the show for an interview."

"And how likely do you think *that* is?"

None. None likely. "You putting in a good word for me couldn't hurt, could it?"

She narrowed her gaze. "Why are you so interested in interviewing Angelo?"

"I don't know much about him. I'd love to know more. If I'm going to ask him stuff anyway, I might as well get a show out of it."

"Just knowledge and entertainment, then? No ulterior motive?"

"Well, more like stories. Vampires have the best stories. That's why I wanted to talk to you—I never would have expected a vampire to work as a stripper. Most of them are so . . . private. Or what's the word I'm looking for . . ."

"Elitist?"

Nailed it. "But here you are, and the Family approves. So what does the Family get out of having one of their own working as an exotic dancer?"

Her smile shined. "It's not always about the Families, Kitty. Sometimes there's no secret agenda, no conspiracy. Not even much of a story. Sometimes there's a stripper who just happens to be a vampire. A radio host who happens to be a werewolf."

She might have had a point. I'd been trying to unwrap Roman's conspiracy for so long, I'd started to see everything as a thread leading back to it. When your only tool is a hammer, every problem looks like a nail.

"And Angelo really is just a guy who was unexpectedly put in charge when he'd rather sit the whole thing out." She shrugged, neither confirming nor denying.

"So you think he's a nice enough guy," I said, not sure I trusted her opinion on the matter.

"To tell you the truth, I miss Rick. But Angelo's not a bad guy."

And that had to count for something I supposed.

We came back on the air, she answered another round of questions. All in all, this show was turning into one of my better efforts.

During the next break, she unfolded from her chair. "This has been fun, but I really need to get going. Thanks for inviting me." She offered her hand, and I shook it, and she gave me a charming little wave before stalking out of the studio.

Matt had to knock on the glass to get me to notice his countdown. On the air in five, and me without my guest. Right. Seat of my pants, here we go.

"All right, welcome back to *The Midnight Hour*. A

little change of plans. My guest, Colette, has turned
into a bat and flapped away. Not really, vampires don't
really turn into bats. They only want us to *think* they
do. Never mind. But I want to thank her for stopping
by and giving us some insight into her world. But this
has brought up an issue I'd love to discuss next. So, a
question for the peanut gallery: Once they turn sixty-
five, how long should working vampires be able to
collect social security? The rest of their lives, like the
rest of us? Are you a vampire collecting social security? I want to hear from you . . ."

Chapter 4

BEN WENT back to work, too, which meant making the business trip to Wyoming. The house was very big and quiet without him around.

This was purely psychological. I'd spent plenty of time in the house alone, when he was out working or whatever. Then, I didn't think about it, because I knew he'd be back soon, or he'd call to let me know where he was. He'd still be in Denver, in our territory. I could listen for the sounds of him returning home.

Now, I listened for sounds that weren't there. The walls seemed to creak, and every car engine or barking dog set my hair on end. I waited for the hum of his car turning into the driveway, a sound I knew I wasn't going to hear. Maddening.

I kept music on to fill the space.

At night, lying in bed alone, the quiet grew much

worse. I left the music on, turned low, to provide a background noise to distract the part of my mind that kept listening for cars, or kept convincing me that an intruder was in the kitchen making off with the silverware. I slept on Ben's side of the bed, my face buried in his pillow, so I could breathe in the scent of him. I berated myself for being soppy.

The next afternoon, I sat on the floor of the office, much as Ben had found me the day before, papers and books piled everywhere, thinking. Pretending to think. I was leaning against the desk, looking at the sky through the window, enjoying the winter sun blazing through, and if someone had asked what I was thinking about in that moment, I wouldn't have been able to say.

While thinking I would work more when I had the house to myself was a nice idea, I'd known all along that it wasn't going to happen, because not having enough time, space, or quiet to work wasn't the reason I hadn't finished the book. I had the problem of too much information, and no clue how to tie it together. I had entire chapters written, and no idea what order to put them in. Did I arrange stories chronologically, geographically, thematically? Biographically, with a framework about how the stories related to me personally? All equally valid approaches. I kept changing my mind.

When my cell phone rang, I jumped like it was a fire alarm, scattering papers and sliding shut the book I'd been pretending to read. I needed a minute of scrambling before I could actually reach the phone, and was surprised when the caller ID showed it wasn't Ben. I shouldn't have been surprised; he'd called last night to say he'd arrived in Cheyenne okay, and I wasn't expecting another call from him until tonight.

This call came from Tom, one of the werewolves in our pack. I may have sounded a little surly when I answered.

"What is it?"

"Um, hi?" Tom was one of the bigger males in the pack—one of the tough guys, the kind who actually made you think of werewolves when you saw him. That he could sound sheepish talking to me usually made me smile.

I settled down. "Hi. And how are we today?"

"Actually . . . we may have a problem."

I straightened, a shadow of fur prickling on my skin and hackles rising. "What is it?"

"I'm up in the mountains, out past Georgetown, and I caught a weird scent. Might be werewolf or some other kind of lycanthrope. Definitely not one of ours."

A stranger, in our territory. We'd had invaders before. Just recently a strange werewolf had arrived for the express purpose of trying to take the pack away from us. I took this sort of thing seriously. With the news about Roman and Antony, my worry pressed on me like a boulder.

"Is it just one person or a group? Did they seem lost? Are they looking for something?"

Tom said, "It wasn't enough to make a trail, not anything I could track. It was almost like they circled around for a while. Maybe they were looking for something."

"And it was fresh?"

"Couldn't be more than a day old," he said. "It was pretty strong—I wouldn't have called if it was just a trace."

I blew out a breath. This could be nothing—someone passing through, getting lost. Or it could be someone with bad intentions. A scouting mission for an attack at some later date?

Either way, I couldn't ignore it. If things went well, we might have a new friend to talk to. If not . . . I had a territory to defend. I started cleaning up in preparation for leaving. I wanted to go there to take a look.

"Just out of curiosity," I said. "What were you doing out that way?"

He paused a moment, then said, nervous, "Um . . . just going for a hike . . ."

"You shifted, didn't you? Went out for a run?" "Going for a run" was a euphemism among werewolves. Tom grumbled a perfunctory, unenthusiastic denial.

"Why exactly did you do this? Full moon's not for a week." Six days, actually. I kept count. We all did.

"I'm not hurting anything," he said, and I could almost see him pouting. "I didn't get in any kind of trouble."

We had to shape-shift on the night of a full moon, but we had the ability to shift anytime we wanted. Or we shifted when we were stressed, angry, frightened, in danger . . . yeah. Part of why we formed packs was so we could watch out for each other. We could gather on nights of the full moon, shape-shift together, make sure we stayed safe—and didn't do anything that might get us in trouble, like hunting people. We could take care of each other, so we didn't shift uncontrollably at other times. Solo shifting kind of defeated the purpose.

"Tom. You know better than that."

"Seriously, I'm not hurting anything. I can handle it."

If I sounded like an irate parent, he sounded like a teenager. I trusted Tom; he was smart enough to go to a remote spot if he was going to do recreational shape-shifting. Of everyone in the pack, he was probably the one who most enjoyed being a werewolf—who reveled in the power and exhilaration of running on four legs, feeling the wind in your fur, hunting for the taste of fresh meat . . .

Most of us tried to ignore how good being wolf made us feel.

"Why don't you just tell me that you had a suspicion something was wrong and went out to patrol under your own initiative?"

"Okay, then. I went out to patrol because I thought something might be wrong."

"Fine. Okay. Good work, then. I want to check it out. I can be out there in about an hour. Can you wait for me and show me what you found?"

"I'll be here."

We hung up and I looked around at my paper-strewn, chaotic office. This could wait another day. Going to see what Tom had found was more important.

I CALLED Ben. His phone went straight to voice mail, which I expected. He was probably in a meeting. I left a message explaining what was happening and that Tom was with me, because Ben would worry if I was on my own. He'd worry anyway, but he'd be reassured that I wasn't running off alone. Then I drove into the mountains to meet Tom.

Denver lay near the foothills of the Rocky Mountains—the Front Range, which rose from the Great Plains like a wall of sandstone and granite. I turned the car onto I-70. The freeway climbed, curving around hills, until I was in the mountains proper. Within half an hour, pine-covered slopes surrounded me. In the dead of winter, I rolled down the window so I could smell the sharp, icy air, laden with the scent of snow and forest. The wind whipped strands of my blond hair out of my ponytail and into my face. South-facing slopes and hillsides were bare of snow, green with conifers rising tall. North-facing slopes had a carpet of white. I'd managed to miss ski traffic heading to the resorts farther west.

Soon enough, I reached the Georgetown exit and pulled off onto the frontage road, and from there to the road that wound into the mountains. Then came a couple of narrow drives, then dirt roads. I felt like I was traveling through time, from the height of civilization to some nineteenth-century village, to wilderness. I ran into patches of ice and snow, but my little car with its snow tires handled the road okay.

On full-moon nights, we rotated between half a dozen semiremote spots in national forest land in the Rockies, or out east on the plains. They had to be close enough to Denver that we could drive there in an hour or two, but far enough away from people that we weren't likely to draw attention or cause trouble. A set of USGS topographic maps marking service roads helped us pick our spots. The best ones had sheltered areas where we could bed down for the rest of the night, open spaces where we could run, and plenty of prey. Deer and rabbit, usually. That was the true purpose of shape-shifting and running on full-moon nights: blood. The need to let our wolf sides loose; the desire to kill that we could only restrain for so long. This one night, we had to send our howling songs to the moon, and let our claws and teeth tear into the weak.

I found Tom's car, a compact SUV parked on the side of the road by a pine tree. I pulled my hatchback in behind his car, then followed his scent through the trees, around a rise, and into a clearing. Tom stood on a slope patched with half-melted drifts of snow, leaning on a tree and looking out into the next valley. He wore jeans and no shirt, and went shoeless. He must have called me as soon as he'd woken up after his time as a wolf and dressed just enough to appear decent. In his thirties, he was as fit and rugged a man as a red-blooded girl like me could hope to gaze upon.

"Hey," I said, coming to stand beside him. I touched his shoulder, a confirmation of contact, a wolfish gesture of comfort and identity. Relaxing, he dropped his shoulders and pressed his lips into a smile. He turned his gaze away, a sign of submission to the alpha of his pack.

"Do you smell it?" he asked.

Stepping away from him, I tipped my face up, found a faint, vagrant breeze, and turned my nose into it. The smells here were thick, layer upon layer of vivid life and wild. I had to filter them out, ignoring the omnipresent smell of trees, forest decay and detritus; the myriad trails of deer and skunk and fox and squirrel and grouse and sparrow, no matter how they piqued my appetite; and more distant scents of mountain snow, an icebound creek.

And there it was, acrid and alien, standing out because it so obviously didn't belong. Wolf and human, bound together, fur under the skin—and something else. There were two distinct scents. I recognized the second one, but I understood why Tom hadn't. This scent also gave me the tangled mix of fur and skin that indicated lycanthrope, but with a feline edge to it, both tangy and musky, making me think of golden eyes and a smug demeanor. This one was female. The wolf was male.

"That other one's a were-lion," I said. "They've been through here, but they didn't stick around."

"Were-lion," Tom said, furrowing a brow. "Really? And they're together?"

"Dogs and cats—sign of the apocalypse. They didn't mark or anything, did they? Just walked on through, like they're scouting without being threatening. You think?"

"No clue," he said. "But it's making me nervous."

"That'll teach you to go off Changing and running by yourself."

"Give me a break," he muttered, but his body language was all apology: shoulders slouched, making him look small and sheepish. If he'd had a tail it would have been tucked between his legs.

That was all I wanted, a little chagrin, a little embarrassment. I might have been the alpha around here but I wasn't much into physical domination. Tom was a lot bigger than I was—he'd beat me in a straight fight. I had to be the leader of this gang without fighting. People usually knew when they'd done something wrong; they didn't need me pointing it out. But I could make them feel guilty. I could rub it in a little.

Now that I'd picked it out, the smell became intrusive, and the muscles across my shoulders tensed. "If they were friendly, they'd come out and show themselves, right?"

"They're probably looking for you," he said. "To meet the famous werewolf queen."

I rolled my eyes. "So if I stand here long enough they'll walk on up and introduce themselves? No. I want to find out what's going on here."

I set off, following the trail the intruders had made. Tom fell into step behind me.

This was one of those bright winter days in Colorado, when the temperature rose enough to thaw out the air and melt some of the snow. I grew warm as we walked, almost needing to take off my sweater, but my breath still fogged. Being outdoors on days like today was a pleasure.

The trail didn't follow a straight line. The two species I'd sensed, wolf and lion, walked together, circling back as if they were searching for something. The backtracking led us south and west. I paused often, thinking I could hear them ahead of us if I listened hard enough.

We continued for over an hour, and the shadows grew longer. I didn't want to be out here after dark, but I wanted the mystery solved. These lycanthropes had to come from somewhere, and had to be going somewhere.

Tom had a worried, furrowed look on his face. He'd ranged off a dozen paces or so—following a different branch of the same trail.

"Find anything?" I asked.

He shook his head. "I don't like it."

The strangers hadn't been hunting, hadn't been marking territory—they really did seem to want to get the pack's attention rather than challenge us. But if that was the case, why not show themselves?

We went on from where we had originally picked up the trail, and Tom's path took him even farther away.

"Hey, Tom, you still tracking both of them?" We were moving to opposite sides of the same slope; in a few more paces, he'd be out of sight.

"Yeah," he said.

So was I. "Let's back up some."

Sure enough, the trail split. They might have taken one path in and another path out. As if they'd arrived, circled around enough to confuse the hell out of us, then left again by another route.

"You think the trails meet up on the other side of the hill?" Tom asked.

"I don't know what's going on. Might as well check it out."

We went back to following the two trails, Tom taking one side and me the other.

Being in the mountains, you couldn't actually see the mountains, unless you got to a peak or open valley where the vistas become visible, big sky and horizon surrounded by hills and snowy peaks. In the mountain forests, the land was a series of slopes, clearings, meadows, creek-cut gullies and washes, and steep rockfalls. Often, you couldn't see more than fifty feet in front of or behind you. The slope Tom and I circled was a rocky bulge on the side of a gentler hill that probably dropped off to a valley or ravine on the other side. I was climbing steadily uphill; he'd gotten farther downhill. We might not meet up exactly on the other side of the slope, but I expected to be able to see him once I cleared the pine trees and outcrops of this particular formation.

He'd only been out of sight for half a minute. I could still hear him, soft breathing, quiet steady footsteps on hard ground. His scent was clear on the air.

Something hit me. Fast and small, like a Ping-Pong ball ramming into my side from behind, accompanied by a sting. Hissing, I jumped a step and reached around to slap at myself—my hand touched something hard and plastic hanging from my side, under my rib cage. I yanked it out, stared.

A dart, with a needle long enough to punch clear through my sweater and into my skin. The plastic syringe attached to it was as long as my hand. Enough stuff had been in there to knock out a bear, probably.

My heart raced, exactly what I didn't want it to do. When I tried to call out to Tom, to warn him, my throat closed up. The sound was a choke instead of the intended howl. I tried to run.

Tranquilizer darts worked on werewolves, as long as they held enough of the drug. I'd seen it. I was guessing whoever had fired this one knew what they were doing, because the dart's impact point started tingling, and numbness spread through my body. My breath caught—the air seemed to have turned thick, and my vision wavered, like I was looking through a fogged window. When I took a step, my legs trembled, and I couldn't raise my arms to break my fall. Again, I tried to shout to Tom, to let out a howl. My voice squeaked like a mouse's.

I fell facedown on a snowbank, trying to get my limbs to move, trying to fill my lungs with enough air to call a warning, and failing. The edges of the world took on a red tinge, then collapsed to darkness.

My last thought: my day was about to get truly awful.

Chapter 5

CONSCIOUSNESS RETURNED slowly.

I spent a lot of time in a half-dreaming fog, like what I felt the mornings after a full moon, waking up and trying to fit back in my human skin. I lay on something cold and hard, and thought that couldn't be right, I was supposed to be home, there was supposed to be coffee, I needed a shower, but first I needed to brush my teeth, which tasted like milk-soaked cotton. My head pounded, my joints were stuck. Ben was supposed to be here, and I couldn't smell him anywhere. My next exhale came out as a whine. I could call—

My phone, usually tucked into my jeans pocket, was gone. Of course it was. I slapped at my neck, pawing for a chain that wasn't there—the chain that held my wedding ring. It was gone, too. So were my shoes and socks. I still had on the rest of my clothes.

I wondered: did my captor get Tom, or had he escaped? If they had caught him as well, where was he? At the moment, all I could smell was the drugged taint in my blood and my own sticky breath. I didn't know where I was or who else might be here.

Who had done this to me? Was it Roman? If so, why hadn't he just killed me?

My breathing, which grated roughly in my too-dry throat, echoed closely. When I opened my eyes, the world came back to me, piece by piece. I was in a small room, and it was dark. Black, really, only a sliver of light creeping in from somewhere. My werewolf eyes were good, even in the dark, and if I couldn't see any details in the room, it was because there weren't any. Bare, rough walls, a dusty floor. I breathed carefully, trying to sense anything through my drugged haze. The air was chilled, full of stone and age. Damp—not wet, but moisture tickled the inside of my nose. I was underground, maybe in a dirt cellar. Or maybe not—cellars didn't normally have granite walls. These walls were solid stone, and I couldn't sense any trace of a building to go with a cellar. No humming power cables or shushing water pipes. No smell of treated, painted wood. No wood at all, or trees, vegetation, people, mice, roaches, or anything. I smelled my own sick scent, the dusty air. A trace of . . . gunpowder? Faint, sulfurous, and old.

I started the process of unkinking my muscles and

peeling myself from the floor. I ached all over, and the spot where the dart had hit me throbbed. Wincing, I rubbed it. Once I was upright, I sat, waiting for a wave of dizziness to pass, gaining a better sense of my bearings. Something about this place made my skin crawl. I scratched my arms through my sweater, trying to soothe an itch that wouldn't go away.

I was still dressed, and I wasn't tied up. So, things could be worse. Way to be positive.

Now, what to do? If I could sense a draft, I could follow it out. But the air was still. I wanted a long drink of water. I wanted to run, I wanted to howl. My options at the moment were limited. I wanted to know more about who had done this to me. One thing at a time.

Carefully I stood, arms outstretched, searching for the walls and ceiling, the confines of the room. Figure out where I was, then where I could go. I had to duck, turning my head because the ceiling was just a touch too low. I squinted into the darkness, and my hand touched gritty stone surface. Now, I ought to be able to follow the wall to . . . something.

Traveling step by careful step, I felt along the wall for any clue, and took slow breaths, trying to filter some meaning from this world. There was dead stillness—nothing for me to hear, no voices of evil kidnappers, not so much as water dripping. The walls were definitely solid—chilled, ancient, no give at all. I was in some kind of cave. However, I wasn't sure it was natural—it seemed too uniform. Artificial, then. A carved tunnel.

My hands itched, and the annoying burn got worse, until I had to shake them, rubbing them together to get rid of the feeling. The more I thought about it, though, the more my whole body started feeling that itch, that slow burn that never got truly painful, but would drive me crazy before too long.

I knew that sensation—silver. There was silver here, low grade, scant quantities found in scattered flecks in the walls, and the more I touched them the worse the allergic reaction would become. Just as they'd known how much tranquilizer to use, my captors knew to paint the walls with silver, to keep me captive, quiet.

No—not a room, a cell, or a cave. This was a mine. They'd taken me to a silver mine, probably one of the hundreds scattered throughout the Colorado mountains, abandoned and forgotten. For some reason, the thought that I was still in Colorado—still relatively close to home—comforted me. I had to find a way out of here and get home.

I continued my circuit of the tiny cave, brushing the wall with only my fingertips, ignoring the building itch. It was just a little silver, it wouldn't kill me unless it got in my bloodstream. This must have been some branch of a tunnel, excavated a short distance, blown out with explosives, then abandoned when it didn't yield high-quality ore. The ceiling arced evenly overhead.

Finally, the stone ended. I touched wood, set perpendicular to the cave wall. I pressed my hands flat against it, felt all over, and didn't feel the burn of silver. Just plain wood. I studied it. A sheet of wood reinforced with two-by-fours had been set across the cave's opening—it might have been a door, but if there were hinges, they were bolted on the outside, into the rock. The inside, the side facing me, had no handle, no lock, no sign of a lock. The wood itself felt solid. I banged on it, gave it a shake, and it didn't budge. There was a gap at the bottom of the door, enough to stick my fingers through, enough to let air in, and a faint sliver of white light, maybe from a lantern. I also found a seam, as if some kind of slot had been cut into the wood.

Bottom line, there was a door. A shut door could be opened and allow escape.

I pounded on the wood and yelled. "Hey! Wanna get the fuck over here and explain yourselves? Hey!" After one last, good hard pound, I pressed my ear to the gap near the floor, waited.

Nothing happened.

I lay on the floor, pressed my nose to the gap, and breathed several slow, deep breaths, hoping to catch a scent of someone, something, anything. Mostly what

I smelled was stone and dusty air, and I swore I could smell the silver pervading everything, tickling the inside of my nose. I sneezed, scrubbed my nose on my sleeve, and tried again, determined not to think too hard about silver anymore. I just had to be careful not to get cut while I was here.

And there they were, the same scents Tom and I had tracked: the two lycanthropes, wolf and lion. They'd lured us out and gotten us. I wished I knew why.

Other scents mingled with the two I recognized. Those I wasn't as clear on. One seemed human enough, but vague. I couldn't even tell the person's sex. The other—chilled. A corpselike cold. Vampire? Or was it just the pervasive cold of the stone masking something else?

That didn't make any more sense than the rest of it.

I spent five minutes pounding on the door, shouting until my voice went hoarse. After the first minute I was pretty sure I wouldn't get a response. But I kept doing it, just to be doing something.

No one answered. I might have been alone in the mine.

This was ridiculous. You didn't drug and kidnap someone, then lock them into a dark room and leave them there for no reason. I wondered where the night-vision cameras were hidden.

This whole place made me itch, and I rubbed my

arms. I went to the middle of the cave, as far from the walls and traces of ambient silver as I could get, and sat. Stared at the door that I very much wanted to be on the other side of.

I could claw my way through the wood, given time and motivation. I had the motivation, but I didn't know how much time I had. I had another problem. I could turn Wolf, dig and chew through the door, and get cut up in the process. Being a werewolf didn't mean I didn't get hurt, it meant I could take a lot of damage and heal quickly. But if I really was in a silver mine, it didn't matter how defunct it was, there could still be traces of silver all through this place, ore that was never excavated, a residue embedded in the walls and even scattered in the dust on the floor. If I cut open my paws, my hands, and if the silver got into my bloodstream, I'd be dead. The bullet half of the silver bullet didn't kill werewolves; blood poisoning from the silver did. Silver-inlaid knives did as well. I didn't know if there was a minimum amount of silver it took to poison a werewolf to death—maybe traces of powder on the floor wouldn't be enough. But I didn't want to be the one to test that threshold.

So any escape plan that might break skin was out.

Cold didn't affect me as much as it did a normal human being, but I started to shiver. I pulled my hands into the sleeves of my sweater, hugged my knees to my chest, and tried to keep my breathing slow and steady. My mind spun, a hamster racing in a wheel that didn't go anywhere.

The pieces of what was happening here didn't fit together. The tranquilizer dart, the efficiency of the strike—I'd never even heard the gun fire, and whoever had the gun must have been downwind because I hadn't smelled anyone that close—made me think military. At one point the army had werewolf soldiers serving in Afghanistan. I'd been called in as a consultant when a unit of werewolves had broken down, its members suffering from post-traumatic stress and unable to control themselves. Out of necessity, the military made excellent use of tranquilizer guns on werewolves in that situation. But if someone in the military had kidnapped me, I'd have ended up in a steel and Plexiglas cell in a hypercontrolled situation in some lab. I'd had a bit of experience with those settings, too. If this had been a military or even some wacky paramilitary situation, I'd have been exposed, plenty of one-way mirrors and closed-circuit cameras watching me. There'd be someone standing there with a clipboard. They'd have had a reason for taking me, even if they didn't want to tell me what it was.

This setting—this was thrown together. This was making use of available resources. This said my captors might not have been working with a lot of time and money on their hands. They could probably get the tranquilizer gun and darts off the Internet, and they used a prison they had at hand rather than building one.

A few choice questions would help me figure this out. I cycled through them a dozen times and didn't find answers. Was Tom here? I desperately hoped he was free, safe, and calling the cavalry. On the other hand, it would be nice to have an ally. I thought about calling his name, then thought better of it. If whoever had done this had missed him, I didn't want them going back for him. Were my captors targeting werewolves in general, or me in particular? If the answer was me in particular, that opened a whole catalog of enemies who might have done this. Who said that having enemies was good, because it meant you'd stood up for something in your life? Ah, I remembered: Winston Churchill. The guy who also said, *If you're going through hell, keep going.* Yes, sir.

Most of all, what I wanted to know was what did this have to do with Roman and his confrontation with Antony? Because whatever Colette said, sometimes all threads did lead back to a conspiracy.

The culprit might be any one of a number of anti-supernatural groups that had sprung up over the last few years, as vampires and lycanthropes and other brands of magic became more visible and more accepted. I made an easy target because of my radio show. Any truly crazy activists would have just killed me outright—I'd gotten plenty of threats. But these guys wanted me for something. And antisupernatural activist didn't mesh with the evidence that at least some of my captors seemed to be supernatural themselves. They could be working for the enemy, but why?

The possibilities I considered got more outlandish. A rabid fan had captured me, *Misery* style, and obsessive games of admiration and torture would soon ensue. Another werewolf pack—one that included a were-lion for some suitably dramatic reason—needed me for some in-person counseling. Flattering, but unlikely. Those folks usually approached me in restaurants, and without tranquilizer guns. Maybe I was being prepared as a hideous sacrifice to some ancient, chthonic god. That had actually already happened to me once, in Las Vegas of all places, so it wasn't entirely outside the realm of reason. But then there should have been candles, burning incense, weird statuary, and chanting. Or maybe I was being collected for display in an alien zoo.

My imagination was getting away from me. My questions accumulated, growing more and more urgent: When would my enemy finally appear? Would there be food and water? Sooner or later, if the door stayed shut and locked, the need for water would drive me to try to break out, danger of silver poisoning or no.

The chill was getting to me, so I got up and paced.

Three steps down the long side of the rocky cell, two steps across, three steps back. Not too cramped, as far as terrifying underground prison cells went. With thoughts like that pressing on me, the pacing didn't do a thing to get rid of the gooseflesh pricking my arms. My head itched, and my lips had pulled back, unconsciously baring my teeth. I hadn't realized I'd been doing it. I pressed my hands to my face, rubbed my cheeks, tried to get the muscles to relax. Appear calm. Not at all like a cornered wolf, no sir.

I had to find a way out of here.

I DIDN'T know much about old silver mines except in the most general historical sense. In the last half of the nineteenth century, prospectors discovered gold, silver, and a collection of other valuable minerals throughout the Rocky Mountains. Industry flooded in, dozens of fortunes were made, cities were built. Mining was still an important industry in the state, but hundreds of antique mines like this one had been abandoned and left to decay. They'd been built with nineteenth-century technology, tunnels blown out with primitive black powder and dynamite, men digging with shovels and pickaxes, hauling ore out with carts and donkeys.

I didn't know how deep a mine like this ran, how many tunnels and chambers it might have, if there was a standard layout or if they twisted randomly depending on where the ore was. I didn't know how stable the arcing stone rooms might be. Not very, was my feeling—hikers and travelers in the mountains were always getting warnings about not venturing into such tunnels. They collapsed a lot, I gathered. If I started worrying about the roof of the place caving in on me, on top of all the other anxieties, I'd freeze completely. So I just didn't think about it.

The darkness was giving me a headache. The strain of trying to stare my way out of a near-lightless cave was telling. Not to mention the fear and anger, with no target to aim toward. I ended up sitting on the floor again and thinking of Ben. He'd find me. Somehow he'd figure out what had happened, come looking, and find me. It was just a matter of time. I could be patient.

I caught myself whispering hurry, hurry, hurry.

IF ONLY I knew how much time had passed. I didn't know how long I'd been unconscious, and I couldn't see outside to know if it was day or night. The timelessness gave me a feeling of mental seasickness, a nausea that crept into my gut. The ground didn't feel firm.

Around the roaring in my own ears, I heard something new—something different outside, breaking the silence of the mine tunnel. Barely there—soft, careful, steady. Slippered footsteps, creeping close. I held my breath. The sound was no greater than that of snow falling. The bare whisper of breath that came with the steps I could hear a little better.

Whoever had approached the door paused just on the other side. I was torn between wanting to shout and wanting to remain as still as possible, straining with my ears and taking deep breaths through my nose, hoping to catch a scent and learn all I could.

The person waited, breathing softly. The smell— female, feline. The were-lion. She'd used some kind of herbal hand lotion recently, and wore clothing of washed cotton.

I rose to a crouch, leaning toward the door. "Who are you? What's going on here?"

The seam I'd noticed in the bottom of the door revealed a panel that flipped open—quickly, loudly. A bottle of water rolled through the opening. I lunged to reach through, to get my hand out there to grab whoever was standing there. But the panel slammed shut on me, and a latch slotted back into place.

Soft footsteps ran away.

"Hey, wait a minute! Talk to me, will you just *talk* to me?" I shouted, slapped the door, rammed my shoulder into it. The board flexed some, but the hinges didn't give, as if they'd bolted this thing into the solid wall with bands of iron. My shouts degenerated into growls of frustration.

Kneeling, I punched at the panel, tried to jam my fingers into the seam, anything I could to pry it open, break it, rip apart the door. Like the rest of the door, it was well made, solidly built and locked into place. It flexed, and with a lot of time and effort maybe I could rip through it. But it wasn't going to give way just by punching it.

I scrabbled at it, until a sharp pain stabbed into my fingertip. I cried out and brought my finger to my mouth, sucking on the wound. Splinter. I could feel it. Wincing, I picked at it in the dark, felt the little fiber under the skin, pulled it out. The pain faded quickly— a wound like that would heal in no time. But the memory of it throbbed. Just a tiny splinter, but it brought tears to my eyes. The stress of it all brought tears to my eyes. Again, I curled up in the middle of the floor, hugging myself, feeling sorry for myself.

My leg brushed against the bottle of water my captor had thrown me. At least, it smelled like water. Just a normal, plastic, store-bought bottle of water. Warm—not refrigerated. It hadn't even come from an ice-filled cooler. Strangely modern and out of place in this medieval dungeon they'd put me in. Like the tranquilizer gun. The paramilitary conspiracy seemed less likely. This wasn't comforting, because it meant I was likely in the grips of some homespun, backwoods conspiracy. They knew what they were doing, and had access to just enough tech to make them really scary.

I wasn't scared. I tried not to be scared.

Vaguely, I thought of hunger strikes. How very nice of them to bring me water, because how terrible it would have been, to go through the trouble of drugging me and bringing me here, then letting me die of thirst. Could a werewolf die of thirst? Probably—it would just take a really long time. Not comforting.

Just because they brought water didn't mean I had to drink it. I could throw it back out—if I could only get that door panel open. Refusing to drink would likely spite nobody but myself. My mouth still tasted of drugs and sleep, my own sour anxiety, residual tranquilizer leaking out of my system. I twisted open the cap, which cracked, the seal breaking. A brand-new bottle, filled with plain water and not poison. They really did want me alive, after all.

I drank a mouthful, swishing the water around to clean out the grime and bitterness. Closed the bottle and saved the rest for later. Then I settled back in the middle of the floor, huddled in on myself, and pondered.

Chapter 6

M Y HEADACHE, spurred by darkness and stress, grew worse, working to pull me into exhaustion. I must have already slept for hours because of the tranquilizer, but I slept again, and more time slipped by. I jerked to wakefulness, scratching my hand on the stone floor, without realizing I'd even fallen asleep in the first place. With the cave's darkness pressing down on me, I wondered if I'd woken up at all. My throbbing head lived in some weird, unconscious twilight state.

I retrieved the bottle of water from where I'd set it by the stone wall—far from the panel in the door, so it couldn't be taken away from me—and drank. The headache dimmed.

The same faint lamplight seeped through the bottom of the door. They'd need some kind of lighting to find their way through the tunnels. With the weight of the air pressing around me, we had to be pretty far underground. Based on the scents I could track, the same set of people had been passing by. Their scents were strong enough, even in the chill, unmoving air of the place, that I imagined them lingering. I wondered if they had some way of looking in here without me knowing. I stared at the door, imagining I was glaring at them with all the challenge I could muster. My Wolf's gaze, amber and terrifying. My lips curled, baring teeth.

Calm down. Heaving a sigh, I made myself relax, rubbed my shoulders to keep them from bunching up. I couldn't afford to shape-shift here, not like this. I couldn't lose control. When my captors finally showed themselves, I wanted to be able to talk to them. To yell at them.

I took another drink of water. And wondered what I was going to do when I had to go to the bathroom, which was going to be soon.

Lying on the floor, I put my feet up against the wood of the door. With my back braced, I pushed with all my strength. The wood flexed; I grew hopeful. Before the plywood bowed more than an inch, though, I slid back on the stone floor. I tried again, pushing until my muscles cramped, and slid on the stone. I could brace, but not well enough to make a difference. I didn't have enough leverage to beat whatever bolted the door in place. I was only wearing myself out.

A drumbeat started. No, a set of drumbeats, from relatively close by—down a tunnel outside the door. Hard to tell, because the sound echoed against the stone. As if rising up from the stone itself. The beat was gentle, steady—the thump of a heartbeat at rest. Not mechanical, though. I pressed my ear to the edge of the door and listened for clanking, clicking, the sound of metal on metal—had some mining equipment been set into motion? But no, this was skin against skin—a hand on the head of a drum. Two of them, just enough out of synch to be distracting.

Something was happening. Something had to be happening. I crept back from the door and crouched, waiting. As soon as it opened, I'd be ready. Not exactly sure what I was going to be ready for, but there you go.

I waited. The drumming continued. Nothing happened.

Human hands definitely made these beats. Over time, the pair of drums grew more out of synch, then back into rhythm. A scattered hiccup of sound, a rumble of thunder put on an endless loop. I started counting beats. Stopped after two hundred. The drumming went on a long time, until my headache grew, my temples throbbing in time with the pounding, on and on.

Yeah, something was happening—someone was trying to drive me crazy. On reflection, that was probably exactly what was going on. So I had to make sure I didn't go crazy. I caught the burr of a growl in my throat. I could decide not to go crazy, but Wolf, I wasn't sure about.

The next hour or so I spent on my back, pounding my feet against the door, shoving into it as hard as I could until I was sweating, gasping for breath. The door must have been braced from the other side; however much the wood bowed, something held it fast. It would have just taken a couple of crossbeams. Those weren't budging.

The drumming continued. While I struggled with the door, it faded to background noise. I could almost forget about it, so much white noise. I had to admire the stamina of the drummers. They lost the rhythm, changed it, picking up a new one to replace the old as they maintained their noise.

I was so preoccupied by the drumming, I almost didn't hear footsteps approach—different footsteps from the ones who'd brought the water. Heavier ones, from a larger person. A scrape on stone that jarred against the drumbeats simply because it was different. My ears pricked, straining to learn more. Holding my breath, I listened to the shallow breathing on the other side of the door. Male—and wolf. He was trying not to draw attention to himself. The skin down my back prickled, fur and hackles stiffening at a potential threat. Strange wolf, strange territory, all of it strange, and we couldn't see our enemy. He was watching us, but we couldn't match his challenge—we could only stare at the blank door.

I stayed still, crouched and frozen, not wanting to give him any kind of clue about my apprehensive state of mind. I kept my breathing calm, even though I felt like I wasn't drawing in any oxygen at all. I didn't shout, though I wanted to.

What the hell did these people *want* with me?

I waited for him to open the door, but he never did. He stood for a long time, no doubt smelling me, listening to me, studying me, the way I was trying to study him. I could stay quiet and calm, but he had to smell the anxiety on me.

The longer he waited in silence, the more I wanted to scream. I wanted my captors to do something, anything. Well, not anything. But I couldn't fight darkness and a barred door. Continually throwing myself against the barriers was only going to make me bruised and exhausted.

I wanted to pace, just to be doing *something*. But I didn't want him to know I was pacing, that the anxiety was getting to me; I didn't want to give away anything.

Then he walked away. Just like that, without a word, without a sign.

This was some kind of test, wasn't it?

A moment later, the drumming stopped. The silence throbbed in my ears, a memory of noise that would take hours to fade. I sank to the floor, lay down, pressed a flushed cheek to the cool stone. Only felt a faint and distant itching from the pervasive trace of silver. Pressed my arm over my head to try to still the throbbing.

So, I'd been kidnapped. Apparently for the express purpose of driving me crazy. Really, that didn't bother me so much.

But what happened if my captors really did manage to drive me crazy—that worried me.

ANYTIME THEY approached, their footsteps began to sound like thunder. I had nothing else to listen for, so when I heard them, they broke through my muddled awareness, sending shocks along my nerves. My now-constant headache throbbed with every hint of noise. I jerked into a crouch and watched the door, glaring at it as if I could challenge it.

The woman, the were-lion who'd brought the water, returned, her steps soft and hesitating. She stopped outside the door and I clamped my mouth shut, to keep from shouting. I wanted to wait to see what she would do. As ridiculous as it seemed, given our respective situations, I didn't want to scare her off by being belligerent. *More* belligerent. The bolt or latch or whatever it was on the panel clicked. The seam split open.

I bolted. Dived forward, hands out toward the gap

made by the open panel, reached through and made a grab. What did I have to lose?

My hand closed on a wrist. I held tight, squeezing. The limb was solid, not particularly dainty. The muscles and tendons flexing under my touch were strong. Bracing against the doorway, I pulled, trying to drag that arm in with me.

She grunted but didn't scream, and yanked away from my grasp; I held on. A tug-of-war ensued. Both of us braced against the door and pulled against the other.

I shouted through the door. "Please, just talk to me! What do you people want? Why are you doing this?"

My nails dug into her skin in an effort to hold on. She scrabbled, kicking against the door and the stone; her voice wheezed with her panting breath as she struggled. She was gaining on me. My reach through the door was past my elbow. My fingers cramped. The sweat breaking out on her skin made her slippery.

"Just say something, please," I begged, my voice squeaking into a higher pitch, tightened by desperation. I just wanted one word.

She won the tug-of-war, her sweat-dampened skin sliding out of my grasp. I shouted a growl, a jagged noise containing all my frustration over the last however many hours. Or days. I kept my hand through the slot in the door, waving, grappling, my fingers hooked like claws. I must have looked like a wild animal.

I expected her to run in a panic, but I heard no footsteps. Her breath came in pants. She was still here, out of reach, watching me. I took a deeper breath and settled, stilling my voice, my body. But I kept my arm outstretched, reaching toward the outside with some kind of hope.

We might have stayed like that for long minutes. I didn't dare pull my arm back in, no matter that she could have stabbed it or cut it off or anything while I held it out to her. This was the farthest I'd gotten in trying to get out of this hole they'd trapped me in. As soon as I pulled my arm back, she'd close the panel over the opening, and I'd be stuck again. I just wanted to hear a word, a single word, a shout or a curse, anything. I didn't want to be the inhuman thing in a cage, not even worth a shred of sunlight. If she would just talk to me . . .

Something touched my fingers. I lay as close to the floor as I could, pressing up to the opening trying to see out of it and into the darkness. I couldn't see her, only her arm, edging into my vision as she nudged an object into my hand. Instinctively, I clutched at it. Plastic crinkled. A cellophane wrapper. At least it wasn't a grenade. I'd kind of wondered. I took a deep breath, trying to smell it—food, it smelled like food. All this struggle over feeding time. Could this get any more ridiculous?

She ducked away, out of my line of sight, and waited. The impasse was well and truly complete—I didn't want to pull my hand in, because she would close the panel. But I wanted to see what she'd given me. She clearly wasn't going to say anything. Since she didn't so much as swear at me when I was clawing at her arm, she wasn't going to speak now. Even with the panel open, I couldn't escape. She could walk away, and I'd still be here, sprawled out on the floor, choking on dusty air, sweaty, chilled, exhausted.

I didn't want to give up. Pulling my hand inside felt like giving up. So did continuing to lie here, exposed and helpless.

"Why won't you people just *talk* to me?" I didn't like the way my voice came out rough, like a growl.

Nothing. Something—fear, power, purpose, whatever—was driving her patience. Me, I wanted to pace, faster and faster, until I could wear a hole in the stone and maybe escape that way. Wasn't going to happen, but that didn't stop the restless burning in my muscles. If I couldn't pace, I wanted to punch something. If I couldn't punch something, I wanted to scream. I wanted to do them all at once. Any of that would show them I was weak, so I didn't. Instead, I gave up. Just this battle.

I pulled my hand back inside.

The plastic-wrapped object she'd given me was a sandwich. The prewrapped deli kind from the supermarket. It even had a label that I couldn't quite make out in the dark. Shit, these people probably shopped at Safeway. Pulling back the packaging, I got a better smell of it—turkey and swiss on whole wheat. All that for a cheap fucking deli sandwich.

A thump and a click, and my "visitor" closed and latched the panel back in place. I was shut in, again. As bids for freedom went, this one had been awfully lame.

I rubbed a hand over my face as tears fell. Just a few, burning on my cheeks. My next breath shuddered. Then I was calm again. I held it together, somehow.

Bringing my hand to my face, I smelled her feline scent. Sensing deeper than that, I tried to find the person underneath. Female, with the ripe undertone of someone living in close quarters for a long time. She wasn't filthy, but she was probably longing for a shower. Sweat, mustiness. A jumbled scent of others, male and female. The wolf I'd smelled before, the chill of the vampire I thought I'd sensed. Whoever they were, they'd been together long enough for their scents to blend, as if they'd become a pack. An eclectic pack, but still.

Her scent reminded me of the werewolf army veterans I'd met, when they were at their worst: beaten down by trauma, at the edge of giving up. This group had been on some kind of campaign for a long time, and they were tired. But they must have also been incredibly determined, to go through all this. To capture me, to keep me here.

I didn't smell Tom on her. The only werewolves I smelled on her were me and the male we'd scented in the forest. I let myself believe that they hadn't captured Tom as well. That gave me hope.

One of my nails had a fleck of blood underneath it; I'd broken her skin. Despite being lycanthropes, my captors must not have been too worried about all the silver in the environment. Or maybe they were. Maybe she'd rushed off to get a bandage. Not that it mattered; a wound that small would have healed already.

I set the sandwich aside with the bottle of water. After a day without food I should have been starving. Mostly, though, I was numb. I couldn't feel anything at all.

Chapter 7

I DISCOVERED, GRATEFULLY, that my little pocket cave sloped slightly downward, away from the door. When I finally gave in and had to relieve myself, I went to the farthest end to do it. The urine pooled there and didn't trickle back to where I was spending my time. Small favors. My jeans around my knees, I'd contorted myself into a crouch, thinking how much simpler this would be as Wolf. If I could just Change, squat to piss, howl at a moon I couldn't see . . .

After pulling my jeans and panties back up, feeling gross and wishing for home, I curled up on the ground, back toward the door, and tried to think. If she wouldn't make a sound while I was digging nails into her arm, how could I get her to talk to me?

Just to be doing something, I started pounding on the door again. "Somebody better come let me out or talk to me or I'm gonna start singing show tunes!" I didn't really know many show tunes, it was just the worst thing I could think of right at the moment. A sad state of affairs.

That only lasted a couple of minutes. My voice was still hoarse from the last round of shouting. Nothing had changed. Not the light, not the smells, not the sounds coming from outside. Except that my prison now smelled like an unflushed toilet. My headache was worse. I curled up on the floor and wrapped my arms around my head, because that seemed to still the pounding in my temples.

If they hadn't taken Tom, then the cavalry was on its way. I held on to that thread, slender as it was. My captors weren't going to kill me, they had no reason to kill me. I just had to hang on.

Somehow, I slept again.

THE TURKEY sandwich was rotting, slowly. It was still good, would still be good for a few more hours, and even then my lycanthropic immune system could handle just about any fun bacteria growing on it. Wolves were fond of carrion, after all. The ripe sandwich and old urine became part of the background odor of the place, and I tried to ignore them. I still wasn't hungry.

But that changed when they offered me something other than an aging sandwich.

A sudden new scent of fresh blood cut through it all and fired my hindbrain, bringing me fully awake. Steaming, rich blood. I could taste it on the back of my tongue. My nerves fired with the imagined flavor. God, I wanted to hunt. Run, break out of here and make my way to open sky, track my prey, rip into it. Flesh shredding, organs bursting within my powerful jaws—

The scent of blood awoke memories, dozens of memories, dozens of hunts in which I'd feasted. Wolf lived for the hunt; it was what we were made for.

The walls of my cage seemed to grow smaller. My imagination, surely. Unless my captors had found some way to move the stone. Maybe they had. Maybe this wasn't a mine at all, but a room, and they were closing the walls on me. Anything was possible. My captors, my enemies, my prey, if I could only find my way out of this cage, I would tear into them all, devour them. I licked my teeth and snarled. I could almost taste them.

Dizziness turned my vision soft, wavering. Might have been hunger, might have been fury.

The smell grew thicker, bloodier. Steaming, the blood rushed from a still-beating heart. I took another long, testing breath. The male wolf was there,

in human form, invading the tiny territory I considered mine even if I couldn't defend it. He had blood
on his hands as well as the fur of prey—rabbit, he'd
slaughtered a rabbit right outside the door. Finally,
my stomach rumbled; I was *starving*. I gagged at the
thought of pouring that blood down my throat. I
needed it . . .

No no no, they were doing this to me on purpose,
this was another manipulation. I should have eaten that
sandwich, just to take the edge off, so I could think
about something other than filling the hollowness in
my belly.

The panel in the door slapped open. I jumped back,
startled, but then lay flat and pressed myself close, to
try to see out. The slight slope to the ground meant a
rivulet of blood ran through the opening toward me.
A thin stream of cooling blood that picked up dirt
and grit as it went. It might even have contained tiny
flecks of silver. It hardly mattered.

I stopped the trail of blood with my finger, let the
thick stuff collect on my hand. Took a good long sniff
of it—I would have smelled it, if it had been poison.
But it didn't smell like poison, it smelled *so good*. I
licked my hand, my tongue spreading to take in every
drop. The taste flared through my nerves. Even after
that trickle was gone, I licked my hand again, tasting
the memory of it. So sharp, perfect, intoxicating.

The man, the wolf, was still there, right outside the

door, holding the slaughtered rabbit. So close, I could just take it. I resisted reaching through the opening to grab the meat from him. That would have made me far too vulnerable; it would have meant entering the territory that he controlled and leaving my own. Had to guard my own small space.

But I wanted to kill. I wanted that meat.

A wet thud slapped the stone as the dead rabbit fell outside the door. Just out of my reach. I could stretch my arm and brush the fluff of its fur but not take hold. They were teasing me. They could, because I was in the cage. Because I had no way out, and I was helpless.

No, let me out, not helpless at all, let me fight—

The bars of a cage inside my gut snapped, shattered to dust. Wolf was free now. She howls, and the piercing sound breaks from my own throat. Her claws slash at the inside of my skin.

I double over, hugging myself, groaning. No, please, not this, I can't shift, I have to keep it together, stay in control. How can I stand up to them if I can't keep myself together?

Finally, it's over. I scream, and all the rage that's been building rips out of me in a throat-splitting howl. Reflexively, I pull off my shirt and sweater, shoving my jeans off in a panicked, violent seizure. Have to get free. The howl just keeps going, a lungful's worth that doesn't stop until I tear out of my own body—

* * *

There is a tiny opening to her cage, and if she fights hard enough, she can break free. She snarls, spit flying. Digs her snout and paws through the opening. Almost fits her whole head through. Almost. Her body flops, back claws scrabbling against rock, trying to push herself out. A male stands outside—an enemy. She can almost see him.

Almost almost almost. She can't do anything. The snarls turn to howls. The sound echoes against rock. The wood of the door bites into her skin, and she can smell the silver in the rock pressing toward her.

A voice from her gut speaks: Calm down. Please be calm. This isn't helping.

She's furious, but the other half of her being pleads. The weaker, two-legged half. This territory is strange, the situation is strange. She doesn't know what to do, so she listens to the calming voice. Backs away from the opening, shaking out splinters caught in her fur.

She lies on the ground, looking out to the dim light. The man is there, the other werewolf. Standing, watching. If she could see his eyes she would challenge him, but she can't. If she could leap at him, she would tear out his throat. She pants, her tongue hanging from her mouth. Blood still stains the ground.

When the man moves, taking a step back, she perks her ears. Tries to guess what will happen next.

Calm.

He kicks the dead rabbit through the hole in the door, right in front of her. She jumps back, stares. Her mind tumbles. It has to be a trick. It doesn't smell like a trick. A soft whine, in the back of her throat. Her other half is silent.

Blood wins out over all.

She eats the carcass, kneading it with jaws and teeth. The blood and flesh sings through her. She forgets about all but the blood and flesh.

Soon it's gone, all of it but a few scraps of fur and bone. Her awareness has collapsed to the space of her own body. She paces, yawns. Wonders where the light is, there should be light, there should be a moon.

Her mate should be here. But no, not in the cage. He's safe, and that's good. But she longs for him, to feel him curled beside her, breathing into the ruff of her neck. The meat feels heavy in her gut. She doesn't want to sleep, but she doesn't have a choice. The walls hold silver. She cringes away from them, curls up in the middle of the floor, her muscles taut. It's all so wrong.

She dreams of running.

I'D BEEN moved. The smells I woke to were different, slightly. While I still smelled the musty damp of underground, the dust and rock of the tunnels, the air had opened up. I wasn't breathing my own waste anymore. A glow pressed against my closed eyelids.

Starting awake, I saw a rocky room with a half a dozen small, battery-run camp lanterns resting on the floor around the edges. I squeezed my eyes shut, rubbed them, opened them again and reveled in the feeling of being able to see something, anything, clearly. This wasn't a cave so much as a junction, a place where two tunnels came together. I was still in the mine; the pale granite walls were even, blasted out by dynamite and hammers. The lamps didn't give much light, and the arcing ceiling was dark, the jagged surface forming weird shadows.

I wanted to believe I was dreaming. But no, I wasn't, because I was naked, and the cold grit of the cave floor bit into my skin. I checked myself for cuts, open wounds. Nothing that I could tell. I was alive, so the silver hadn't gotten to me yet. But I could still sense it, in the itching on my spine.

While propping myself on an elbow, I stayed low, curling up, sheltering myself as best I could. I didn't know where my clothes were. I didn't know where I was in relation to the cave I'd been in before. I looked around for an exit, for a hint of sunlight. Didn't see anything. Two tunnels leading out, that was it.

Four people stood on the far side of the space, maybe twenty feet away. Two women, two men, one of whom was old, decrepit. My nose flared, taking in their scents. I sneezed. Too much to process all at once.

While I'd slept off my Wolf, they'd brought me here so they could have a look at me. No—I realized what had really happened. The rabbit, and being out of that cage, were a reward. Finally, I knew what they wanted from me. They wanted my Wolf.

Chapter 8

I HARDLY DARED move, not knowing what would happen when I did. Not really wanting to know. I stayed calm, kept my breathing steady. I wasn't in a strong position here; I couldn't rip out all their throats at once, however much I wanted to. I stayed low to the floor, crouched protectively, and stared. Finally, I had a good look at my captors.

They were not what I expected, especially in the Gothic atmosphere of the cavern. They were startlingly . . . normal. Standing to my left against the far wall was the woman, the were-lion who'd brought me the water and sandwich. She was muscular and beautiful, with silky black hair knotted into a braid, sharp features, and bronzed skin. Middle Eastern, maybe. She made me think of deserts. Her clothing was simple, casual—a knit tank top and peasant skirt that had seen a lot of washing. She went barefoot. Her expression was neutral—not giving any sort of reply to my challenge.

Next to her stood a powerfully built man—the wolf, the one who'd taunted me and driven me to shift. He wore jeans, boots, and went shirtless, showing off an impressively sculpted chest. He worked out. I thought he might have been Indian, deep brown skin, a round face. A frown to bring down mountains. His dark gaze matched my own. He'd accept any challenge I gave him. Wolf didn't like him.

To my right stood the other woman, and she was human, but her scent was so mixed up with the others she came across as something in between, neither one nor the other. Average height and build, hollow cheeks and tired eyes. Not getting enough sleep or food. Pale, with dirty blond hair tied back in a ponytail. She wore a tunic-type shirt over jeans, and three or four pendants on leather cords around her neck. Not pendants—amulets, cast in metal or made of twisted wire. A pentacle, a Thor's hammer, a couple of others I didn't recognize but were clearly symbolic of something. She was probably some kind of magician. Her hands were clenched at her sides, and her breathing was fast—she was scared. She wouldn't meet my gaze.

Then came the fourth one, the ancient one, standing effectively in the middle. My nose flared at his smell, which was cold, corpselike, preserved. He was the vampire, but unlike any vampire I'd ever met. He wasn't pretty, well dressed, or haughty. Calculating, yes, with his stony gaze and iron demeanor. Powerful, I didn't doubt. But his skin was gray, wrinkled, like paper left out in the weather. Bald, he wore a shapeless shirt and drawstring pants that made me think of hospital scrubs. He might have been ancient, or he might have simply been through hell and lived— sort of—to tell the tale. He also wore some kind of amulet around his neck, but it was too small for me to make out. If the vampire was up and about, night must have fallen. Which night, I still didn't know.

Here they were, the international werewolf kidnapping squad. What an eclectic, unlikely group of people. My curiosity about them and how they'd come to be working together almost won out over my extreme annoyance and my deeply buried fear. I wanted to make some jab, some clever and pointed remark. Something that would give me a tiny bit of dominance, however small. But my voice was stuck, my tongue dry and thick. Wolf still stared out of my eyes; I wasn't fully human yet, and the words wouldn't come. My arguments were building in my throat and would come out as a howl if I couldn't get them out as words. My lips opened, baring my teeth. All I had was Wolf's body language.

I was naked, exposed, weak, and I hated it. If I just ran, I wondered how far I would get.

The vampire took a step forward and drew a breath to speak. I held my ground—what little ground I had. Stared at him, without meeting his gaze. I had to stay out of his power. I wondered if he'd enslaved the others somehow, or if they were here voluntarily. This was the first time I'd really thought of a vampire as *ancient*. My usual, traditional first question for vampires—how old are you, really?—died. It seemed pointless here. Irrelevant. Knowing the answer wouldn't get me out of here.

"We gather from the far corners of the world on a dire quest. Finally, we can strike the blow that I have been preparing against the enemy for centuries . . ."

If I expected an explanation or an apology—something straightforward and rational, in other words—I was disappointed. The answer to who would want to kidnap me: crazy cult. I still didn't have any idea what *kind* of crazy cult it was. And I still had no idea what they intended to do with me, or what I'd have to do to get out.

The vampire continued intoning his story, chanting a practiced speech. He had an accent, but it was light, clipped, hard to place. He spread his arms to me, a patriarch welcoming a child into the fold.

"You—you are the heir to a great spirit, to the

mother wolf who nurtured an empire, whose statue stood in the Forum for centuries, a symbol of such untold strength and loyalty—"

"What?" I croaked, finally able to make my throat work. I didn't know whether to lurch to my feet or fall over entirely, so I just sat there. "You mean like the *Capitoline Wolf*?"

I might have handed him a birthday cake, the way his face lit up. He smiled, a hideous expression on his cracked face and thin lips. "You understand. The fates are with us." He tipped his head back, as if beseeching the heavens in prayer. "You are our Regina Luporum. You truly are ready to join us."

Huh?

My laugh came out as a hiccup. Then the dam burst, and I doubled over, pressing my face to my arm, trying to stop the hysterics. Really, it was too much. I was laughing so hard, I thought I was going to throw up. That would have been cute.

The vampire blinked at me, nonplussed. The others were looking back and forth among themselves, obviously confused. But what had they expected?

"I'm sorry," I managed to gasp. "That probably wasn't the reaction you were looking for. But actually I'm not sorry." Now it was the gobsmacked looks on their faces making me laugh. On the one hand this was all spooky and terrifying, with dim lamps and dark caves and monsters and blood. On the other hand . . . Yeah, what else could I do but laugh?

"You are Regina Luporum," the vampire declared.

I hiccupped again. My stomach hurt. "You're not serious," I managed to gasp. That was a joke, it had always been just a joke.

"We've brought you here to fulfill your role. Your fate," he said.

"Who the hell are you people?" I asked.

"Your destiny," said the vampire, in a tone that suggested he thought this was obvious.

I stared. Sudden gooseflesh covered my skin, even though the temperature wasn't that cold. The cave was insulating. But I was naked and vulnerable. I did have a clearer idea of who my enemy was, though: fanatics, of unknown origin and purpose. Small comfort that they seemed to need me for something *not* involving blood sacrifice and death. I couldn't shove my mind past the *crazy* part.

"I don't understand," I said, fiercely as I could manage. Wolf was present, glaring out in challenge. My teeth were bared. That didn't seem to make a difference. They were all very good at maintaining neutral expressions. They had a plan, and so far I hadn't done anything to disrupt it.

"You will," the vampire said, turning a cracked and ominous smile.

"Like hell," I muttered. If they wanted to keep me here, they'd have to work for it.

Likely, one of the openings in the cave led out, and one didn't. Fifty-fifty chance. I looked at them both, trying not to give away that I was looking, and made a plan. Neither exit had an obvious slope, up or down. The whole place was flat, so that didn't help. The two lycanthropes stood near the left-hand tunnel, which meant my chances of reaching it before they stopped me were slim. I might be able to fight them both off, but I didn't want to bet my freedom on it. On my right, the human magician stood. Her, I could flat outrun. Of course, the vampire would probably be able to stop me no matter what. Unless, just maybe, his ancient, wizened appearance meant that his strength and re-flexes had also decayed. I could hope.

I couldn't prepare, I could only *go*.

I launched, running as I stood, stumbling forward and letting gravity do the work. Still cramped and woozy after shifting just a few hours ago, I hadn't had a chance to stretch and unkink my muscles. Couldn't think about it. Just aimed myself at the tun-nel and ran. Didn't look behind me, only saw my cap-tors' reactions out of the corner of my eye. Appearing startled and determined, they came after me. I had to be faster.

And hope this was the tunnel that would take me out of the mine.

Leaving the wider space, I escaped into darkness, under an arcing passage of stone. Two parallel steel lines imbedded in the tunnel floor formed a pathway— rails of a former oar cart system. The tracks glittered, covered with a patina of rust and crystallized minerals, running through the previous chamber as well. They gave me a path to follow.

The ceiling became lower and cut into my speed. I suddenly wished I was Wolf, able to cover this ground in seconds. Then the tunnel began to slope— downward. A bad sign, but I was committed. Maybe it only sloped down a little way before sloping back up. Please . . .

The tunnel opened into a chamber, roughly round and lit by another of those battery camp lanterns, giving off the palest glow, just enough light to be able to navigate by without crashing into the rough-cut walls.

I slid to a flailing stop in the middle of the room, looking around, desperate for an exit that wasn't there. It was a dead end. Fifty-fifty chance, and I picked wrong.

Trapped and panting for breath, I noticed the markings on the floor. Dark lines and curves drawn in precise patterns, symbols placed at regular intervals. I could just make out more symbols on the walls, and amulets of metal, bone, and wood secured in place, corresponding to the marks on the floor. I stepped softly, following the track of the pattern, tracing with my gaze until the whole of it became clear—a five-pointed star inside a circle, about fifteen feet across. Traditional European arcane symbolism. This was a magician's ritual space.

Maybe I'd spoken too soon about the sacrifices.

Footsteps pounded into the room after me, the four of them fanning across the entrance to block my escape. I was trapped. But I stood my ground, staring back at them. Not ducking a millimeter in the face of their challenge.

The white woman, the magician, drew up the rifle-looking gun she'd been holding hidden by her leg, and fired. I turned, an instinctive move to protect myself rather than an attempt at escape, which would have been futile.

A familiar punch and sting hit my shoulder. Snarling, I yanked out the tranquilizer and threw it away. Too late, it had already delivered its dose, and the tingling spread through my chest and arms. Stumbling, I retreated to the back wall. Started to press myself against it, but itching stopped me. There was silver here, just as there was silver everywhere.

The magician loaded another tranquilizer dart and fired again. Woozy now, I was more concerned with getting away from the wall than with dodging the shot, which suddenly seemed like a distant thing. On the ground, I was aware of flopping like a fish, scraping my skin. Then I couldn't move at all, and they were all there, looking down at me. I couldn't read their expressions, however much I wanted to see anger, regret, annoyance, sadness, anything.

I faded out altogether, still confused, unable to figure out how to solve this riddle.

I EXPECTED to wake up back in the cell, the cubbyhole where they'd first put me. I hoped they'd put me there, because my clothes were there. They wanted my Wolf, which meant they wanted me naked, and I was sick of being naked. But the pervasive light and open space meant I was back in the tunnel, the antechamber to the ritual space. And still naked. The grit of the floor dug into the skin of my thigh, shoulder, arm, cheek. I smelled of earth, like I'd been buried.

The vampire was speaking. Intoning, rather, in the formal diction of a poet or a storyteller, like he had before, but this time he recited from a story.

"May the Roads of Enkidu to the Cedar Forest mourn you and not fall silent night or day. May the Elders of the broad city of Uruk-Haven mourn you. May the peoples who gave up their blessings after us mourn you. May the rivers of silt and waterfowl mourn you, may the pasture lands mourn you . . . May the bear, hyena, panther, tiger, water buffalo, jackal, lion, wild bull, stag, ibex, all the creatures of the plains mourn you . . ."

The others stood around him, their heads bent in prayer. This was like being in a church service, but for a religion I'd never encountered. I should have been praying along out of politeness, but I was too baffled. I remained still, quiet, hoping they didn't notice that I'd woken up.

"I mourn for Enkidu, my friend . . . the swift mule, fleet wild ass of the mountain, panther of the wilderness . . ."

I couldn't tell how much time had passed since they knocked me out. It must have been the same night, if the vampire was still here. I might have been out for a few minutes, a few hours. It might have all been a part of a dream. Why was he reciting from the *Epic of Gilgamesh*? This had to be a dream.

The vampire continued, "Enkidu, the first beast, wild man of the hills who guides all who come after. The greatest warrior, the greatest friend. We remember, we tell the tale, how great Gilgamesh tracked the wild man through the hills. Gilgamesh, king of men, challenged the king of beasts to battle, to see which of them would rule all, for they were evenly matched and only battle would decide. But Enkidu could see the prowess and dignity of the other, and so yielded his claim to any crown of man or beast.

Willingly, Enkidu followed Gilgamesh and became his guard."

I knew this story, but I'd never heard a version of it like this. In the original Sumerian version, Gilgamesh and Enkidu became friends. One didn't serve the other. Enkidu was on my list of possible werewolves. Another possible hero for me.

If I hadn't been a captive audience, not to mention naked, I'd have been fascinated by the way the vampire's voice echoed in the tunnel, and the way he changed the story to suit whatever arcane purpose he had in mind. Instead of being fascinated, though, my dread built.

"Gladly, Enkidu gave his life to save Gilgamesh, taking into himself the weapon meant for the other. Gilgamesh could not be spared, but Enkidu knew his sacrifice would be celebrated—"

"No," I said. I couldn't take it anymore. So much for them not noticing I'd woken up. They probably started this because I'd woken up. It was about *me*. And here I was thinking this couldn't get any crazier. "That's not right, that isn't how the story goes. Enkidu knew their quest had gone too far, that they were in trouble, but Gilgamesh wouldn't listen to him. Enkidu died cursing Gilgamesh, and nothing Gilgamesh did overcame his grief at losing his best friend—"

"We honor Enkidu's sacrifice," the vampire said, glaring at me, because who was I to say his version wasn't right? Maybe he'd been there. Or maybe it was just a story.

But this wasn't right. The story of Gilgamesh was about hubris. The point of the vampire's retelling seemed to be that all powers, even the wildest, will bend toward a righteous goal—a righteous leader. That we must defer to the leader. Him.

The vampire spread his arms, encompassing the others in a fatherly gesture. His tone changed, becoming commanding, decisive. Story over, on to phase two. "You—do you stand witness for Enkidu?" the vampire said.

The werewolf answered, "I stand witness for Enkidu."

"Do you stand witness for Sakhmet?"

"I stand witness for Sakhmet," said the were-lion.

"Do you stand witness for Zoroaster?"

"I stand witness for Zoroaster," said the magician.

Then the vampire looked across the cave at me. "Do you stand witness for Regina Luporum?"

I didn't say anything.

Impatient, he repeated, "Do you stand witness for Regina Luporum?"

"That's not even a real story. It's something Marid made up." And Marid was twenty-eight hundred years old. How old did a story have to be before it was "real"?

"What is your answer?"

"You call me Regina Luporum, you say I'm some

kind of queen. Is *this* how you treat a queen?" I gestured to myself, naked and grubby, hungry and thirsty, woozy from the drugs they'd pumped into me.

Appearing anxious, the werewolf stepped forward. His jaw was taut, and his eyes held a desperate blaze. He glanced at the vampire, as if asking permission or looking for a reaction. When the vampire remained still, silent, the werewolf spoke.

"We had to break through to your wolf side. Your primal self. Your *true* self."

"You think this is it, do you? Well, fuck you."

Could have heard a pin drop, as they say. I wasn't sure what response they expected from me, but verbal rage obviously wasn't it. Which meant they probably didn't listen to my show. Oh well.

"You people have to let me go. I don't belong here. Please," I said, because surely it couldn't hurt.

"But we need you," the were-lion said. Like the wolf, she had a desperation to her that disturbed me.

The werewolf took hold of her hand, squeezed, and she settled. The two of them had never moved more than a handbreadth apart, not since I'd been watching.

"Then tell me what you need me *for*," I said.

"To play your part," the vampire said. He moved closer, staring. He was trying to catch my gaze, but I knew better than to be caught. I focused on his leathery neck, or on the others, pleading with them, as if I could beg them to help me. As if they'd go against the leader.

"I can't play my part if you won't tell me what it is. What's your plan—blood sacrifice? You going to gut me over your circle in there and read my entrails?" That sounded plausible enough to make my breath catch. I glared to hide my fear.

"Oh, no," he said, smiling. "We need your *life*."

And what did that mean?

He continued in a steady voice that was probably meant to be calming but instead came off as condescending. "We can't reveal meaning to you. You have to *understand*. Listen to your instincts."

My instincts were telling me to wrap my jaws around his throat and rip into him with Wolf's fangs. I had to clamp down on a sudden roiling in my gut, as Wolf stirred and tested the bars of her cage. We were already naked, it would just take a tiny push to set her free . . . I continued breathing calmly, locking that cage as tightly as I could, keeping Wolf still. I didn't want to shift again and lose control of what I could say.

The vampire's lips pressed in a thin smile, as if he knew what I was thinking. He knew what buttons to push. He was thinking he could bring out another dead rabbit and trip my circuit, forcing me to Change. I couldn't let that happen.

Instead of starting another bloodbath, he came to

within a few paces of me, just out of reach, and crouched, bringing himself to my eye level.

"You *will* understand," he said, his expression full of sympathy and righteousness.

But I hardly heard the words. Up close, I got a better look at the amulet around his neck: a coin on a leather cord, ancient and bronze. A Roman coin. The image had been defaced, mangled by hatch marks, smashed and misshapen.

A coin of Dux Bellorum, defaced. Which made him one of the good guys. Didn't it?

"Where did you get that?" I whispered. I leaned in, resisting an urge to reach out and touch it. Maybe it was something different. It only looked like a Roman coin and would turn out to be plastic or wood. It was just old, not defaced.

Confused, the vampire tilted his head. I had interrupted his speech. He didn't seem to know what to say next, and regarded me as if I had sprouted wings. He had probably expected me to be awed by him, and afraid.

"I know where you got that," I continued. "You got it from Dux Bellorum."

His eyes widened in shock, anger, something. He wrapped a hand around the coin and backed away from me.

I wasn't sure what reaction I'd been expecting. I had hoped—optimistically, it turned out—that he would tell me about Roman, about how he knew the other vampire, how he'd acquired the coin, what he knew about its power. I wanted to have a goddamned conversation.

I pressed on. "You know him—you've met him. Where? How? You got away from him. You wouldn't have marked it up like that otherwise. I've met Roman, I've faced him myself. What can you tell me—"

Grimacing, he stood in a rush and marched out. He took the tunnel to my left—the *correct* one. I wondered where he was going. No, I actually didn't much care what the guy did. But I'd pissed him off. That was good. Nice to know he had a weak spot I could leverage.

The blond woman, the magician, gave me a shocked look, then ran after the vampire. Leaving the two lycanthropes staring at me. They were holding hands, almost bracing against each other.

Them, I matched gazes with. Straight on, full of challenge. I might have been sprawled on the floor naked, but I was better than this and I let them know it.

"Gosh," I said flatly. "What did I say?"

Of all the wonders, the werewolf smiled.

"You do understand," he said. "You do know what we're battling." He said this with awe and hope. The woman raised his hand to her mouth and kissed it. I might have just handed them the map to buried treasure, the way they acted.

I suddenly wanted to take a nap. Another one, hard rock for a mattress or not. The fuzz in my head had become too thick to muddle through. But I tried.

"This is all about fighting Roman? You maybe think if you let me in on the secret I might actually be able to *help*?"

"It's—it's more complicated than that."

Wasn't it always? "Let me go. Just let me go."

"We can't do that."

I growled in frustration. The pair turned and left the chamber as well, and I was alone. They hadn't left a guard, they hadn't chained me up. So I stood and ran after them—what was to stop me?

Answer: another door, a few feet down the tunnel, bolted into supports drilled into the rock. The whole place was compartmentalized; they could lock me up anywhere.

On principle, I screamed and banged on the door a few times. This one wasn't any less solid than the one to that first cell. But I didn't waste breath and energy lashing out any more than that.

I curled up on the ground next to the door, hugged myself, and waited.

TIME PASSED and the door opened, scraping against the stone floor. I started awake and wondered if I could grab the door, haul it the rest of the way, tackle whoever was on the other side, run hard, find my way out of the tunnels—

The door opened just a few inches, and it closed again quickly, just as soon as the were-lion shoved a bundle through. I could smell her, sense her moving quickly, but then she was gone again. I blinked, trying to figure out what had happened. My nose flared, smelling. She'd left a pile of clothing. My sweater, jeans, panties.

I wondered what the catch was.

Maybe she was being nice. Maybe I actually had an ally in this place. Or maybe this was a good cop/bad cop ploy. I'd put my trust in her—she kept giving me things, after all. Water, food, clothes. I was supposed to cling to her, and they'd use that trust to manipulate me into doing . . . whatever they were trying to do. Or maybe I was overthinking this.

I didn't much care what the ulterior motives were, I was putting my clothes on.

Chapter 9

I HAD LIGHT at this end of the tunnel. I had room to
move around. And I felt a million times better being dressed.

I went exploring.

The antechamber, more of an extrawide part of the
tunnel, didn't have much to it. It was small, the remnant
of mining activity. A vein of ore might have been dug
out, and this and the adjoining cave were what was
left. The old rails ran straight through, out the other
side. I couldn't guess how deep underground this was.
Air must have been coming in from somewhere, because I was still breathing. It smelled musty, like chalk
and silt, but not stale. The walls shimmered, and in
some places had rounded mounds of colored rock,
places where the water seeped through and deposited
minerals in strange colors, patterns, and pencil-thin

baby stalactites. I had no interest in touching the walls more than I had to, leery of the silver there.

I went down the short tunnel into the ritual chamber, picking up the lantern there to study the room and its details better.

In a panicked moment, I wondered if the circle and star on the floor had been drawn in blood. I didn't *smell* blood, but I was starting to not trust my senses. After kneeling and studying the markings, I saw they were black, thick, and opaque—ink or paint of some kind. Decisive, indelible. Dozens of symbols marked the floor and walls, their shapes and shadows bending strangely in the light as I brought the lantern close and moved it across. I recognized some of them in the most general sense—there were zodiac signs, Greek letters, Roman numerals, shapes that might have been Egyptian hieroglyphs, words in what I thought was Hebrew. I didn't know what any of it actually meant, except that they were Western in origin—Judeo-Christian, Greco-Roman. Medieval alchemical stuff. Whoever did this—the woman magician?—must have taken hours to draw it all.

Amelia would have known what all this meant. A pang of homesickness struck, along with gratitude that my friends weren't here and in danger. I could be rescued, or I could break out on my own. I didn't need to share the whole experience. I had a sudden, horrible thought: Tom wasn't here, they hadn't captured him.

But maybe they'd killed him instead, and that was why the cavalry hadn't come yet. Tears fell; I brushed them away. I'd get out of this, I would. Tom was fine, everyone was fine, everything was fine.

Continuing my circuit of the room, I found objects hanging from spikes driven into the walls at five places, corresponding with the points of the star on the floor. Amulets, talismans, whatever. They looked antique, with that worn and aged patina that very old items had. Again, I recognized some of them in the most general sense—a Maltese cross, an ankh. But I couldn't have said where they came from or what they meant, and if they meant anything in relation to each other.

I raised the lantern, trying to make out the cave's ceiling, but it was too high for the light to reach. A black depth, that was all.

This was a hodgepodge of symbols and ritual, from Europe and the Middle East. If I had to guess, I'd say this was all done by an overactive history student playing at magic. They'd stand around wearing black velveteen cloaks, speaking in pig latin. But the four of them had looked so deadly serious.

Having seen what real rituals, real power could do, I was not feeling good about what rituals they might be performing here. Especially since they seemed to think they needed me to continue whatever the hell it was they were doing.

The outer door scraped against the stone floor again. I thought of hiding, but where would I go?

I went back through the tunnel to the antechamber, faced the door, and waited. I still had the lantern in hand. Maybe I could use it as a weapon.

The werewolf and were-lion entered; I smelled them before I saw them. The door scraped again, shutting this time. Probably not locked. If I could overpower them both, I might have a way out. What were the odds? I set down the lantern.

They emerged from the tunnel into the chamber. We stared at each other. It was like none of us knew what to say.

"I don't suppose if I asked nicely you would let me go," I said finally. My voice scratched, my throat aching from all the shouting and dehydration. So much for sounding tough. At least with my clothes on I had an easier time standing tall and showing my dominance. Perceived dominance.

"It's daylight," the werewolf said, gesturing backward to some theoretical exit. "Kumarbis is asleep."

I didn't know what that was supposed to mean. Did that mean I could go? Would they really let me go? "Kumarbis—the vampire?" I asked.

The woman, the were-lion, nodded. "This is our chance to explain this to you—"

"About time," I muttered.

They moved forward, reaching to me—and I took

a step back. They looked like attackers, coming to finish me off at last.

"Please, don't be frightened," the were-lion said. Her voice was light, beautiful. If we were having coffee in a hip bistro I could have listened to her all day long. But we weren't. "We're not going to hurt you."

"I don't believe you," I said. I itched, I had to move, so I started pacing back and forth along the back wall of the chamber, my bare feet scraping on cool stone. Rapid steps, my hands opening and closing into fists.

The two of them moved closer together, flinching back from me. I must have looked pretty crazy. But I had to let Wolf bleed out a little, or I'd scream. So I paced.

"I'm sorry about this. We're both sorry," the man said. He had a crisp accent that I couldn't place. "Does that help?"

"Only if you let me go now."

"We can't do that."

"I didn't think so."

"If you'll stop, sit and be calm, I'll explain," he said. He sounded oh so rational. I didn't trust him, how could I? March six steps, turn, march six steps, glaring at them the whole time.

"Please," she said in that melodic voice.

Their body language shifted; they turned away from me, lowered their gazes—not showing submission, but not offering a challenge. Giving me room.

I slowed. *We have to run . . .*

Not yet, not when they were between us and the door. Finally, I stopped. "How the hell do you deal with all the *silver*?"

It had started to feel like bugs crawling on my skin. I kept looking over my shoulder and checking myself for open wounds. I couldn't tell what was paranoia and what I ought to be truly worried about.

The man said, "Most of the silver here isn't pure. It's ore, at a low purity, or it would have been taken out decades ago. The rock here won't hurt you, unless you eat it or rub it into an open wound."

Somehow, this was less comforting than it should have been. "I can still feel it."

"You just have to ignore it," he said.

So not helpful. "But *why*? Why put yourselves through this?" Why put *me* through this . . .

"Protection," he said. "It's a magical defense."

Against what? Was that supposed to make me feel better? My questions were starting to turn circular. "Okay. Fine. But what about . . . what did you do to Tom?" Their confused expressions made my stomach drop. "The other werewolf who was with me. My packmate, Tom."

The woman got it first and nodded. "We left him behind. We didn't hurt him, he's fine."

I wasn't sure I believed her, but what choice did I

have? "Okay. Now, explain the rest of it. What's going on here?"

They glanced at each other, a secret communication between two people on very familiar terms. They were together, I didn't have a doubt. That line about dogs and cats living together surfaced again, briefly. They made their silent bargain, drew their mental straws. The werewolf was the one who spoke.

"There's a great evil, a powerful adversary—"

"Let me guess: the vampire Gaius Albinus, known as Dux Bellorum or Roman."

He only showed the mildest shock. I'd already announced that I knew of the ambitious, globe-trotting vampire. He probably wouldn't believe how much I knew.

"Yes."

"And what does that vampire—Kumarbis—have to do with Dux Bellorum? What does any of this have to do with him? What's going on here?" I bet I could ask that question a hundred times and never get a straight answer.

The werewolf drew a breath and spoke slowly, as if searching for words. As if he'd never really had to explain this before. "Kumarbis has the knowledge to destroy Dux Bellorum. Zora has the power, the spell. But she needs five people to work her magic—the right five."

The right people, representing different aspects of
the supernatural. I'd spent enough time around this
sort of thing that it almost made sense.

I chuckled; it was the only way I had to insult them.
"You're probably thinking I should be flattered. You've
kidnapped me, humiliated me, but it's to save the
world so of course it's all right."

He raised his hand in a calming gesture and shook
his head. Was he actually blushing? Embarrassed? "I
wouldn't ask you to think that this is all right. I only
ask for your understanding—"

My voice shook with anger. "This is *not* how you
go about earning someone's understanding."

The were-lion jumped in. "Kumarbis believes if
you know too much before the time of the ritual, your
mind will close. You won't become a true avatar.
You must let the spirit of your predecessor fill you.
You can't force it."

"Avatar, what do you mean, avatar?"

"We're more than just the right people," the man
said. "We're avatars—representatives of the divine.
That's why Kumarbis needs us. It has to be us, the five
of us, and no one else."

Avatars of the divine, figures from very ancient
stories. There was a kind of power in that, I supposed.
Symbolic, if nothing else. This all felt like a terrible
joke.

"Do you really believe that?" I asked. "You can't

believe it, or you wouldn't be here explaining it to
me. Apologizing to me." Because that was what they
were doing, essentially.

They didn't answer.

If I was behind the microphone at my studio, and
I'd gotten a call during the show explaining this in as
serious a tone—I wasn't sure how I'd respond. It
would depend on my mood. I might have humored
him, picked at his explanation, pounced on details,
encouraged him to dig himself deeper. I might have
mocked him outright and then hung up on him. I
might have just felt sorry for him.

I wanted to pretend like I was hosting my show,
so I could rake them over the coals of my sarcasm.
But for all the time I'd spent unconscious over the
last day or so, I was too tired. Not to mention my life
was pretty much in their hands. Best not make them
too angry.

I sighed. "Can you at least tell me your names?"

The werewolf nodded. "I am Enkidu. She is
Sakhmet."

Oh, give me a . . . "That's what *he* called you—those
aren't really your names."

"They are now," he said. "We are their avatars. We
speak for them."

"And you are Regina Luporum," said the were-lion.

"I'm Kitty," I said. "I will always be Kitty. Kather-
ine Norville, Kitty."

"Kumarbis is hoping to convince you otherwise." His tone didn't invite doubt that Kumarbis would succeed.

"Kumarbis—is that his name, or is he supposed to be an avatar, too? I've never even *heard* of any Kumarbis—"

The werewolf hurried to explain. "Kumarbis is a god of the Hittites, a father-god, a source of power."

"I don't believe this," I muttered. "This is crazy."

"It isn't all crazy," said the werewolf, Enkidu. "I believe that Dux Bellorum is evil and means the world ill. And I believe Kumarbis and Zora have the power to defeat him, and that they need us to do so. Does anything else matter?"

A million other things mattered, but I was at a loss for words. I didn't know how to argue his beliefs, his dogma.

"Truly, we mean you no harm. Please believe that," said the woman. Sakhmet, I supposed I had to call her.

I curled my lip and growled.

"We'll let you rest now," she added. Her partner nodded, and together they turned back to the doorway. Too late, I realized this was my chance, and it was vanishing. I ran, head down and legs working, carrying me across the room and to the door in seconds. But they were lycanthropes, too, and they were ready. And not drugged, sleep deprived, dehydrated, and nervous. They slipped out and shut the door behind them, just as I crashed into it.

Wouldn't do me any good, but I pounded on the wood and screamed after them anyway. Wordless shouts of denial. Probably a lot of curse words, or maybe just a lot of noise. Then I sank to the floor, curling up on myself, my forehead resting against the wood, because I was getting really tired of this.

I hugged myself, grateful to have my sweater back. Like I could burrow up inside of it and have some bit of comfort. If I buried my nose in the fibers and took a deep breath, I imagined I could smell a hint of home, and Ben. Which somehow made the situation worse, because I couldn't think of a way to get out of this. Except to stay close to the door and wait for my chance to fight my way out.

Chapter 10

AFTER THAT, I started telling myself stories.

The research I'd been doing for my book, all the stories I'd been reading and analyzing, flooded out of my hindbrain and to the front of my memory. The *Epic of Gilgamesh* was one of my favorites. *Not* Kumarbis's version. The ancient Sumerian tale is famous for being one of the first articulate, literary, and, most important, *recorded* stories in human civilization. Like most of the stories coming out of the first 90 percent of human civilization, this one's about a mighty king who is part divine and can do no wrong. Except he's also arrogant and oppressive, and the gods decide to create another person who will be a match for him and take him down a peg: Enkidu.

Enkidu was the reason this was one of my favorite

stories. He was a wild man who lived in the mountains, clothed in fur like one of the beasts, drinking with them at the water holes, and generally representing all that was natural and uncivilized about humanity. He also had a habit of rescuing animals and sabotaging hunters' traps, so one of the hunters brought a temple prostitute into the mountains to seduce Enkidu and lure him into civilization. That's right—sex soothed the savage beast. She also taught him about language and clothing, and brought him to the city, hoping that he could stop Gilgamesh's dominance. As expected, Gilgamesh and Enkidu fought, and then, seeing in the other a true equal, became fast friends. Maybe even lovers, depending on the interpretation you agreed with. They went off and had many fine adventures, battling monsters, hunting for treasure, angering the gods, all that good stuff.

The *Epic of Gilgamesh* does not end well. Another common trait of epics. There's a price for all that glory, and it's usually loss. Heartbreaking, unendurable loss. Enkidu dies a slow, terrible death, not in battle, but by the whim of the gods. Gilgamesh is inconsolable. I wonder if this says something about civilization in opposition to humanity's wild roots: the wild cannot survive. If I were to take the analysis further, from a purely literary, symbolic standpoint, I'd say that lycanthropy isn't a curse—it's a reminder of what humanity used to be. Of what we lost. We used to be able to talk to wolves. And now we fear them as monsters or worship them as paragons.

Enkidu's strength came from the opposite source of Gilgamesh's strength—one was wild and the other was a king, one preferred mountains and the other preferred cities. But the world needed both to be in balance. Together, they were unstoppable. The metaphor was appealing to a werewolf like me.

Enkidu, if he had been a real person, must have been a Rex Luporum.

My friend TJ—one of the first werewolves I ever met, one of the ones who found me after the attack that infected me and helped bring me into the Denver pack, the one who held me and comforted me during my first full-moon night of Change—used to tell me that lycanthropy could be a strength, if I knew how to use it. If I accepted and controlled it rather than fought against it. This was hard to remember sometimes when I thought of all I had lost because of being a werewolf. When the full moon approached and blood lust rose up in me and I wanted to rip off my clothes, howl at the sky, and flee into wilderness, never to return. But I had gained so much by being a werewolf. My career, my life, my friends. My husband. It could be a strength. Wolves weren't monsters—they were hunters, careful and intelligent. They stalked with great patience, and defended their packs with ferocity. That was the strength I chose. Enkidu's strength. Enkidu, both man and beast, the first such being to cross from the wilderness and choose civilization over the wild. He did it, the stories said, for love. Or at least lust. Translations could be tricky sometimes. He was one of the characters from myth and legend I classified as maybe a werewolf, and I looked up to him.

Now I thought how *dare* this man, this kidnapper, call himself Enkidu. What did he know about the ancient hero? What made him think he could claim such a legacy for himself?

I fell asleep again. Sleep was easier, so while my mind was a shivering wreck, my body took over, and I curled up on the hard ground, rigid with tension.

When I heard voices, I wasn't sure if they were real or if I was dreaming them. This whole situation felt dreamlike. The lines were starting to blur.

"We can't keep tranking her," said a male voice. Enkidu, I supposed I had to call him. He was on the other side of the door, a little way down the tunnel.

A woman whose voice was less familiar spoke. "How else can we control her until the spirit enters her?" She spoke quickly, nervously. The magician— had to be. Zora—Zoroaster. The hubris.

The frustration in Enkidu's voice was plain. "And what if it doesn't? She's too strong to just give in to your . . . your brainwashing. That's the whole point of recruiting her!"

"I need more time."

"She will not wait quietly. She'll find a way to break free, I tell you."

"Which is why we have to use the tranquilizers—"

"Talk to her. If we could just explain—"

"No! Then she'll never truly understand."

I really was awake, I decided. I tried to focus, wishing I still had that sandwich. And the water. If I played along, I bet they'd feed me. I wondered when they'd think of bribing me with food. And I didn't mean slaughtered rodents that would bring Wolf charging forward.

"This is ridiculous," Enkidu muttered.

"You know what's at stake," the magician said. "If this doesn't work, all is lost."

The dynamic here was strange. The vampire was obviously the one in charge. But during the day, when he was asleep, who among his followers was leader? That seemed to be up for debate.

I didn't want them tranquilizing me again. But I also didn't want to just give in. My brain was starting to misfire over the dilemma. I was hungry, but even if I had food I didn't think I'd be able to eat, I was so anxious. I might have whimpered a little.

"Regina Luporum is awake," said the were-lion, Sakhmet.

They fell silent, listening. I imagined us, me on one

side of the door, them on the other, listening close. Waiting for somebody to do something.

I called, "My name's Kitty."

"You see? She's not ready," hissed the magician, as if I couldn't hear.

"We can't wait forever," Enkidu hissed back. "She has friends, and she'll be missed."

Damn straight. But if I could get out of here without dragging them into this mess, I'd do it. Just open that door . . .

I heard movement, and Sakhmet stepped close to the door—I could smell her. Inches from me now, she said, "Regina Luporum, are you hungry?"

"Kitty," I murmured, on principle. I knew what this was—they'd keep calling me Regina Luporum until I answered. I wouldn't play along.

But I really needed some water.

I backed away from the door. A bolt slid open, and the door pushed inward. I was a good girl and didn't do anything crazy—all three of them were there, blocking the way out.

Sakhmet crouched and offered me a bottle of water. I took it and smiled a thanks. Probably drank it down a little too eagerly and with less dignity than I would have liked. Dignity, ha. These people had all seen me naked, who was I kidding? My hair itched. I scratched it back, trying to brush it out with my fingers as well as I could.

The three of them watched me apprehensively, waiting to see which way I would jump. So I didn't jump. I sat quietly, clutching my bottle of water, and gazed up at them with big, harmless eyes.

"You shouldn't be here talking to her like this," Zora muttered at Enkidu. "You'll ruin everything." He glared at her, but didn't argue. Even in the faint light, I could see the lines of indecision marking his face.

I focused on Sakhmet, who was closest to me, at my eye level, and regarding me with something like pity. *She* would talk to me, I bet.

"How did you all meet?" I asked softly, nonthreateningly. I was doing the show, trying to coax a story from a reluctant interview subject. Invite her to tell me her story, assume that she secretly *wanted* to tell me her story. Most people only needed a sympathetic ear to start talking about themselves. "You and Enkidu—you've known each other awhile, I can tell. How did you two meet?"

She didn't talk, not right away, so I shrugged, played gee-whiz naïve. "It's just you're an interesting group of people, you know? People usually stick to their packs, but here you all are, working together."

Sakhmet gave a thin smile, glancing over her shoulder at the others. "I met . . . Enkidu, first. When we were younger. I was a college student in Cairo." She seemed about thirty—my age. Enkidu was probably a few years older. So this might have been ten years ago, maybe less.

"Were you already a lycanthrope?" I asked gently.

"Yes, but not for long. I was attacked. It was stupid, being out by the river after dark," she said, wincing at the memory. "I survived, and there were those who took care of me—"

"Sakhmet, come away from her, we should not be talking to her!" Zora hissed.

"We're just talking, we're not hurting anything," Sakhmet shot back.

"What about you, Zora? How'd you hook up with this crowd?" I asked.

"It's not important," Zora said. "Our stories— irrelevant." She stomped toward the door, sat on the floor with a huff, crossed her arms, and stared at us. Baby-sitting, it seemed like. Zora was a bit of a freak, wasn't she?

Sakhmet sat with her legs folded, graceful, her skirt splayed around her. Her smile was thin, serene. "What happened to me, what you call lycanthropy—it isn't a curse, I came to realize. It's a blessing. Thousands of years ago, my people worshipped gods and goddesses with the faces of animals. Those of us who are both human and animal—who is to say we're not messengers of those gods? We share their images, we are part of them."

Easy to persuade her then that she was an avatar of

the lion-headed goddess Sakhmet. She was Egyptian, and in ancient Egypt she might have been a priestess, draped in fine cloth and jewels. I wondered where those animal-headed gods had come from. Had the ancient Egyptians known about lycanthropes?

Had everyone known, once upon a time, and then just forgotten? People stopped believing the stories were true.

If Zora was baby-sitting, Enkidu was standing guard, lurking near Sakhmet, shoulders stiff like raised hackles. As if he expected me to leap at her, snarling, even though I was acting as unthreatening as I knew how, without going so far as to roll onto my back and show my belly. My gaze was lowered, I sat with my knees to my chest. Just people telling stories.

"What about you?" I said, nodding at him. "Where are you from?"

He wouldn't stop staring at me, which made me nervous. But not any more nervous than I already was, so I ignored him. He waited so long I didn't think he was going to answer, when he finally said, "Kashmir."

"And how did you two meet?"

He glanced at Sakhmet sidelong, and she won a smile from him. Ah, that was a good memory, then. "I wandered for a long time," he said. "Then I found her."

Even in the dire setting, they produced a glow of affection. Whose heart wouldn't melt? If we'd been anywhere else—New Moon, maybe, sharing a pitcher of beer—I'd have basked in it. If I could just get these two away from everyone else . . .

"How'd you meet her?" I said, nodding at Zora.

No smiles for the magician. "Kumarbis found her," Enkidu said. "Before he found us."

The vampire had recruited them all, then. What did he know that had started all this? Did he really have the power to stop Roman?

From a certain point of view, I couldn't fault them. They were allies banding together, just like me, Rick, Alette, and all the others. They just had a different set of tactics. I kept bugging Cormac to learn the secret of Dux Bellorum's coins because I wanted a magical weapon. A silver bullet, if you will. If he'd come to me and said, "All we need to do is kidnap various avatars of various powerful mythological figures," I'd have thought he was crazy. *He* would have thought he was crazy. But if that was what I'd have to do to stop Roman, could I do it? No. I would have called them all up on the phone and talked them into it. Why couldn't they have just *called* me?

They were gathered around me. If not relaxed, at least not in a fighting mood. I had an audience, and I'd warmed them up. Time to push a little.

"What do you know about Dux Bellorum?" I asked.

Some hesitation. Enkidu's gaze darkened. Again, Sakhmet answered first. "He is old. Not one of the oldest vampires, but very old. He craves power, and many have flocked to him hoping to share in his power. But I—we—believe his intent isn't to share power, but to enslave. His allies will be beholden to him and under his dominion. The rest of us . . ." She shook her head, making the implications clear: the fate of Dux Bellorum's enemies would be unspeakable.

"Dux Bellorum will not succeed," Enkidu said. "It's why we're here. We cannot fail."

I could argue that, but this wasn't the time to argue about the merits of their plan. It might have been a perfectly good plan. But I wasn't at all impressed with their implementation of it.

"Have you ever seen Dux Bellorum?"

Enkidu said, "I did, once. I was . . . spying, I suppose you might say, among the werewolf pack outside of Mumbai. I suspected that they served Dux Bellorum, but I didn't know. Until the night I saw him in a marketplace. A serious man, with short-cut hair, pale skin. Glaring like the world had insulted him. Very out of place, but he commanded the wolves. The whole pack had gathered, and they all bowed to him, submissive, groveling. He gave money to the alpha—the pack served him as mercenaries, but I don't know what exactly they did for him. I was too new to share that information with. But I left them that night. The vampire saw me in the back of the alley where we had gathered, trying to stay out of sight. He saw me, saw through me, as if he could guess I was an enemy. As soon as he was gone, I ran. The alpha chased me, hunted me. I escaped, and I will never forget that night. Dux Bellorum—he frightened even me."

"You never told me that they hunted you," Sakhmet said, touching his arm.

"I didn't want you to worry."

"I'll always worry." She frowned, chastising him, and he bowed his head.

"You aren't wrong about Roman. I've faced him down a couple of times," I said.

"We heard rumors that you had," Enkidu said. "It's how we know you are our Regina Luporum."

Somehow, I managed not to roll my eyes. The times I'd met Roman in person, I hadn't had any more ambition than getting away from him alive. Much like Enkidu. That I'd succeeded had as much to do with luck—and incredibly good taste in friends—as anything. Moving on.

"You're targeting him. That's the point of all this, right?" I gestured around the musty and unlikely setting. "To bring him down, destroy him."

He nodded once, with the confidence of a crusader going into battle.

In the end, the success of their plan depended on

how much they really knew about Roman. And I suspected that few of us knew as much about him as we thought we did.

I said, "I've had some . . . I wouldn't call it evidence. A hint, a suggestion. A credible implication that Roman didn't start the Long Game. He isn't really the one in charge. There's someone else, another figure. A Caesar."

For a moment, they stared at me in apparent disbelief. Even Zora lifted her head from the sullen pout she'd been in. The very idea was ridiculous, of course. Except that it wasn't.

Enkidu furrowed his brow. "What proof do you have?"

An offhand comment made by a trapped demon of uncertain and unlikely origin? She came to Denver on a mission to kill a vampire priest—I was still getting used to the idea of a vampire priest, of vampires working for the Vatican, but apparently it was all true. She succeeded in her mission and would have gotten Rick and me, too, if Cormac hadn't stopped her. We all assumed that she was working for Roman. She laughed at this and claimed that Roman wasn't the one pulling her strings, implying that someone else was, which opened a whole new world of paranoia, didn't it?

"I don't have any proof," I said. "It's just something to think about." Any uncertainty I could plant in them might be useful. Or might get me killed. Whatever. In the meantime, I had so many more questions. "Do you have any idea how Kumarbis knows—"

A noise, the familiar sound of a wood door scraping on stone, echoed down the tunnel. The three of us lycanthropes started, raising our heads, pricking our ears.

Zora noticed our alertness and brightened. "He's awake."

He. Kumarbis, the vampire. Master of this little shindig. Could I get *him* to sit and talk with me?

The others gathered themselves, straightening, turning away. We were done here, it seemed.

"I'll go to him," Sakhmet said. As she passed Enkidu, he held her arm and leaned in. Their kiss was gentle, soft, full of obvious comfort passing between them. My heart ached, seeing it. Where was Ben, how freaked out was he, coming home to find me missing? At least two nights had passed. He'd be home now, never mind how many times he'd tried to call.

The were-lion padded down the tunnel toward the noise, presumably the vampire's lair, where he slept out his days. To feed him, I realized. He needed blood, and they provided.

Enkidu must have seen the understanding in my expression. "We take turns," he explained. Which made a twisted kind of sense, but I must have looked sour. Dismayed, even.

"You'll take your turn soon, when you join us," Zora said.

I shook my head in denial. Never, not in a billion years.

The magician took hold of the door in order to close it. Desperate, irrational, angry, I leapt forward, grabbed the edge, and held on. I didn't want them to close it, I didn't want to be shut in, not anymore. I wanted to keep talking, and I wanted them to listen. I wanted to get out.

If I'd been fighting over the door with just Zora, I'd have won. She was small, weak, and I was a were-wolf. I could tear her to pieces. But Enkidu took hold of the door as well and hauled back. I scraped along the floor, trying to anchor the thing with my body. He caught my gaze, glared a challenge, and I snarled back. He wanted to fight, and we could fight this out.

After one last mighty shove, he yanked the door, caught me off balance, and I let go just before it would have slammed on my fingers. Letting out a frustrated growl, I glared at the slab of wood, since I didn't have anything better to glare at.

On the plus side, I wasn't any *worse* off than I was a few minutes ago.

I had to come up with a plan. Any plan. I had to develop telepathy so I could call for help. Or—they had to have my cell phone stashed away somewhere, didn't they? If I could get out from behind the locked door, find my cell phone, get to a place where I could get a signal—probably out of the mine, which I ought to be able to do if I made it that far. Then call the cavalry. Simple.

Simple as stone.

Chapter 11

IF KUMARBIS was awake, night had fallen. Was this the second night I'd been here, or third? I didn't know, but the number mattered to me. Counting time seemed important. I'd seen the vampire once, then he slept, and now he was awake. Call it the second night, then. I'd been here two full days, at least. Or was it three?

Two.

The tunnel system in the mine must have been complex. The group was living here, they had separate chambers, they'd built doors and created rooms. There was a place to lock me up, a place for the vampire to sleep. The others must have had rooms as well. They had to be storing food and water somewhere, and using something other than unobtrusive corners of various caves as toilets. Assuming I found a way to break out and avoid my captors, how long would it take me to search the place? How did I find my way out? With my nose. I just had to find the draft of fresh air and follow it. I hoped.

First thing I had to do was figure out how to get past the door. Well, that was easy. Plan A: Wait until someone opened it, then start running, see how far I could get. Satisfying, but probably not effective. I wouldn't have time to look for my phone in that scenario.

Plan B: Win their trust so they'd let me out of the room *and* leave me alone to go exploring. On further thought, it might even be easy; I'd just have to start pretending to agree with them. Easy, maybe, but the idea left a sour taste in my mouth. I didn't want them to think they'd convinced me. Brainwashed me. But if it meant getting out of here . . . I could turn my mind in circles for hours thinking of this. Hunger had become a dull ache, and lack of food was affecting my thinking. The next time Sakhmet appeared, I'd ask for food.

Once again, steps approached, and the door scraped open. I backed away, because I wasn't ready and didn't think about charging until it was too late. Next time for sure, right?

The vampire came in, alone. He shut the door behind him and stood, blocking the way, studying me. Him and me, all alone. I buried a growl.

He might be able to pass for human in poor light,

but people would look twice at him and maybe wonder what disease he was suffering from. He was stooped, wizened, his spine was hunched, and his joints were gnarled. Leathery wrinkles covered his face; in anyone else I would have called it sun damage. His appearance wasn't old so much as worn out. Even flush from his recent feeding, he appeared ashen. He'd seen some hard times. Periods of starvation maybe. Lack of blood wouldn't kill a vampire right away, but it would cause something like decay. This vampire was decayed.

I wouldn't get any closer to him than I had to. He approached, and I backed away, keeping the same distance between us. Straightening, I squared my shoulders and lifted my chin. He could smell my anxiety, but I didn't have to act scared.

"You are strong," he said, sounding pleased. "I knew you would be."

"Then why do you think you can force me to do what you want?"

"When you understand, you won't need to be forced."

The mangled coin around his neck kept drawing my eye. I wanted to know more, I had so many questions. "How old are you?" I asked on a whim.

He narrowed his gaze, curled his lip. An expression of disdain. "We brought you here to make you understand. To show you—"

"Understand what? Maybe I could understand if you'd actually explain to me what you're doing." I should have just shut up and listened. But I was angry. I didn't like being lectured at.

"You *will* understand."

"Yeah, all you have to do is keep saying that, over and over," I muttered. We could keep this up all day. "Help me understand. You wear one of Roman's coins. Why?"

"I took it from him."

"It means you served him—"

He scowled. "I never served him." He actually sounded offended.

I took a calming breath and tried again. "How do you know him, then?"

"It's enough that I know how dangerous he is. We must stop him."

"I agree," I said. Kumarbis tilted his head as if startled. He must have thought I just argued on principle. "How are you going to do that?"

"It is not your place to ask, only to join the battle."

That made me think of Antony, and all the other casualties. Kumarbis wasn't wrong—this was a war, and maybe he'd been fighting it longer than the rest of us, but that didn't put him in charge.

"That's just typical vampire superiority garbage," I said. "You're a vampire, I'm a werewolf, so you expect me to line up like a good little foot soldier. It's crap

like that that's got me fighting Roman in the first
place. You want my help, treat me like an ally and not
cannon fodder. Too many people have already died
fighting Roman."

He stretched his crooked hands and his lips pulled
back to show yellowed fangs. He seemed so broken,
but ropy muscles flexed under the leathery skin. He
was still a vampire, and I couldn't underestimate his
strength. I wondered how hard I'd have to push him
before he got physical.

"No one knows Gaius Albinus better than I do."

I believed him. He'd been around for most of that
history. Roman was a bogeyman among vampires, a
Machiavellian figure manipulating them and their
Families around the world in order to bind them under his own power. The few facts: he was two thousand years old, had been a Roman soldier in Palestine,
had traveled across Europe and Asia over the centuries. His followers wore the bronze coins, which had
some magic that connected them. Defacing the coins
broke the spell. I had spent the last several years trying to identify Roman's followers, and to find others
who knew about him and opposed him. I had my own
band of allies. But none of them knew about Kumarbis. What did Kumarbis know that we didn't?

"What can you tell me about him?" I asked.

"Only that we must stop him. Nothing else is important."

It was like pulling teeth. Sharp, pointy teeth. I said, "Do you know Marid? Ned Alleyn? Alette, Rick—Ricardo? Do you know they're trying to stop Roman, too? If no one knows him better than you, they could really use your help. That's the whole point, we're supposed to be working together."

He shook his head. "What they think they know doesn't matter. I am the only one who can stop Gaius Albinus."

We had a saying around the radio station: the minute you thought no one else could do your job, it was time to give up that job. "You can't do it alone," I said. "You need help."

"I have everything I need here, now that you are with us."

"You know so much about Dux Bellorum—even what can stop him—why not just tell me?" I paced, just to be moving. I had to burn the anxious energy somehow, either through moving or through howling. The howling might come in a minute.

"You'll learn what I know—when you are initiated into our mysteries."

"I don't want to be initiated into any mysteries. Sorority rush was bad enough."

He put his hand on his heart—his dead, still heart—in a strange gesture of calm. Like a saint in a medieval painting. Closing his eyes, he said, "Be comforted, wolf. Regina Luporum. You'll understand everything, in time." He turned to tap on the door. One of the others must have been on the other side, to unlock it.

"Wait!" I reached for him as the door cracked open.

He turned back to me, waited as I had asked. But I didn't know what to say that I hadn't already said.

"Are you hungry?" he asked, after a pause. "Of course you are. I will have Sakhmet bring you food."

Then he left, and the door shut behind him.

Maybe it was time to figure out a plan C.

I DIDN'T know any stories about Regina Luporum. About the wolf who adopted and cared for Romulus and Remus. Only that she was there, like any number of nameless mother wolves in any number of stories. Although the mother wolf who adopts Mowgli in Rudyard Kipling's *The Jungle Book* is named Raksha. *She* gets a name. She is the overlooked power, the unnoticed linchpin. The unspoken prologue to every story. I had to give credit to Kumarbis and the others for acknowledging her and giving her some power. But I didn't have to trust the stories he told about her.

Mythology was filled with queens. A queen of the wolves would only be one in a long line of them. Like Inanna, Queen of Heaven, goddess of sex and war, who was pictured flanked by lions. There's a story about Inanna traveling to the land of the dead, the underworld, just like most epic heroes seem to do at one time or another. At each of seven gates she is forced to give up an item of clothing, a jewel from her collection. And she arrives at her destination naked, stripped of all wealth and identity at the darkest part of her journey.

She spent three days underground, then she escaped. She was reborn. She reclaimed all that she'd lost. Like all good heroes do.

TIME PASSED strangely. My eyes were getting tired, even my Wolf's supernatural night vision straining in the dim lamplight for so long. I paced, just to have something to do, just to keep my blood flowing through tired muscles, so when the chance to run came, I'd be ready. Even though pacing made Wolf anxious. She was so close to the surface all the time now, ready to spring forth, to burst free. *To defend us, when the time comes.*

I was circling the antechamber for what felt like the hundredth time, trying to think. Sakhmet was my best chance for escape. All she had to do was leave the door unlocked the next time she brought me water. I could get her to convince Enkidu to leave the door unlocked. Escape in a way that wouldn't implicate them. Make it look like I broke out. They already knew it was the right thing to do, I was sure. I didn't think they were afraid of Kumarbis. So what was stopping them from doing the right thing?

They believed Kumarbis and Zora, believed they could really do what they claimed. And they would keep trying to convince me of the same.

On the other hand, I could beg and threaten. My pack and mate would come looking for me. A dozen raging werewolves, along with the vampires from the Denver Family, would swarm the place, seeking revenge in their effort to rescue me. My allies were ruthless and implacable, and Kumarbis and his cult didn't have a chance, no matter how powerful they were. Maybe that would convince them to let me go.

I'd try that. Plan C.

The sound of the door scraping on stone was familiar enough that it shouldn't have made me jump, but it did. Every noise, even a familiar one, meant something was happening, something I couldn't predict. What amazing new fun interaction did the gang have planned for me this time? The mind boggled.

I was tired of jumping at noises.

I stepped carefully toward the door, watchful and hesitant. The smell of blood and meat filled the air, the sound of wet flesh slurped against the floor, and the door scraped shut again.

He'd promised me food. Right. And here I thought he might actually have meant something my human side would consider food. I crouched to study what Enkidu—this smelled like him—had brought me. Fresh kill, only an hour or so old based on the stickiness of the blood. Large, with a tawny hide: the entire hind leg of a deer, ripped off the rest of the carcass.

Oddly, my next thought was Wolf's: *Enkidu and Sakhmet are good hunters, to be able to bring down deer.* I shook that away. Tried to clear my mind. But my mouth was watering. As far as Wolf was concerned, Kumarbis had made good on his word to feed us.

My human side was human enough that I didn't think I could eat the raw flank of deer in front of me. Not with my flat molars and my modern sensibilities that had grown up on macaroni and cheese out of a box, along with other technological wonders. A rare steak looked appetizing . . . this was ambiguous. *You are weak.* Yes, in some ways. In others, no. *Hungry, need to eat.* I couldn't argue. Wolf would have no problem eating the flank.

Even if I ate the meat raw with my human mouth, I'd still be feeding Wolf, who was perfectly fine with the idea. Ecstatic, even. At least I hadn't shifted at the first smell of blood, the first glimpse of the bloody carcass. I still had some control. Should have made me feel better. But they'd known I wouldn't be able to eat this as a human. If I wanted to eat, I'd have to choose to shift. This was part of the plan.

They didn't want me, they wanted Wolf.

I curled up on the floor, trying to think while Wolf whined her incessant logic at me.

In the end, I decided that if I was going to do this, it would be my own choice, under my own control. I wasn't going to shift in a rage-filled panic like I had last time. I could do this calmly, sensibly even. I had a choice. Or I could pretend I did.

I took off my sweater, jeans, panties. Folded them neatly, put them out of the way next to a craggy piece of rock where I could find them again when I was ready. Kneeling, keeping my balance with a hand resting on the stony ground, I breathed steadily, calming myself. I was hungry, and this was the solution to the problem. Made perfect sense.

The Change hurt less when I didn't fight it, when I let it slide over me like water pouring through a channel. I imagined a cage in my gut where Wolf lived, where she slept behind bars. As I let out my next breath in a long exhale, I imagined the bars disappearing, the cage opening, and Wolf sprang free. In a wave of tingling pinpricks, fur sprouted along my arms and back. My fingers bent into claws, and my muscles spasmed as the bones under them began to change.

Like water . . . Without a sound, I closed my eyes,

arced back my head, and the Change passed over me
in a wave—

—*when she opens her eyes, she sees the world in a*
sharp light. The scent of meat fills her. It's why she's
here.

She pads over to the carcass. Suspicious, she
noses it all over, searching for tricks, for proof that
this is a trap. But it only smells like good, fresh deer.
She noses under the skin and rips into flesh. Settles
in to devour as much of the feast as she can, because
she doesn't know when she will eat again. Or if it
might unexpectedly vanish. The meat should taste
good, but she's anxious, eating too quickly to enjoy
this. She's alone, here. Cornered. No pack to keep
watch with her.

She has almost finished the flesh and starts crack-
ing and gnawing on bones when a noise catches her
attention and her ears prick up. In front of her, the
door scrapes open. The enemy has come. Her hack-
les stiffen, fur standing straight up. Her muscles
brace. Her claws click against the stone as she backs
away.

Their scents reach her, alien and uncertain. Four
of them, all different. Her lips curl from her teeth
and her throat burrs a growl. They've brought more

light with them, a glare that fills the space, hurts her eyes. But she can't look away. Ears flattened, tail straight, she stares at them, challenging. If they try to hurt her, she will mangle them all.

"Oh, she's beautiful," says one of them, female, smelling of feline, of musk and desert.

"Dangerous," mutters another. Male. Another wolf. She hates him.

The group approaches and she backs away, keeping her distance. She can only back so far, and when they corner her, she'll strike. She will not let them corner her.

Of the other two, one is cold. He smells of carrion without being rotten. She keeps her distance from him. The other, another female—this one smells of prey. Fear, sweat, trembling. Weak, she stands behind the others for protection.

She stares at the prey, and the curl in her lips feels almost like a smile.

"Here," says the cold one. "We'll start from here. No need to frighten her."

For a moment, the door beyond the group stands open. A faint touch of mountain air seeps in, and her nose quivers, taking in the taste of freedom. But the door closes again before she can rally herself to escape.

Too slow, too late. Her muscles are stiff from standing rigid, from spending days locked in this

*cold, stone-filled space. Her mind burns. The blood
of her meal coats her tongue; part of the haunch still
remains, but she's no longer hungry. Now, she wants
only to escape. That, or devour the enemies standing
before her.*

*She has to move. Circling back, she paces, follow-
ing the wall, hoping it will run out, lead her to some
wide open space where she can run, but it doesn't. It
loops back to the start, to the enemies and their dron-
ing voices. They stand their ground, don't try to stop
her from moving. But she has no path around them
without going through them, which seems unwise. So
she paces. She can still taste blood and wants more.*

*On the next loop, she ducks and charges, mouth
open. Her claws scrape on the ground, her muscles
pump—running feels good. She sees through a haze
of anger. The cold one, whose voice has ice and smoke
in it. She aims for him.*

*The wolf steps in her path. She plants her jaw on
his raised arm. His skin rips, she tastes his blood. He
shoves her back, redirects her, slams her into the cave
wall. Pain stings her shoulder. Writhing, she twists
out of his grip, falls, finds her feet again.*

*He braces, arms spread, standing between her
and the others. He's ready to fight. Blood drips down
his arm; she tastes drops of it that smear on her tongue.
There's a tang of fear—from the lion, who comes
forward and wraps cloth around his arm.*

She remembers: traces of poison are everywhere here, imbedded in the walls. They wouldn't have to rip out each others' hearts, merely poison each others' blood with traces of metallic stone.

His teeth are bared; so are hers. She won't back down from the challenge. Softly, she growls.

Stop. We can't win.

She stands, legs rigid, panting.

Calm, calm. We must stay calm. We have to wait them out.

The cold one speaks. "We have gathered to raise power, in order to do battle with great evil. We invite Regina Luporum to merge her power with ours. Now, in your truest form, see with your wolf's eyes what we do here, see the power we have already gathered . . ."

She glares a challenge at him; the cold one meets her gaze, and her focus tumbles. The world turns to fog, and she cannot look away.

His tone is like singing. This makes her think of howls, of her pack under the full moon's light, surging pure and ever skyward. But the cold one's singing is broken and grates on her nerves. At the start, she almost understands what he says. Her two-legged self strains to listen. But as the chant goes on, her head aches, and it becomes meaningless, like everything else about this place. She doesn't understand, and her other self fades to a distant influence.

A murmur in the back of her head urges, listen, listen, *remember what they're saying, we have to understand what they're saying . . .*

They know things, they have the key to what this is about, but she doesn't understand.

The others speak, telling their parts of the muddled flood of voices. They are not speaking her language, she is not part of their pack . . . but she could be . . . they are letting her in by telling their secrets.

She is so tired.

The haunch of deer is taken away. The cold one and the small human prey leave the room. They are careful to shut the door. But the wolf and lion linger.

She settles, lying with her head resting on her paws. Still watching them, full of confusion.

"Will she be all right?" the lion says.

"She'll go to sleep soon enough," the wolf answers.

"That's not what I mean. What if Kumarbis is wrong and she never joins us?"

"We have to show her that his is the way. That's all."

Her ears prick forward, listening. Almost, she understands. Almost, she wishes she can answer them. Let me go, why not just let me go . . .

But they, too, leave, and she hears the metallic click and slide, and knows it means the door is locked again.

She picks herself up and paces again. The track she walks is familiar. She's made a clear trail in the dust and grit on the floor. If she paces forever, maybe she can wear out the stone and carve her way to freedom. If she doesn't wear her claws to stubs first.

She would fall asleep walking if she could.

Chapter 12

THE ISLAND OF DOCTOR MOREAU is one of the more modern takes in a long line of stories about beings who cross the line between human and not. I'd always thought that Moreau himself was the least human creature in the story. A confession: I started reading the H. G. Wells novel thinking it would be quaint and cute, like a lot of Victorian literature that was meant to be startling and horrifying, but really wasn't to our modern, jaded sensibilities.

What a lot of people don't realize about the story because they've just seen the movies is that most film versions only cover the first two-thirds of the book. In the novel, Prendick is stranded on the island for another ten months, having to coexist with the horde of devolving man-beasts. Having to become like them in order to hold his own among them, while maintaining enough of his humanity to be able to build a raft and escape. The end of the novel—the part that's meant to be truly horrifying to anybody who reads it, no matter where or when they live—shows Prendick rescued and back in London, among the teeming mass of humanity. And he can't tell the difference between them and the tormented beasts he left behind. This was a common theme of H. G. Wells: the idea that humanity is just a very short step from utter, uncivilized chaos.

Some of the worst people I'd ever met didn't have a lick of supernatural about them. Technically, they weren't monsters. But they were, surely. You can only judge people by their actions.

I WOKE up on top of my clothes, which gave me a weird jolt of happiness. They hadn't taken my clothes! Instead, I was nested in my own familiar unwashed body odor, which gave me a strange sense of well-being. They really didn't mean me harm, they really weren't going to hurt me, maybe they weren't so bad . . .

I sat up and stewed, trying to remember everything that had happened after I'd turned Wolf. Trying to dredge from those fuzzy memories some solid nugget of information. Sometimes, my stretches as Wolf passed in a haze, my human mind unable to hold on to memories gathered through animal senses. Other times, I remembered so much, entire scenes, thoughts, images, and people. The less stressed, the more calm I was, the more I could remember. Wolf had only heard their words as the mumbling of lesser, weaker, two-legged beings. My subconscious was not helping.

One memory stood out: Sakhmet and Enkidu were sympathetic. I could talk to them, maybe even get through to Kumarbis. I remembered him looking at me. He was so hopeful.

After a quick stretch I got dressed. They'd cleaned up the deer haunch while I'd slept. Some blood remained smeared on the floor. It smelled dirty and rotten now, not at all appetizing.

I curled up on the floor, resting my head on my bent arm, trying to think. Kumarbis had spoken for a long time, so that all the words ran together. He'd been telling stories, I thought, stories that I would have loved to hear, but in a foreign language for all that I could tell. It was all fuzzy, growing more fuzzy by the moment.

Even if Tom hadn't been able to look for me or get help, Ben would be on the warpath by now. He'd call Cormac, and Cormac was a professional in hunting down werewolves. Between the two of them, they'd find me, I was sure of it. I beat down any arguments to the contrary before they could bubble into my awareness. They'd find me. Among the hundreds of abandoned mines scattered in the mountains, hundreds of miles from anywhere . . .

And what would he tell my mother? Was it Sunday yet? Mom usually called on Sunday, updated me on the whole family . . . my dad, my sister, her kids. They must have known I was gone, they must have been so worried about me. I didn't want to get wrung out from crying, so I squeezed my eyes shut and didn't cry.

I must have fallen asleep again. I hadn't meant to, and I didn't like what it meant. The exhaustion was getting to me, I was losing energy. It wasn't that I was giving up. But sleeping was so much easier than trying to think, when my brain hurt and my heart ached.

The door scraped on stone. My eyes were closed, stuck together almost. I thought I was dreaming, but my back and shoulders were stiff from sleeping on the ground; the feeling was visceral, not at all dreamlike. Footsteps padded, and I smelled Sakhmet and Enkidu. I took far too long a time gathering myself, opening my eyes and struggling to a sitting position, not even able to get to my feet before they were standing in front of me. My reflexes were dull, my awareness drained. That was probably the point. They were wearing me down, slowly. My anger over it had become dull and distant, like an old bruise.

Sakhmet knelt, putting herself at my level. Condescending, I thought. She wasn't worried about me being dominant or putting herself in a submissive position compared to me. I was the prisoner, we all knew it.

"Your wolf is very beautiful," she said, smiling kindly.

Part of me warmed to her. Of course, I wanted to say. Sometimes I thought Wolf was the most beautiful part about me, sleek and wild, full of strength and focus.

Instead, I muttered in a dry, croaking voice, "She's also really pissed off." Sakhmet revealed another bottle of water, which I accepted. It was like she knew exactly what I needed. Creeped me out a little.

I took a long drink, which seemed to clear my mind, and splashed some on my face, which cleaned out my eyes and woke me up. My anger settled. I could see the pair of them a bit more clearly.

They stood shoulder to shoulder, totally familiar, not just comfortable with each other, but drawing comfort from the other.

"How much do you remember?" Enkidu asked.

I knew what he was asking—how much did I remember from being Wolf? Complicated question. After my latest nap, the memories were even more blurred. Or it could have been that everything was going blurry. I had to get out of here.

I shrugged. "You know how it is. The deer was pretty good. Thanks for that, I guess. But the rest—you came in here and talked. Kumarbis was explaining something. Wolf wasn't interested in listening. You guys maybe want to fill me in?" Hey, it was worth a shot.

They glanced at each other, exchanging one of those telepathic married people secret messages. Sakhmet looked away first. "I told them you wouldn't remember. Our animal sides—speech is like the chatter of birds to them."

"*My* wolf understands," Enkidu said. The edge in his voice seemed due more to frustration than to anger. He had shadows under his eyes, as if he hadn't been sleeping. Sakhmet just looked tired, slouching. "I've worked hard, to make sure I remember what my wolf sees and hears. I thought you would be the same—that your animal side would hear *better*."

He said this as an accusation, but I wasn't rising to that bait. "My Wolf understands when friends are talking," I said. "She listens to her friends."

Sakhmet leaned close to whisper to him. "She has no reason to listen to us." He bowed his head, acquiescing.

I licked my lips and spoke carefully, testing words. "He's asleep, isn't he? Kumarbis. It's daylight again. You only come to see me like this during the day."

"He doesn't want us speaking to you at all, when he isn't here," Sakhmet said. "He wants you to learn from him."

"Why? What hold does he have over you all?"

"He is right," Enkidu said. That simple.

"You're all *nuts*," I said. To their credit, they didn't argue with me. "Look, I can't play your game if you don't tell me the rules, and I can't buy into your little cult if you don't convince me you really have some kind of power. Beyond kidnapping radio personalities and cutting yourselves off from civilization. And those aren't powers, they're pathologies." I had to stop and take several deep breaths. I'd winded myself with that speech. God, I was a wreck. I drank more water, but it didn't help.

I tried to creep away from them without actually going anywhere. A sort of hopeful leaning. They were blocking the exit again.

Sakhmet said, "We're here to explain. At nightfall, we'll bring you to the ritual chamber. You must wait quietly—please tell me you'll wait quietly."

I rolled my eyes. "You couldn't coerce me, so now you're just asking me to be a nice little cooperative prisoner? You should have tried being reasonable in the first place."

She leaned forward. "We never wanted you to be a prisoner at all. I wanted to come see you at your office, to explain everything—"

"She wouldn't have cooperated then, either," Enkidu said. "She would have written us off as crackpots."

"We'll never know, will we?" She glared at him.

"Well. Here's your chance. Better late than never. Explain."

Enkidu knelt, turning his gaze away from me. He was still stiff, anxious. If he'd been a wolf, his ears would have been flattened, his hackles up. But he was forcing his body language into a more peaceful stance. He was trying to set me at ease. Not possible, and though I probably should have appreciated the effort, I wasn't feeling generous. I just kept staring at him.

"Sakhmet is right," Enkidu said. "I believe if you understand what's happening, you'll cooperate. Kumarbis and Zora don't need to know what we've told you. If you're with us, it's enough. So I'll tell you, but you must let me speak, while we have time. No interrupting—just listen."

He said it admonishingly. Even after a couple of days he knew me that well. Just to prove that I could listen quietly, I nodded and kept my mouth shut.

"What has happened so far," he explained, "has been to bind you to the group. To align our powers, draw us together, so that when Zora performs the final rituals, we are as one. Our spirits will be united, and greater than the sum of our parts. This will make the rituals more powerful than anything Dux Bellorum has faced in all his years. This is why your cooperation is so important. If we are not united, we will fail.

"Tonight, we will gather and Zora will perform the first half of the ritual. The purpose is to locate Dux

Bellorum. We cannot strike at him until we find him. But we will find him. This will prove to you that Kumarbis can do what he says he can do. Tomorrow night, the second part of the ritual, Zora will open a doorway to Dux Bellorum, and we will kill him."

Just like that. A much more attractive plan of attack than the "wait and see" we'd decided on after Antony's death.

"Defeat Dux Bellorum," I said, only half sure. Do X, Y, Z, and all will be well. It couldn't be that easy. Could it?

What if it was?

They lured me with the tantalizing bait they thought I'd be most interested in—defeating Dux Bellorum. Like that alone would make me trust them. How could I ever trust them, after all this? The enemy of my enemy . . . they hadn't killed me yet . . .

He continued. "You must have an open mind. When we gather tonight, don't argue, don't fight. Once you see, you'll believe."

That had an ominous ring to it. "You all are on a schedule, aren't you? There's a time limit to this thing." Zora must have been watching the stars, the turning of the planets—how long to the full moon? Four days? Three? I could feel the pull of the waxing moon. Was *that* the time limit? Lycanthropes were at their strongest on the full moon. Zora needed us at our strongest, without us actually shape-shifting. Playing it close as she could, using us at the peak of our power but not beyond it. It was a dangerous strategy. Would I still be here when the full moon forced me to Change? I desperately hoped not. "The full moon?"

The glanced at each other, and Sakhmet said, "I told you she'd understand."

That this was making sense probably said something not very comforting about my state of mind. "There's more," I said. I thought carefully, marshalling my awareness, trying to get this right. "Kumarbis knows something—something specific, not just a general hunt-down-bad-vampires ritual. This is all built around that, isn't it? He's the one who can defeat Dux Bellorum because . . . why?"

Enkidu pursed his lips, and I waited very, very quietly, because he looked like someone who wanted to talk.

"Do you know who Dux Bellorum is?" he asked finally.

I furrowed my brow, confused at the question. "He's a vampire, old. From ancient Rome. Calls himself Roman. What do you mean, who is he?"

"Where did he come from? What's his origin?"

I shook my head.

He leaned in, his voice hushed to a paranoid whisper. "Kumarbis made Dux Bellorum. He's the vampire who turned Gaius Albinus, two thousand years ago."

A long, stretched silence followed this declaration. I turned the words around, not sure I made sense of them. It all started here. All my questions about Roman, Dux Bellorum, answered at last. The mystery, solved. Roman was so old I hadn't considered that the question of where he came from—how he was made a vampire—might even be relevant. Apparently it was, and I couldn't help but think this was all Kumarbis's fault. All of it. Antony died because of him.

"How?" I asked, full of disbelief, maybe even horror. "What happened?"

"We don't know all of the story," Sakhmet said softly. As if we had to keep our voices from echoing. "But Dux Bellorum—before he became Dux Bellorum—betrayed Kumarbis. He, Roman, has done terrible things. Kumarbis feels responsible."

"I can see why he might," I murmured. "A few days ago, right before you . . . brought me here, I got word that a friend of mine died fighting Roman. Antony went after him, and Roman killed him."

"That is what the battle has been for you, hasn't it?" she said, her rich gaze full of sadness and understanding. "Like throwing yourself against a wall and never breaking through."

Something in me deflated. My shoulders slumped; I rubbed my eyes, keeping back tears. My whole body felt like grit. If she'd offered to give me a hug then, I might have fallen into her arms.

"More like trying to beat up a storm cloud," I said, and she smiled.

"Right here, we can finish Roman once and for all," she said, and this time, the light gleaming in her eyes belonged to a warrior. To a goddess of war, a lion in battle. "You can avenge your friend. You can avenge everyone who Roman has hurt."

What a tantalizing possibility.

We all looked over just before we heard the footsteps pad through the doorway, when we smelled Zora enter the tunnel. Like everyone else here, she smelled ripe; she hadn't showered in days. But she also smelled of herbs, candle wax, and chalk. The tools of her trade. She appeared in the tunnel, holding up a battery-powered lantern, which gave her the appearance of a ghost in shadows.

"What are you doing? You shouldn't be here!" Holding her cloak around her, she glared at us with wide, indignant eyes.

"We're making sure our plans don't fall apart," Enkidu said.

"But—you know what he said. You'll ruin everything! You don't trust him, you never trusted him!"

Sakhmet spoke soothingly. "No, Zora, it isn't like that. Please, calm down."

"Then what are you telling her?"

Enkidu glared. "We are ensuring that *your* ritual will go smoothly."

"That isn't your place. She is like you, an avatar and a conduit, you don't understand anything beyond that, and you cannot *make* her understand. That's for me and Kumarbis. You should wait, that is your part in this."

"We've been waiting too long already," he muttered.

Zora demanded of them, "What did you tell her? How much damage have you done?"

"You know," I drawled. "You could talk to me. Direct, like. 'Cause I can hear you and all."

She looked at me, about as startled as if I had just slapped her with a wet fish. I wasn't a being to her but a tool, and tools weren't supposed to talk. What did you do when your tools weren't particularly happy about being used? She was probably having a bad week, wasn't she? Not as bad as mine . . .

In a hurried, flustered movement, she shook herself out and looked at Sakhmet and Enkidu. "We'll discuss this outside. Come."

She marched to the end of the tunnel, stopped at the doorway, turned to glare. Enkidu bristled, his werewolf's gaze returning the challenge, but Zora didn't seem to notice. These people were all dominant in their own ways, trying to tread lightly, and not particularly succeeding. The cracks showed.

Enkidu finally sighed. "Fine."

Sakhmet took his hand and squeezed; the gesture seemed to soothe him. To me she said, "We'll calm

Zora down. You should rest, to prepare for tonight. Drink more water." She was trying to be comforting. Trying to help, I could see that.

Hand in hand, Sakhmet and Enkidu joined Zora, and the argument picked up as they went through the doorway. Zora ranted. "She must stay open to be a true avatar, you don't understand, you haven't truly understood, not ever, you're both *mercenary*—"

"Zora, will you *please* calm down," Sakhmet said in a long-suffering tone.

Their voices traveled down the outside tunnel, echoing until I couldn't hear them anymore. They were carrying the argument elsewhere, far enough away that I couldn't eavesdrop. Too bad for me.

I stared after them for a long time, and at the door at the end of the tunnel. My sleepy, angry, anxious brain felt slow, and had to churn through the realization before it clicked. When it did, my heart pounded so hard I went dizzy for a moment.

They'd left the door at the end of the tunnel unlocked.

Chapter 13

THEY SHUT the door, but I didn't hear the bolt slide into place. *Oh, please . . .*

Oh so quietly, I pulled on the slab of wood—and it opened. Wincing, I froze. Waited, listened. But no one was coming, they hadn't heard it. I had to hope that Enkidu and Sakhmet were arguing with Zora so loudly they wouldn't hear the door scraping on the stone. Inch by inch, I eased the door open, just enough for me to be able to slip through the opening without scraping any skin on the silver-tainted mine wall.

And just like that I was outside.

More of the battery powered camp lanterns sat on the floor of the tunnel at intervals, spaced far apart. They gave off tiny auras of muted white light, so the space was still dim, the far walls and ceiling lost in darkness. But I could make my way well enough. The tunnel beyond the door was exactly like the ones I'd seen so far, nothing holding up the mountain over us but arcing granite, parallel rusted steel tracks curving along the floor, leading away. A historical curiosity. Any ore carts, spikes and hammers, drills, whatever other tools would have been used to dig out the mine and carry out ore had been cleared out long ago. A coating of white and red minerals splotched the walls in places. The place felt like a tomb.

I stood there far too long, studying the hallway, gaining my bearings. I had no idea how far underground I was, or which way to turn. I'd made that mistake before. Sakhmet and the others would be back soon, so whatever I did I had to hurry.

Closing my eyes, settling my racing heart, I tipped up my nose and took a long breath, learning as much as I could from simple air. Then another, to confirm what I thought—hoped—the air was telling me.

A draft, very faint, stirred down the tunnel. I smelled fresh air, coming from my left.

I ran.

The tunnel branched once. I hesitated at the fork, knowing my window was short, which meant I didn't have time to make a mistake. But the trail of fresh air continued, and I kept going, until the floor sloped up in a gentle grade. I stopped encountering lanterns—but light remained. The spot of sunlight ahead looked like treasure, brilliant and longed-for. Tears filled my eyes, and I rubbed my face.

The mine entrance was small, a curved passage opening out of the hillside like a mouth. A field of bare gravel sloped away from it, and beyond that granite outcroppings and forest. I paused there, my eyes shut, my arm up to shield my face from too-bright sunlight. Gasping for breath, I coughed as my lungs filled with the clean scent of pine trees, snow, and mountain air, so startling after the close smell of the mine. Even better, the air smelled like Colorado. The Rockies, lodgepole pines and Douglas fir and all the rest. Colorado dirt and sky. Home wasn't that far away.

I was out, I was free. I couldn't believe it. I huddled by the entrance, shivering. I was barefoot, and my toes nestled into gritty dirt and snow. My eyes took a long time getting used to the light before I could open them fully and figure out where I was. And what to do next.

By the way the sun slanted, it must have been afternoon. Golden light stabbed through the trees of the forest that dotted the mountainside. A recent snow had fallen; clean white blanketed the ground. The slope of the old tailings pile—waste rock from the mine— was visible, a triangle cutting down the hill and bare of trees. I could start walking, but to where? I could be hundreds of miles from anything resembling help, a gas station pay phone or road with any traffic, a town of any size. My werewolf self could walk that far, even barefoot in the snow, no problem. I might be a wreck at the end of it, but I'd recover.

The air must have been cold, but I didn't feel it. I just felt . . . confused. If I really did have a chance to stop Roman—if Kumarbis and the others really could stop him, and needed my help—I couldn't walk away from that. Could I? Antony hadn't turned away from the chance. *Avenge your friend,* Sakhmet's voice whispered to me. I'd never been one for revenge—much. But the idea of stopping Roman, of keeping him from ever hurting anyone again—*that* was attractive. It seemed a fine way to honor what Antony had given up. Antony must have thought the chance to stop Roman was worth risking his life. Could I do less?

Ben would disagree with me. He would say that trusting strangers and uncertain magic wasn't any better a plan of retaliation than waiting for better information. We already had allies, I didn't need to charge into an iffy situation with these guys, guns blazing. But Kumarbis *made* Roman; if anyone could stop him, he ought to be the one.

Then why hasn't he before now?

God, I wanted to talk to Ben so badly.

If I could stop Roman, I had to try. If I failed—not just that, but if I died trying, vanished utterly, and

Ben never found me and never learned what happened to me—would he ever forgive me? It wasn't just my life I was offering to sacrifice, I realized.

I wanted to laugh and cry at the same time. The thought of giving up Ben was more difficult than the thought of giving up my own life.

I might never get another chance like this.

Maybe I could find where they'd hidden my phone.

I sat on that tailings pile for what must have been a long time, torn between the world outside and the one in the mine. My skin itched, like someone was watching me. The others would find me any second now.

Sunshine made the snow look like scattered crystals. The air was still, not so much as a tree branch creaking. A bird, a crow or a jay or something, was calling in the distance, and the rough sound echoed. I had never smelled air so clean. This must have been what snow-covered mountains at the start of time smelled like. What a beautiful afternoon. At the mouth of the mine, with the world spread out around me, forest and distant mountain peaks and wide open sky, I could believe I was the only living soul in the world.

I should have looked for my phone before racing out of there. Assuming I could get a signal way out here, I could have at least texted Ben: *wait for me, forgive me*.

Assuming Kumarbis and crew weren't all actually

crazy after all. Go through the first ritual, see if they really knew what they were doing, and if it looked like they were full of it—I'd gotten out here once, I could do it again.

In the end, I couldn't give up the chance. Not just to stop Roman, but to learn everything I could about him and his plans. I couldn't walk away from the stories.

Nevertheless, I had a really hard time going back into that tunnel. The darkness became absolute just a few feet in, so that the tunnel seemed like the mouth of some legendary creature, eager to swallow me whole. I took a deep breath to still my pounding heart. Enkidu and the others still hadn't come after me. I had a little time. Phone, I was looking for my phone, so I could try to find a signal and call Ben to tell him I was alive and about to do something crazy stupid. This wouldn't surprise him; I'd done crazy stupid before. I usually had my support team backing me up.

But if Ben wasn't here, he was safe, and that was good. If this worked, I could save Ben, Cormac, the pack, my parents, my family, everybody. I could do this. The risk was worth it. After one last look at the forested hillside, imprinting its smells in my memory, I walked back into the darkness. The stone chill of it tickled my nose.

Stashed somewhere in the mine were my shoes,

phone, wedding ring, and other bits and pieces I'd had in my pockets when they grabbed me. A used tissue, maybe. I just had to track the scents. Easier said than done. The days of people traveling back and forth through the tunnels mashed up any scent I could follow. Vampire, lycanthrope, magician, stuff—it smelled like a pervasive mess. I explored, going down tunnels. I'd left the sunlight behind and entered the lanterns' ghost light when I found a trail that smelled strongly of myself and then a heavy door with bolts and a hinged panel on the bottom. This was the cell they'd first used to hold me. I didn't want to look inside; I was already far too familiar with it. I couldn't smell that anyone had been in here recently. I moved on.

They must have storage space somewhere, where they were keeping bottled water, food, who knew what else. They'd probably stashed my stuff there. Another room had to be Kumarbis's. Probably in the deepest, darkest tunnel, with no chance of sunlight reaching it.

The gang found me first. When running footsteps approached, I decided to hold my ground. Breathing calm into my body, keeping my chin up and face neutral, I waited.

Enkidu arrived, loping out of the dark. "Kitty—Regina Luporum!"

And there was a slip of the tongue. How much of this avatar thing did he believe, really? I wondered what their real names were, all of them. When I didn't run or flinch—or react at all, really—he slid to a stop.

"What are you doing?" he said, hand on his head, like he wanted to pull out his hair.

"Looking for my phone," I said. "You want to tell me where you put it?"

He was sweating, his heart was racing. Had I actually scared him by running off? Or was he just really pissed off? A little of both, by the nervous scent of him.

"You—you didn't leave," he said.

"Yeah. Made it all the way outside. It's a beautiful day out."

"You came back."

"And I may yet come to regret that," I said. Never mind, moving forward.

My returning to the tunnel was almost worth it just to see his expression of stark bafflement. He'd probably thought he had a crisis on his hands.

Sakhmet and Zora trotted up the tunnel after him and seemed just as shocked to see me standing still, regarding him calmly.

"I don't understand you," Enkidu said.

"Likewise. So, can I have my phone back?"

"No," he said. He shook his head, as if trying to shed his confusion.

"Oh, well. Never hurts to ask."

Probably intending to bodily escort me back to the main chamber, he grabbed my arm. I pushed away, showing my teeth, rasping a growl. Because he was also a dominant wolf who couldn't back down from a fight, he snarled back and lunged. I ducked, shoved into him with my shoulder, knocking him into the wall, and the fight was on. Three days of stress erupted. He turned, and we went after each other, arms out, fingers bent like claws. My Wolf growled with delight. No ambivalence, no decisions. Just claws, teeth, and blood.

"Stop! Stop it, both of you!" Sakhmet shouted.

Enkidu broke away from me, bowed his shoulders, ducked his gaze—the body language of a puppy who knows he's done something wrong. His beloved had spoken, and he obeyed.

Wolf hesitated, because her instincts said you didn't attack someone showing all the signs of standing down. I trembled, wanting to strike, knowing I shouldn't. My breath came in growls. All he had to do was look at me funny and I'd be on him again.

Sakhmet moved into the space between us. She was tall, regal in her skirt and tunic. Her skin shone like mahogany in the faint light. Her movements were fluid, feline. Her stance said I could try to fight her, but she could hold her own against the best of them. Sakhmet, the warrior goddess, the lioness of Egypt.

I didn't lower my gaze, but I let myself relax. I backed off a step.

"You're all animals!" Zora muttered. She stood a few paces away—reasonable safe distance—her hands on her hips.

I couldn't help it; I giggled. Doubled over, tried to stop laughing, but that only brought on hiccups. I was crazy. They were crazy. We were all crazy. I'd go ahead and blame that on Roman, too.

Sakhmet regarded me calmly, maybe even with pity. "Regina Luporum, will you come with me, please?" She held her hand out, careful not to touch me, not to even get close enough to where she might touch me by chance. I stepped forward, and she moved down the tunnel, gently encouraging me.

Eventually we made our careful, suspicious way back to the wide tunnel before the ritual chamber. Sakhmet escorted me through the doorway while the others waited outside.

"Zora would want me to lock the door on you, so you don't go snooping around. But you came back. I don't think you'll leave again, but will see this through to the end. Am I right? Can I trust you, and leave the door unlocked?"

"You all have asked me to trust you," I said. "It's only fair."

"Promise me that you'll wait here, until we all

gather at nightfall." Her eyes gleamed, and she wore a sly, catlike smile.

The words shouldn't have pressed down on me. It was my imagination—the ambient silver, itching at my skin. But I couldn't deny: the idea of making a promise had a physical weight here. Magic saturated the tunnels, the stone. Zora and all her rituals and symbols, Kumarbis and his history, all the stories they'd been telling and plans they'd been making. In this place of magic, a promise meant something. If I made that promise, I couldn't go back on it, and I couldn't even say why. They were only words, weren't they?

"I promise," I murmured.

She left me there, closing the door behind her. She didn't lock it.

I slumped to the floor, hands resting loose in my lap, my mind an odd blank. Nothing to do for it, then, than to wait for night to fall and see if this ritual actually worked.

Chapter 14

RULES OF the underworld: don't eat pomegranate seeds. Don't eat or drink anything the fairies give you. When you enter through the gates, you must remove all your clothing, all your possessions. You must bring an offering of blood to the shades who dwell there, especially if you want to ask them questions. When you leave the underworld, don't look back, not for anything.

When Inanna passed the seventh gate and reached the heart of the underworld, she wept at what she found, and all that she had lost. Hubris had brought her to this plight. Divine intervention brought her out.

She had to find a replacement to take her place in the underworld. But her servants had been loyal to her, and she was loathe to repay their kindness by sending them to the land of the dead. Her friends had mourned her, and they, too, she would not ask to take her place. But her husband, Dumuzi, had been at leisure and without care during her time in the underworld, and so she condemned—

No. Ben was looking for me. He'd never give up on me. The only reason he hadn't found me yet was that he had too much ground to cover, too many places to search. But he was trying, I knew it. I had faith.

The underworld doesn't always mean death, it isn't always the end. Sometimes, it's the beginning. The Hopi tell stories about the beginning of the world, the transition from the previous age to this one, the birth of civilization. Humanity first lived underground, and one day Spider Woman—messenger of the creator, herself a creator of life, a weaver of knowledge—led them through caves to an opening that emerged into the world we know. The underworld, the old world, is the womb that gave birth to humanity. The journey from under the earth is the journey from ignorance to wisdom.

You traveled to the underworld so that you could emerge reborn. With new wisdom, new power. One way or another, I would emerge from this with what I needed to protect what I loved.

But right now, I didn't know what I was learning here.

Chapter 15

I WAITED FOR nightfall, which seemed to both come quickly and take forever. Sitting in the middle of the antechamber, arms around my knees, I dredged up stories from my memory, myths and fables, lost knowledge and lessons learned. I tried not to think about my cell phone and how many messages from Ben it had on it by this time.

When the outer door opened, I flinched, startled, even though I shouldn't have been surprised. I'd been expecting them, hadn't I?

The four of them filed in. Kumarbis led.

Wolf itched; we were sitting, they were looking down on us, so I climbed to my feet, squared my shoulders. Didn't look Kumarbis in the eye because whatever else he was, he was still a vampire. But the others—I met their gazes, waited for their reactions.

Enkidu was neutral. Sakhmet gave me a comforting smile. I wasn't much comforted. Zora kept ducking her gaze, looking away. I wondered if she realized she was doing it.

Kumarbis's arrival meant night had fallen again. The third night. Too long. It hardly seemed to matter anymore. He'd been around for over two thousand years, time probably didn't mean anything to him.

I wished I could skip forward to when this could all be over. But I stood tall and didn't look away.

Kumarbis intoned in his ritual voice, "Tonight, we speak in praise of Regina Luporum, also called Lupa Capitolina." The others bent their heads, as if in prayer. "Tonight, we tell *your* story."

I perked up, trying to focus. My latest hero: I could see her, in the picture of the statue I'd printed, snarling and protective. The story Marid had hinted at, of the founding of Rome. The queen of the wolves, who stood up for her kind. Was I anything like her? How could I be?

The vampire continued. "She is not only the defender of the weak, but the savior of an empire. She shows us how by defending the needy, one may become the mother of an empire. What glory for her! Even should she die, as the one of whom we speak died. When the enemies of Romulus came for him, she put herself in their way and fought to her death to stop them. As all mothers will die to protect their children.

She saved the life of Romulus, who went on to glory, and so we celebrate her sacrifice . . ."

This wasn't right. I knew, because I'd just done the research. "That's not what happened, not according to the stories. Romulus killed his brother over power. What would their mother have thought of that? How is that protecting the pack? The wolf, the Capitoline Wolf, she saved them, but she didn't die for them. They didn't have enemies, they had an argument, and she was out of the picture by then." At least, the stories didn't mention her after that.

He bowed his head, a wry smile on his face, the expression of a teacher confronting a recalcitrant student. "The stories are corrupted, unreliable. I know the truth of them. I've *seen*."

I gaped. "Seen, as in witness? Are you saying you were *there*?"

"I have seen the truth of the stories."

Maybe he really had been there at the founding of Rome. Maybe he really had seen. Or maybe he was a standard demagogue, offering his interpretations as ultimate truth. Like someone calling in to my show, declaring their opinion of the One True Path.

"Or maybe you're winging it, like the rest of us."

"It is the place of mothers—even foster mothers, or those who play the role of mothers—to die for their children."

Oh for the love of . . . "A woman should be able to be a mother without being a martyr," I said.

Again, he offered a condescending smile. "Wouldn't you die to save your children? Or for a cause you believe in? I see your courage—I think you would."

Having children had become such an abstract concept for me. I couldn't have my own, but Ben and I had talked about adopting. Someday. When life got less crazy. Like, when I wasn't being kidnapped by weird revenge cults. But this wasn't about children. It was a red herring, a bad argument.

This was a discussion about sacrifice. I'd come back here because I was willing to make that sacrifice, if I had to. But I wouldn't be doing it for Kumarbis.

"You're way too eager to fit me into that slot," I said. "My plan right now isn't to become a martyr. That time may come, but not yet."

"You have a destiny," Kumarbis said. "Zora has seen it in her visions, we all felt it when you arrived here—"

"—when you kidnapped and dragged me here."

He took a deep breath, the better to lecture with. "You are here for a reason, but more than that you are what you are for a reason. Regina Luporum called to you, guided you—it is your destiny to become her heir. It was your destiny to become the wolf that you are."

"Are you saying it was my *destiny* to get attacked and torn up and turned into . . . *this*?"

They all, all of them, stared back at me like it was obvious. In their world, of course these things happened for a reason.

"Yes," the vampire said.

My teeth were bared, my muscles stiff. I leaned forward, aggressive. The bars around Wolf's cage were dissolving, turning to air. "That was the worst night of my life," I said, my voice low to keep from screaming. "I was raped by a frat boy and left in the woods and shredded by a werewolf—where the *hell* is the destiny in that?"

It was only slightly gratifying, seeing them flinch at the word *raped*. Zora had pressed herself against the tunnel wall.

Attempting to be soothing, Kumarbis said, "There is power in pain—"

"Fuck you." The words turned into a howl, and I doubled over, clutching my gut. A million needles stabbed my skin, fur about to burst through, and my bones ached, struggling to change. We could do it, reach out claws, launch ourselves at the vampire's throat and tear into flesh. We'd do a lot of damage before they stopped us. In that moment, all we want is to do damage, fierce and bloody.

But I held on tight, I kept hold of her leash and kept myself together. Breathed slowly, thought calm thoughts. Took myself out of this place and conversation. A peaceful clearing in summer, sunlight in trees, birdsong. Green growing things and peace. My breathing slowed, Wolf retreated, the bars returned. Wolf came out when I called her, not when they did.

Sakhmet moved between us, hands raised, calming. "Kumarbis, please let her be. Regina, are you calm?"

I straightened, rounded my shoulders. Came as close as I could to meeting the vampire's gaze without letting him trap me. Zora glared fearfully. She was the most vulnerable one here—at least she was smart enough to recognize it.

However, nothing fazed Kumarbis. "You show the power of Regina Luporum at every turn. You truly are her avatar." He bowed his head, in a show of respect that I didn't believe.

Even rolling my eyes wasn't worth the effort. Not that Kumarbis noticed my annoyance. He saw what he wanted to.

I hadn't thought about Zan, the wolf who attacked and infected me, in a long time. I thought about that night, sure, but I didn't spend much time thinking about *him,* the person. I wasn't sure I could remember what he looked like, man or wolf. He was a young guy, early twenties like I had been at the time, working odd jobs and trying to get by when he wasn't being a werewolf, which he seemed to enjoy. Now, he was dead. So were Carl, Meg, and TJ, the old pack, the werewolves who took me in and made me what I am. That was a chapter I'd happily left behind, and my only regret was I hadn't been able to take TJ with me. He'd died so I could escape. Him, I remembered clearly, gratefully. He'd had a chance to run, and he didn't. He risked his life for me. Yes, I understood sacrifice.

And if TJ were here, he'd probably kick my ass for not running away when I had the chance.

That all seemed like such a long time ago.

Kumarbis whispered to Zora, who nodded and began bustling around the antechamber, gathering up a bag of items she'd stashed against the wall, lighting candles, dousing the camp lanterns, until all that was left was flickering, natural flame. The handful of yellow will-o'-the-wisp lights left the rest of the place in shocking, complete darkness. When Zora moved her candle, the faces of the others appeared like misshapen ghosts. Their eyes blazed.

"One more step remains in your initiation, before we can perform our ritual," Kumarbis said.

In the corner of my eye, I saw Zora, her back to the rest of us, take off her shirt and pull on a long white tunic. She moved quickly, searching her bag for more items, making additional preparations, letting loose her ponytail, adding chains and jewelry to her ensemble.

The others lined up in front of me. "What?" I

asked, wary. I thought that meant the ritual, the one they kept talking about, that Zora was obviously preparing to lead. But they weren't making any motions toward the ritual chamber. So what else did they want? Did I dare ask?

"You join your blood with ours," Kumarbis said.

Typical ritual stuff. Blood oath, I slice my hand, then what? My mouth was sticky, and instead of the snarky question I was thinking, I simply blurted, "How?"

They didn't say anything, but Sakhmet gave me the cue. Her brow furrowed and she winced as if embarrassed as she glanced at me, then at the vampire. Vampire, blood . . . he had to be getting it from somewhere. Shit. *We take turns,* Enkidu had said.

Finally Zora turned back to us, and she had transformed herself. The floor-length tunic shone in the candlelight. Her blond hair was loose, hanging almost to her waist, and held back from her face by a gold-colored metallic band. She wore a New Age shop's worth of amulets around her neck, arms, and waist. I had to admire her theatricality, but if she was trying to impress me, she failed. I'd seen Cormac work spells with bits of string he'd pulled from the pockets of his leather jacket. No more theatricality than changing a lightbulb. I knew which one of them I trusted more.

But this wasn't a spell, was it? It was a *ritual.* It was a *lifestyle.*

I wasn't one of them, I wasn't *with* them, the taking turns didn't apply to *me,* did it? But I had come back into the mine, I'd returned to help them . . . I was already shaking my head. "I only feed my friends, and only when they need it."

"We are your friends," Kumarbis said.

"I'm thinking we may have different definitions of the word."

"Then we are allies," he said.

Was he wrong? I didn't know. I was cornered again, surrounded, with them making demands. My resolve was fading, after all that talk of martyrdom. I'd fed vampires before, wasn't a big deal, and arguing was so tiring. But in my gut, Wolf was howling. *This is too much to give . . .*

I lunged before I realized I was doing it, hands out, curled, open mouth aimed for Kumarbis's throat. It wouldn't taste good, but it sure would be satisfying . . .

Enkidu and Sakhmet both rushed forward, grabbed my arms, yanked me up short, and held me fast while I thrashed, snarling.

"Stop it, stop it! You'll ruin everything!" Zora cried, hands pressed to her head.

Sakhmet's voice was next to my ear. "Calm, be calm, please. We need you for this. Please." Her voice was soothing, like a purr. She and her partner had braced and weren't going to budge. I could wrench my arms out of my sockets, and they'd keep hold of me.

But she kept whispering, and Wolf settled, retreating back to her cage.

I trusted Sakhmet. I listened to her.

"We're out of time," Zora continued, pleading with Kumarbis now. "We need to do this *now,* or we'll miss the proper phase and have to wait until the next full moon."

Sagging in the lycanthropes' arms, I stopped struggling and stared ahead like the caged wolf I was. "I am not staying here for another month. We'll do this now."

Zora stomped over to me, brave now that I was restrained. She brought herself close enough that I could have bit her nose off with a well-timed snap. I just grinned at her.

She said, "If you want to learn about Dux Bellorum, if you want to see him destroyed, then you must be initiated of your own free will. If you want to see our true purpose, then this is the only door into that realm."

You must bring an offering of blood, if you wish to ask questions . . .

I had to remember why I was here. I relaxed, straightened. Tentatively, Enkidu and Sakhmet loosened their grips. I had to focus. Refocus. I didn't bolt.

"I want to know about Gaius Albinus," I said.

Kumarbis said, "He is a force of evil, with plans for domination—"

"I know that!" I glared. Kumarbis blinked, taken aback. He'd probably never had anyone interrupt him before. At least not for a bunch of centuries. "Tell me about the man. You turned him. You knew him when he was mortal. I want to know how you met. How you decided to make him a vampire. Can you tell me that?"

Now he was in the same place I was—cornered, resisting. Having to give to get what he wanted. Good. Let him see how it feels.

He licked his lips, drew breath in order to speak. "How—how do you know? Who told you that?"

"I guessed," I said, before Enkidu could fall on that sword and get himself in trouble by admitting he'd told. "You have his coin. You're old. Very old. You haven't had an easy time of it, have you?"

I must have been just vague enough to make sense, because he nodded. His face sagged into a long expression of sadness as his gaze turned inward, to his own long, uneasy history. Then he gave his head a deep bow, a show of respect. "You have the insight of Regina Luporum. You truly are her avatar."

I did not roll my eyes. Guy could rationalize anything he wanted to. "Can you tell me about Gaius Albinus? I want to know what happened when you met him."

Seconds ticked on. The others stared, holding their breath.

"Submit, and I will tell you," he said finally. I expected him to leer, but he didn't. He was making a deal, and he was serious.

The tension in the place was at a constant pitch, so I didn't notice it anymore. Like the smell of rock, the itch of silver. But I felt a spike, all of them watching, wondering which way I'd leap. My eyes burned, my gaze intent, haunted.

I'd already gone all-in, hadn't I, when I turned around and came back underground?

Kumarbis nodded, and Enkidu and Sakhmet stepped away. Then, I stretched my arm to him. My left arm. When I'd done this before, she asked for my off hand, out of politeness. The memory of Alette sparked an image, a scent—I could almost smell her, clean and chilled, in the startlingly domestic setting of her Washington, D.C., townhome. The sensations were so visceral I almost choked. Maybe she'd come and rescue me from this.

I clamped down on everything, every memory, every emotion, every reaction, so that I could hold my arm steady. Not so much as a tremor shook me. I set my jaw and stared, determined.

Kumarbis stepped forward and took my hand. His touch was gentle, more gentle than I expected. As if he realized how close I was to losing it, to freaking out and giving Wolf permission to get us out of this. His skin was rough, calloused. I wondered—was the rough skin preserved from his former life? Or maybe this was part of him simply not caring about appearances. He wasn't an aristocrat. He didn't need to be an aristocrat.

He moved so he was standing next to me, but at an angle to better cradle my arm, which he handled like it was a piece of glass, fragile and precious. Petting the skin, stroking his thumb along the inside of my forearm to warm it, to bring the blood to the surface. He knew what he was doing, to calm his . . . donor. Not victim. In other circumstances, his movements might even have been seductive. Some vampires I'd spoken to told me that a willing, aroused victim tasted better than one who struggled. That was why they did what they did, acted the way they did. Attracting, luring, rather than hunting. Most vampires I'd met were very good at it. I thought again of Alette, and wished I hadn't. I didn't want to remember her when I remembered him, and this.

My stomach churned. I'd either eaten too much, or not enough. I looked away, squeezed my eyes shut. I hadn't meant to, but it was either that or panic.

When his lips, as rough as his hands, brushed the inside of my wrist, I almost decided that feeling him was worse than seeing him. His movements were amplified in my imagination. The lips stroked along the tendon, to the base of my palm, and back. He tightened his grip on my arm, tucking it under his own to stabilize it. His tongue darted, tasting my skin. I clenched my fist, tried hard not to yank away. His story had better be worth it.

When he finally bit, I hardly felt it. I'd been so tense, waiting, so overwhelmed with anticipation, that the pain of his fangs in my skin lasted only a second. His lips closed over the wound, and he drank. I kept my eyes shut, my head craned away from him, and waited.

He shouldn't have needed much. Vampires didn't need to kill their prey. They only needed a few sips to survive—more, to be strong. But I was a werewolf, and he could take a lot more from me than he could a normal person without hurting me. I was pretty sure he'd take advantage of that. I should have eaten more, so I'd get through this easier. Asked for another bottle of water. I should have done a lot of things.

My sense of time was shot to hell. I didn't know how long he drank from me. It seemed like far too long, but then any amount of time would have felt too long.

His mouth lifted, and cool air chilled the wet spot on my wrist where his lips had been. I sighed, relaxing in spite of myself. Over, it was over. He licked the wound twice to speed the healing, then let go of me and moved away, until he was standing just out of my reach.

My arm fell, dangling at my side. I sat slowly,

because I was afraid I'd fall over. Cross-legged, I left my arms resting on my legs and sighed. Let the dizziness pass. I felt like a little kid getting a shot. I stretched, rubbing my arm to put some life back into it. It tingled. Blood loss—he'd taken a lot. But the wounds—two little circles, hardly bigger than bug bites—were already scabbed over, turning pink. Another reason vampires liked feeding from werewolves—rapid healing. Fast food. Ugh.

Sakhmet crouched and put her hand on my shoulder. I didn't even flinch away. I was too exhausted to feel anything. She offered me a bottle of water, which I desperately needed after this. As she'd well known. Den mother. I smiled at my own joke.

"Are you all right?" she whispered.

"I'm feeling a little drained," I said. That choking sound was Enkidu, standing behind her, sputtering. He either thought it was funny or horribly disrespectful. Or both, that was okay, too. She only smiled, rubbed my shoulder, then left me alone. I drank, downing almost the whole bottle of water.

"Your blood is now combined with all of ours, in me," Kumarbis announced. Like I should be proud. "Now, our circle is truly complete, and we may perform our rituals."

This wasn't over yet. Of course it wasn't. Zora was lurking at the edges of the antechamber, scowling.

Impatient, probably. I was holding up her party. Whatever.

"I want my story," I said. "If I really am part of the circle—I want to know what you know. You want me to trust you, give me the story you promised."

He closed his eyes, bowed his head, nodded. Then, he spoke.

Chapter 16

I AM VERY old. I'm not sure how old. I have spent stretches of time when I was not as . . . aware as I should have been. Always, I managed to survive. But . . . I was not old, once." Kumarbis spoke with something like wonder in his voice, as if he could not believe that he had ever been young. Though when he said "not old," why did I think he meant a century or two? A span of time that would have been forever to the rest of us. "I don't remember what it was to be mortal. My life then, who I was then, has not been important for a very long time. I feel myself a creature who came to being out of nothing.

"I was made what I am now in the mountains of Anatolia. I was made, but not claimed. Attacked and abandoned. I could have been destroyed as a demon. Perhaps I should have been, times being what they were. But Fate took me in hand. I had a destiny. I must have had a destiny."

The others, even Zora, settled on the stone floor, gathering around the vampire in a semicircle, watching him with intense focus. Something about the warm light of the candles, the ancient scent of the granite, made me feel as if we had traveled back in time to those ancient mountains. Kumarbis's voice itself had altered the flow of time, and we were in the ancient world.

"When the Roman Empire rose and spread, it seemed new to me. I traveled, studying it. The Romans—they had very good roads. I traveled, looking for . . . purpose. I had so much power—I could have set myself up as a god in some small village. Others of our kind did so. But that seemed too obvious, too easy. If one of our kind was a god alone, how powerful would two of us be? Or all of us? A pantheon of the supreme undead. That is how we were meant to be. An empire of our own, like others that had come before, but this one would last, ours would be eternal, as we were. What Rome dreamed of but could not achieve. I traveled, spoke to others, tried to show them my vision. But I could not sway them. They were satisfied with their tiny, inconsequential kingdoms. I—I was not meant to be an emperor. But there was another.

"Something . . . something guided me to Palestine

and the Roman occupation there. Like a voice in the wilderness. That's how the story goes, I think. A voice in the wilderness calling me. There were so many in those days putting themselves forward as prophets, as preachers, promising a better world to their followers. I thought one of them might be my worthy partner. But no, one by one they failed, they fell. Then I found this man, this centurion. He was one of hundreds, thousands of soldiers I had seen. I shouldn't have been able to pick him out of a crowd. But I did. I saw him and knew he could be powerful. That feeling I had, that voice, had steered me true."

He smiled, triumphant at the memory. He had entranced himself into returning to that distant past. To distant glory.

I had a million questions. What had those other vampires been like? The ones with the tiny kingdoms? How had he survived all those years, without a Family or a place of his own? Did he have rivals, with the same thought of gathering allies? Was this the start of the Long Game? What about this feeling, this instinct? I kept my mouth shut, because I didn't want to distract him. I didn't want him to decide not to finish.

"I avoided the Master of Jerusalem, made my way through the city on my own. I met the man known as Gaius Albinus. Befriended him, even. He was a serious young man, ambitious. His career was everything to him, and he was destined for high rank, for accolades. The Empire was built on the shoulders of thousands of men like him, who worked for the good of the whole because it meant success for themselves."

So far, Kumarbis hadn't said anything I didn't already know about Roman. He was still serious and ambitious. But I did have a hard time thinking of him as young. Maybe all old vampires gave off that impression.

"I knew, somehow, he was destined for more. He was greater. Everything in my being said so. I could make him immortal, and he would be invincible, unstoppable. Together, we could do . . . do anything."

The story had taken on the tone of a confession. He wasn't just explaining, he was apologizing.

"He . . . needed time. He required persuading. But he saw my vision, in time. Eventually, I convinced him."

"You attacked him," I said. "He didn't choose."

There was a long pause, made heavy by the silent weight of stone.

"Yes," he said finally, facing the ground. His head was bent, his shoulders slumped. He wouldn't look at any of us.

I could almost feel sorry for Roman, in spite of myself. A minute ago I would have said the guy didn't deserve any pity at all. But this, imagining him as much a victim as any of us . . . No, I didn't pity him, but maybe I understood him a little better. Him and his war.

My friend Rick also had been turned against his will. Rick and Roman were nothing alike. Or maybe they were two sides of the same coin. Rick was still out there, fighting his crusade against Roman with the Order of Saint Lazarus of the Shadows, the Vatican's order of vampire priests. I wondered if the order knew about Kumarbis. I had a feeling they didn't. Everyone else had been tracking Roman himself, but I'd found the other end of the thread, and was following it forward to the beginning. Maybe the key to defeating Roman lay in his origin. This had been worth the blood the vampire had taken from me. Worth returning to the mine. But there was more.

I wanted to shout at Kumarbis that this was his fault. The Long Game, Dux Bellorum, the man Roman had become. All his scheming, all the people he'd hurt, the vampires he'd made, the conspiracy he'd gathered to himself. It had all started here, and I had only one question.

"Why?" I asked finally. "Why did you need to turn Gaius Albinus, to make him invincible? For what purpose?"

The vampire sighed, an affectation. An expression of resignation. "It seemed . . . necessary at the time. It was so long ago. So much has happened since then, I hardly remember why."

Now may we kill him?

Wolf was mocking me. Such a kidder.

I curled my lips, baring my teeth. Wolf expressing her opinion. Kumarbis didn't even flinch. He said, "I remember one thing—as soon as it was done, my certainty left me. I took care of Gaius Albinus, watched over him as had not been done for me. I still . . . he was like my son, a son I could never have. But he was so angry. What else could I do but take care of him and hope for the best?"

Gaius Albinus, Dux Bellorum, was the general. Caesar was the true emperor, pulling the general's strings. I hadn't thought that Kumarbis might actually be that Caesar. No, he was something else. A pawn, maybe. The same strings had yanked on them both. *Those* were the strings I had to follow. I was pretty sure I wouldn't be happy with whom I found at the end of them.

I waited, and Kumarbis continued. "We had a falling-out, years later. Of course we did. You could have guessed that."

The pendant around his neck indicated that at one point he'd signed on with Roman. Been one of his allies in the Long Game, linked to him, commanded by him. Without his mystical voice guiding him, the Long Game must have seemed full of purpose, and Roman's drive inspiring. At one time, he'd been willing to follow.

Something had made him leave, obviously. I could imagine a number of scenarios. I put myself in Roman's place, regarding this man, the vampire who'd made him, who must have seemed weak and purposeless to his regimented, ambitious mind. He would have punished Kumarbis, maybe indirectly. Kumarbis, who felt so much loyalty, however misguided, would have put up with it until . . . My imagination failed me. To be a fly on that wall, all those hundreds of years ago.

Kumarbis saw himself as a father, even now, to this ragged little band he'd collected. He probably slotted me easily into the role of rebellious teenager. The trickster whose chaos balanced order, who would find the solution, accidentally or otherwise, to all their problems. Like Coyote in the stories. He wouldn't listen to me, he'd only pay attention to the role he'd constructed for me in his own dusty brain.

The one thing he was right about: he might very well know Roman better than anyone in the world. Now, what did I do with that information?

"Now you fight against him," I said. "You did more than leave Gaius Albinus, you changed your mind about the whole mission, about the Long Game. Why did you stop believing in uniting the vampires?"

"I could not convince the Masters of the cities to unite, but he did. At first I admired him. I thought *I* had inspired him. He was carrying out *my* plan. But he . . . he went to places I could not follow. He found lore I had no knowledge of, he brought the beasts under his influence—"

"Beasts," I said. "Werewolves? Lycanthropes?"

"And more, creatures that even in centuries of wandering I hadn't known existed. I never asked so many questions as Gaius did. He knew, I think he understood, that if he could become this monster, this creature that we were, then all the other stories must be true. All the magic in the world must be real. He wants to be master of it all, so that he can destroy it all."

Not rule, but destroy. It didn't even surprise me. In the washed-out lantern light, in the depths of this cave, where the air smelled cold and the shadows seemed alive, anything was possible, anything at all. All the stories came to life.

Kumarbis gripped the coin around his neck. "When he made this, the first of the coins, I saw what he would become. Where his ambitions lay. I followed him still, I wore the coin because I had nowhere else to go. I had been alone for so very long, you see. You cannot understand how long I was alone."

No, I couldn't. My sympathies swung wildly, from one to the other, to both. They'd both been wronged, they'd both made mistakes. I couldn't feel anything anymore.

"But you left," I said. "You left, but you didn't stop him, back when he wasn't so powerful—"

"I wore his coin," Kumarbis said simply. "I could not harm him. Leaving was difficult enough. Breaking the bond, marring the coin, nearly destroyed me. I don't know of anyone who's done it since."

Anastasia had done it. She'd been called Li Hua when she lived in China at the time of Kublai Khan, and Roman had bought her as a slave from the conquering army. He'd turned her, she'd served him—and then she'd escaped. She was the one who'd explained the coins to me. And Kumarbis had never had a clue about her, or anything else that had happened after he left Roman, I was betting.

"How? How's he going to do it? Destroy everything?" I said. Only one of many obvious questions. But the one I really had to know, if I wanted to stop the man. That artifact, the one Roman was looking for—the Hand of Hercules—did Kumarbis know about that?

"Does it matter? If we stop him, it won't matter—"

"Yes, dammit, it matters!"

His body seemed to creak with the deep breath he took. "We will stop him, and the point will be moot."

He didn't know. Chuckling, I scratched my itchy, unwashed hair. The vampire didn't move. Didn't stand up to announce that he was finished, that he'd carried out his part of the deal and we were done now. This was still story time, and he was still waiting for my questions. Maybe I had some journalistic interview chops after all.

I said, "You could have had power. You could have gathered followers, like Roman has. But you never settled, never founded a Family of your own—why is that?"

"I was not meant to stay in one city, to rule over mundane matters. I was not meant for power. I learned that then. If I could have been Master of my own Family, I would have succeeded all those years ago."

He'd tried to be a Master and failed. Or rather, stopped trying when he realized continuing would probably get him killed. Failed Masters were destroyed, they didn't escape with their undead half-lives. He'd succeeded in surviving. Might have been the only thing he'd ever succeeded at. Finally, in the end, I did feel sorry for him.

"I'm sorry," I said. "For everything you went through."

He bowed his head in acknowledgment. "And now, there is nothing else to tell. It is time. Zora, we must prepare."

When he climbed to his feet, he looked like a figure of bone, wood, and leather unfolding, stretching and groaning, a carving come to life, but it was only my imagination, building on stories. I didn't actually hear his dry skin creak, or see puffs of ancient dust rise from his joints as he straightened. His movement only seemed like it should be accompanied by such effects. Even after drinking my blood, which should have made him flush, he seemed faded.

Zora came to his side, took his arm, and he leaned on her as they made their way to the ritual chamber.

"Come," he said over his shoulder to the rest of us.

I had to remind myself this wasn't a story. I was here physically, and this was real. I was still processing what he'd told me. It all made such weird sense. I would love to hear the story from Róman's point of view. I probably never would, and that made me a little sad.

Enkidu and Sakhmet waited for me to pull myself off the floor. She was at my shoulder, as she had been since the vampire had fed.

"Are you all right?"

"Yeah," I said, sighing. I looked at her. "Had you heard any of that before?"

"It's more than he's ever told the rest of us," Sakhmet said. "It—it happened so long ago, it's hard to think that those events still impact us. Are still driving this."

"That's all of history," I said, gathering the motivation to haul myself to my feet. "Vampires just put a face on it."

Chapter 17

THE RITUAL chamber had been transformed. Zora must have been busy in the day or so since I'd last been in here. While I'd been asleep, she'd been preparing.

She moved clockwise around the rough-hewn walls of the room, using a candle to light torches set in sconces drilled into the stone. Five torches, for the five points of the star painted on the floor. The flames produced more light, orange and churning, than I'd yet seen in this underground world. I looked up—and up, and up. What I hadn't noticed before in the darkness: the mine extended upward, a vertical shaft that must have followed the vein of ore. A tower of open space, outcrops of rough granite wavering in the light. Boards lay across the space at irregular intervals, and a couple of ancient, desiccated wooden ladders were

propped against the stretches of stone, as far up as
the light allowed me to see. Miners had worked here,
once upon a time, climbing ever upward in search of
wealth. The surface of the wood glittered with that
ever-present patina of precipitated minerals.

I gazed in awe, as if I stared up from the nave of a
cathedral. The lofty space of a holy site, carved out
of what people called living rock. The air seemed to
pulse with the rhythm of my breathing. Black smoke
trailed upward, to infinity. There must have been
some unseen cracks or fissures to the surface, provid-
ing ventilation. The chamber smelled of pitch and
incense, sandalwood and sage. Oily, hot, pungent. I
blinked, my eyes stinging from the smoke, squinting
to try to adjust to the changing light. I put out my
hands, afraid I was going to get dizzy. I was still
hungry, dehydrated. Nothing I could do about it but
hang on.

Arriving at the top point of the star, Kumarbis
wore a serene smile on his face, hands folded regally
before him. He might have been a statue, or a figure
from an ancient frieze. He might very well have been
the model for one of those stone kings, with his broad
face and determined gaze. He had on the same pale,
loose shirt and pants he'd been wearing. Only Zora
was dressed as some kind of otherworldly priestess.
Thank goodness she wasn't making us all wear white
robes.

Kumarbis nodded at me and said, "Regina Luporum, will you join us and take your place in our circle?"

Zora pointed at a spot, one of the branches of the star. I didn't recognize any of the markings there, nothing that particularly meant "Regina Luporum" or anything else. It could have been scribbling, random symbols copied from a Wikipedia article. If I asked Zora what the symbols meant, would she know? Or would she tell me I couldn't possibly understand? I wanted to remember this, the symbols and patterns, everything, so I could ask Cormac and Amelia about it later.

I'd wanted to know what all this was about. Fine. This was it.

"We won't hurt you," Sakhmet whispered as she moved past me to her own place on the circle. Her smile was meant to be reassuring, and in spite of myself, I was reassured. I liked her. If only we could have coffee together in my favorite diner and have a normal conversation. This setting was damaging my judgment.

When Zora finished lighting torches, she joined us in the circle. Five points to the star, a place for each of us to stand. Kumarbis, then me, then Zora, then Enkidu and Sakhmet. I could see their faces, watch their expressions. They all showed calm, but their bodies were tense with anticipation. I scented their sweat, which gave the air a ripe, musty odor. *We are the sacrifice.* The sudden thought might not have been wrong, either. I was well into the cave, away from the tunnel. I'd have to get past Kumarbis to escape. That was probably intentional. Or was it critical that Regina Luporum stand in *this* spot and no other?

I was supposed to be concentrating on the ritual. I was supposed to be cooperating. I was feeling dizzy, slipping out of my own body.

A B-grade horror flick featuring an ancient magical ritual might have done something similar to what Zora cooked up. She brought her toolkit with her and worked industriously, scooping dried herbs out of a wooden box, putting them in a brazier, pulling crystals out of a velvet sack, along with sticks and wands and carved symbols, little sphinxes and Eyes of Horus and Ganeshas and Chinese symbols that I felt like I should have recognized.

I wanted to say something, to poke at her and the obvious theatricality of what she was doing. Like she wasn't sure exactly what worked so she was going to try it all. But I kept quiet. My jaw hurt, I clamped it shut so tightly in my effort to keep quiet.

Then things took a turn. The next item she drew from her kit was a dead bird—an all-white dove, stiffened, eyes missing. It smelled musty rather than corpselike. Mummified. Next, a sheet of yellowed paper, or maybe parchment, that appeared to be blank.

And a jar, containing a very much alive mouse, peach size and gray, skittering up the sides of the glass. There appeared to be holes punched into the lid. These three items she placed in the center of her ritual space, on top of a spiraling shape that must have had some specific meaning.

She moved around the circle, placing crystals and totems, little piles of herbs and salt, sprinkling us all with water from a copper bowl. I blinked and winced when the water hit my face, suppressing a growl. I hoped the others understood the heroic efforts I was making here to be good and quiet. I entertained myself by imagining what Cormac might say about all this, and I decided he wouldn't say anything. He wouldn't have to; the smirk on his face would be epic. And what would Amelia say? I didn't know her as well as I knew Cormac, but I imagined she'd be smirking just as hard. The two of them got along for a reason.

I needed to stop thinking about Cormac and Amelia, and how they could help me if they were here. But I also needed to remember as many details as I could about all this, so I could tell them, so they could help me ferret out the meaning of this. I had to have faith that I would be able to talk to them about this later. So I tried to pay attention to the details they would want to know. The dove, the mouse, the torches, the symbols. My vision was swimming from the smoke.

Zora was saying prayers under her breath. A consecration, I realized. A cleansing, a blessing.

She went to Kumarbis last, leaving talismans for his place on the circle, saying her prayer. Last, she held out her hand, and he pulled the coin on its cord over his head and gave it to her. Like giving the bloodhound something to scent.

Was it crazy that this was starting to make sense?

She placed the coin in the center circle, with the dead dove, the sheet of paper, and the live mouse. Finally, she returned to her place on the star and circle, raised her arms, and began to chant. "*Munde Deus virtuti tuae,* confirm thy power in us, oh spirit of the world, confirm thy power against our enemy, may his paths be uncertain, let the spirit of the world persecute him, El, Elohim, Elohe, Zebatth, Elion, Escerchie, Adonay, Jah, Tetragrammaton, Saday . . ."

And so on. She moved from English to Latin to languages I didn't recognize. Probably Hebrew and Arabic, and a few others besides. Whatever language, whatever she was saying, she spoke like she meant it, and her conviction brought a strange weight to the room, as if the air grew thicker, and breathing grew more difficult. Enkidu's and Sakhment's chests moved visbly; they, too, were taking deeper, more purposeful breaths. Enkidu's expression was set, frowning, determined. He watched Zora as if he could make her succeed by force of will alone. Sakhmet, also determined, full of faith, was watching Enkidu.

Kumarbis wasn't breathing at all, because he didn't need to. Of all of us, he was relaxed, arms loose at his sides. His head was tilted back, and he smiled. It was a look of triumph. He had been planning this for centuries, and finally, *finally,* his great scheme was coming to fruition. Of course he looked triumphant. So, what would he do if nothing happened?

Because apart from her chanting, the wavering light of the torches, and the psychological influences that prompted us to think we'd entered another world, nothing was happening. Movement kept catching my gaze—a spark of reflected light in the thumb-size crystal she'd put on the ground in front of me. The pale yellow stone was catching the flickering light of the torches and throwing it back at me. Swirling patterns in the air were only smoke, writhing, thickening. The burning incense drifted, gathered, growing dense. The light from the torches played against it. I could almost imagine I saw shapes in the light and shadow, the haze in the air. Claws and legs, fangs and black eyes.

Zora's voice became ecstatic, as if she really was getting off on this. "The window opens, spirit of the world, give us the strength to tread on serpents, to smash the power of our enemy, that none may hurt us. The window opens, spirit of the world, show us our enemy!"

So help me, I saw something in the smoke, with eyes, looking back. Something male and wicked. I could almost smell it—cold, like stone. Vampirically cold, weighted with age and purpose. It seemed to look around the circle, studying each of us. Marking us, for future reference.

Wolf braced as if cornered. We wouldn't scream, we wouldn't run, because it wouldn't do any good. We would face it and fight.

This was the power of suggestion at work, nothing else. This was Plato's Allegory of the Cave, and we were trying to draw meaning from half-perceived images, building worlds out of shadows. But Wolf's hackles were rising, a shivering down the back of my spine that told me *something* was watching us. The urge to run grew. *Yes, let's, please.* I ought to listen to Wolf more often.

Kumarbis's eyes were closed, his arms spread, basking in the radiance of the ritual. Enkidu's jaw was taut, and he held himself in the rigid stance of a cornered wolf. He was feeling much like I was, then. I gathered he didn't know what to expect out of this ritual any more than I did. He had committed to all this without knowing details. Did that make him loyal, foolish, or both? Sakhmet also watched the patterns in the smoke, but every now and then she glanced at

Enkidu, and her fingers clenched as if she wanted to reach out to him and take his hand.

Zora moved to the center of the circle. In one hand she had a dagger, a clearly ceremonial piece with a slender, shining blade and a carved bone handle. Kneeling before the collection of items she'd placed there, she opened the jar and grabbed the flailing mouse. She held up the mouse in one hand and dagger in the other, beseeching the smoke rising into the expanse above us.

"Show me our enemy, show me the future!"

She dug the point of the dagger into the mouse and wrenched, splitting open the tiny body. Expertly, as if she had done this before, or often, she twisted the knife again, digging out a brick-red chunk of flesh the size and shape of a peanut. Its heart. The mouse squealed, a brief and shockingly loud sound. There was surprisingly little blood.

She dropped the mouse and ate its heart. Still hot. Zora chewed twice and swallowed. The body of the mouse was still twitching.

I stared, too shocked to react. The torches crackled and sparked. Zora's eyes were closed, and she clasped the dagger before her, point down. A few drops of blood dripped onto the paper.

By then, we were all holding our breath. I thought I heard a voice, a murky sound to go with the smoke and shadows. A soft, mocking chuckle. It didn't come from any of us. Zora's chants had spoken of defeating our enemy. But someone was laughing at us.

I caught Enkidu's gaze, tried to ask the question—who?—but he gave his head a small shake. "Zora—" I growled at the magician, questioning.

Her eyes opened, she looked up, jumped to her feet, and held out the blood-smeared dagger as if she might actually use it to defend herself. But there was nothing to attack, and even the laughter faded until I thought I'd imagined it.

Her tunic flapping around her legs, she turned back to her place on the circle and raised her arms. Shouting, she repeated chants from the ritual with a tone of defiance. More smiting of our enemy, along with words of banishing.

The only way I knew it was over was when she sat heavily, dropping the knife and putting her head in her hands. The smoke remained, drifting upward, and I continued to see patterns, whorls and spirals reflecting the shapes drawn on the floor. The torches still burned, and the stinging smoke and weight of expectation remained. The hair on the back of my neck stood up.

We stood around the circle, blinking at each other.

"What happened?" I said finally, breaking the quiet with the suddenness of shattering glass. Felt stupid doing it, but somebody had to say something. "Something happened, right?" I couldn't be sure anymore.

Maybe I was still tranquilized and dreaming all this. Except I didn't think my imagination was that good. My nose flared, picking up the scent of fresh blood. The mouse carcass, little more than bits of flesh and mangled fur, still lay in the middle of the circle. The smell made me oddly hungry.

"What did you learn?" Enkidu asked. Demanded.

Zora looked exhausted. She held her hands, stained with blood and soot, like they were newly discovered treasure. Like she was surprised this had worked, heaven help us.

"Zoroaster?" Kumarbis prompted, and at this she looked up, nodded. She crept to the center of the circle and retrieved the piece of paper, read the bloody pattern smeared on it, and nodded.

I expected a fortune-teller's vague pronouncement. A brooding man seeks your destruction, great changes loom in your future, your lucky numbers are two and twelve, and so on, yadda, whatever.

Zora spoke in an even, matter-of-fact tone. "He's in Split, Croatia, in the old town, the ruins of Diocletian's Palace. Very near his own origin. A place of healing and power for him. He thinks it's a place of safety, so his defenses are few. This is very good for us."

"How the hell—" I clamped my teeth shut before I could finish the outburst. Zora *knew,* the ritual worked, they were *right*.

Kumarbis laughed, the low victorious chuckle of a

supervillain, though he probably didn't hear it that way. "We have him. Finally, we can stop him. Thank you, thank you all." The vampire's eyes were half lidded, his lips curling back, showing fang. He might have become emperor of everything, as happy as he looked.

If Zora could use magic to find Roman, then maybe she really could stop him by zapping him with magic from five thousand miles away . . .

We have to get out of here. This is crazy. Kumarbis might have been right, but Wolf still didn't trust him. *He knows where we are, he knows what we're doing.*

Zora had opened a door, and the door allowed access both ways. If we'd found Roman, he could just as easily find us. The urge to flee became fierce. Antony hadn't been dumb, he hadn't been reckless. He wouldn't have confronted Roman if he hadn't thought he had a good chance against him. And he'd lost. What chance did we have?

The others didn't seem worried. They began to march out of the ritual space and back to the antechamber. Zora moved like a queen in her palace, her chin up, her tunic flowing around her, gold ornaments glinting in torchlight, as if they sparkled with their own light. Were they really gold, were they really ancient, or were they some cheap knockoff posing as ancient sacred artifacts? And did it matter, if they really were magic? The questions made me tired.

She retrieved the coin from the ritual space, returned it to Kumarbis, and processed with him back to the antechamber. The high priest and his acolyte, so imperious and serene, so sure of themselves. He was righteous, she was proud to follow him. We, the pack of lycanthropes, followed.

Back in the main chamber, Kumarbis turned and bowed to us all. "Dawn approaches. I must leave you. Tonight, our final ritual commences. We are close, so close. Thank you, all of you, for your help, your power, your blessing. Zoroaster. Sakhmet. Enkidu. Regina Luporum." He bowed again, eyes closed, head bent low. The show of gratitude was profound, genuine.

It almost made staying mad at him hard. *Almost.* He believed. He really, really believed.

"Wait a minute," I said, my words dropping like a china plate on a tile floor, breaking the mood, causing even me to shiver. I had to get out my thoughts, no matter how awkwardly. "You're right. I see that now. You're right, you really can do what you say you can do. I believe you." Saying it felt like I was giving over part of myself, carving out a piece of my own flesh. Admitting they were right about *me.* "But you're missing something."

"We've overlooked *nothing,*" Zora insisted.

"Zora," I said. Wincing, I revised the thought. "Zoroaster. The one who speaks for Zoroaster." I was absolutely no good at this ritual thing. Regina Luporum, hah, not even. "You opened a door, you saw Dux Bellorum—but doors open both ways. He can find us just like we've found him. He's in Split right now laughing at us." I flashed on the memory of my first day here, grabbing Sakhmet's hand through the slot in the door, desperately holding on in our tug-of-war. Roman could do that to us.

But everyone looked at her. Even Kumarbis looked at her, waiting for her response.

Her expression wrenched itself into a kind of fury, puckered, glaring. "We're safe here. I've protected this place, I've cast many spells, I've built many shields. No one can find us, no one can harm us. We're safe!" She spit the words, and her face flushed. In her robes and finery, she looked like she was playacting. I couldn't laugh, though. I felt a little sorry for her.

Kumarbis looked back at me. "You see? We are safe. Tomorrow, we can strike."

"Antony!" I said, making his name an exclamation. A call to arms, however incomprehensible. But I had gotten their attention. "My friend Antony. He was Master of Barcelona, but he was one of us—one of my allies in the fight against the Long Game. Like Ned, Alette, Anastasia, Marid . . . Rick." And what would they say if they could see me now? God, I could really use some help here . . . "Antony knew that Roman was in Split, and he went there to kill him. He thought he could kill him. He failed. He was destroyed. You can open a door to try to kill him, but you'll be going in blind. He *will* defend himself."

"And so will we," Kumarbis said, just like that.

"Before he died, Antony said Roman was in Split looking for something, an artifact or a spell or something, called the Hand of Hercules. Maybe it's a weapon, maybe it's something else, I don't know. You say you know Roman better than anyone—do you know what it is? Hand of Hercules, the . . . the Manus Herculei—"

Kumarbis's eyes widened in a show of recognition.

"You know!" I pressed. "You know what he's looking for, you know what it does."

He might not have realized he was speaking. "It was what caused our falling-out. It was why we parted ways. He sought a different kind of magic than I did. Not Hercules. Herculaneum. He was going to Herculaneum, looking for . . . something." His gaze went distant, dredging up two-thousand-year-old memories. He looked like a lost old man, nothing more than that.

And where the fuck was Herculaneum? It was all I could do to keep from screaming at Kumarbis, What? *What was it?*

I kept going, the tension pouring out in words.

"The next ritual, the second half tomorrow night—what's going to happen, exactly? You know Roman, you know what he's capable of, exactly how powerful he is—so how are you going to destroy him?"

The staring at me went on for another minute. I had gone so thoroughly off script they didn't know what to do with me. It was as if I'd done something unseemly at a dinner party and they couldn't look away. Finally Zora turned to Kumarbis—waiting for permission. Only when the vampire nodded did she turn to me and speak.

"The ceremony will gather the power to destroy Dux Bellorum, then open a door so the power will reach him. You will see it when it happens. You will understand." Her eyes were round; her raised hands, explaining in vague gestures, trembled. She was on the edge of breaking. Of insanity. Maybe her power demanded insanity.

"And when Roman hits back?"

Sakhmet put her hand on my arm, squeezed my wrist. I jerked away, bared my teeth. We were cornered. *Get out, now.* Too late for that.

"Regina, please," Sakhmet said.

"Please what?" I shot back. Please stop, please help, please wait? Please be patient, this could all still work out. Wolf didn't think so.

She looked at me, her golden gaze narrowed. Like

a cat on the hunt. "Please have faith. You've seen what we can do."

Enkidu added, "We represent five different aspects of power. By uniting our wills, our strength, we can overcome Dux Bellorum's defenses. We've already located him, we can strike while he is weak, while he doesn't know who or where we are. The next ritual will direct our united force to him, and destroy him magically."

I said, "There are others . . . he's got magicians working for him, vampires and lycanthropes, just like us. And did I tell you about the demon? She's working for the same person, thing, whatever, that Roman is. *That's* what I'm trying to say—what if we go through all this and it still isn't over?"

Zora glared at me, furious. I was almost taken aback. "You're wrong! You're an animal, you do not understand!"

We could tear out her throat . . . I put my hands on my temples, squeezed. Had to keep it together.

"Regina," Kumarbis said. "It's all right. It's going to be all right. You believe, you would not feel so strongly if you did not. But you must trust that this, our ritual, our plan, will work. Please."

That was what all this was about, after all. It wasn't enough to have me here, I had to be a willing—enthusiastic—participant. And if I didn't believe, and the ritual failed, they could point the finger at me, it would be my fault. I had no way to win this.

What could I do? What did I believe in, really?

I nodded, because what else could I do? Even though this wasn't faith, in the end. It was fanaticism. "But you—we have to be ready to defend ourselves. Roman isn't going to take this quietly."

The vampire—he gazed at me, a smile shifting the deep lines in his face, like a cracked leather mask coming to life.

"The very fact that you question us, that you urge us to such vigilance, proves to me that you are Regina Luporum. You *are* queen of the wolves, and we are fortunate to have you with us. Your guidance will see us through, I have no doubt."

My arguments fell silent. What could I possibly say after that?

Before I could flip out any more than I already had, Kumarbis gathered his dignity again, straightening, gazing on us all with the beatific regard of a priest. "I must think on this, and dawn approaches. I suggest you all rest for the day, as I will. Good night, my dear friends." He departed the chamber for his own quarters, to sleep out the day.

"I will attend him," Zora said, and followed. She was welcome to it.

That left the three of us, regarding each other as if we'd just survived a tornado. We'd been through something, we weren't sure what, and we couldn't quite believe we'd survived. And this was just the beginning.

I let out a snarl and started pacing, that same track, back and forth along the far wall of the antechamber.

"He's right," Sakhmet said in her gentle, diplomatic voice. "We should rest."

Finally, I pointed down the tunnel after Kumarbis and Zora. "Are they crazy? Do they really think they can just sneak up on a guy like Roman without any consequences? Who do they think they are?"

Enkidu sighed and said, "She is the avatar of Zoroaster, and he is . . . Kumarbis."

Because that made so much sense. About as much sense as a werewolf named Kitty. This wasn't about sense, it was about gut instinct and magic, and as much as I wanted to go after Roman and rip out his undead heart myself, this didn't feel right. This felt like a trap. I stopped pacing and laced my fingers in my hair, which had become hopelessly tangled and greasy. "Right, right, like you're the avatar of Enkidu and you're the avatar of Sakhmet. And why you all, and not the avatars of . . . of Shiva or Hermes Trismegistus? How do you know the real Sakhmet isn't running around somewhere—"

"Because it's a story," Enkidu said, identifying the fundamental problem with the whole enterprise. If you believed hard enough, worked hard enough, could you make the stories real by force of will? Were the ancient gods and myths only metaphors, or was there something more behind them? Could they have it both ways? According to the story, Enkidu and Gilgamesh battled giant scorpions in the cedar forest, and what about any of that made sense?

But what if they really had?

My smile felt bitter, exhausted. "Except there's really a Sun Wukong and Xiwangmu, because I've met them. And maybe they're just really powerful people who called themselves gods and convinced everyone else that they were right. But in their case I'm pretty sure the stories are about them, not the other way around. They didn't borrow their identities from the stories. Kumarbis is cobbling together whatever he can because he doesn't know what else to do. He's making it up as he goes along, and Zora's making it work because it gives her power. Where did Kumarbis find her?"

"She was telling fortunes in Istanbul," Sakhmet said. "She had a reputation—she was real, she was the fortune-teller the creatures of magic went to for help. That was how Kumarbis found her and recruited her. Named her the avatar of Zoroaster. We don't know where she's from. We think she's American, but how she came to be in the Middle East, practicing such powerful magic, we're not sure."

Another story I'd love to get on the show. I

wondered what I'd have to do to make that happen. Pay with more blood, probably.

"What does Kumarbis expect is going to happen?" I asked.

Sakhmet said, "The final ritual will destroy Gaius Albinus, Dux Bellorum."

The first ritual had worked—I *knew* it had worked. Why shouldn't the second? And what would be the cost?

Enkidu said, "You say you have met gods. Real gods, not avatars. Chinese, yes? The Monkey King, the Queen Mother of the West."

"You know some mythology."

"I've read a few books," he said, with a crooked half smile. The closest thing to a smile I'd seen on him. "Tell me, how is that possible?"

"I don't know," I said. "Right place at the right time. Or wrong place, depending on how you look at it. But they had power. I believed." I'd come to believe so much over the last few years, since doing the show and meeting people like Kumarbis. But I couldn't believe *him*. Sun Wukong had inspired me. This . . . this was something else entirely.

Enkidu's gaze turned downcast, somber. "We've lost so much of the power that we had in ancient days."

Sakhmet added, "Once, long ago, our kind were worshipped as gods. We were revered."

"If we still had some of that power," Enkidu said, "Dux Bellorum would not be as strong as he is."

"And that's why you're here?" I asked. "To get back the power of the gods?"

They didn't answer. They must have known what it sounded like from the outside. But still, they kept on, because . . . because what else could they do? If they had any hope that these rituals could defeat Roman, or at least give them the power to defeat Roman, they had to stay. That, I understood.

"You can't do what Zora's doing—you can't work that kind of magic that pokes and prods at someone without drawing attention. Scrying, searching—it works both ways. We might have learned something about Roman, but you can bet he learned something about us. If we know where he is, he might also have discovered where we are and what we're doing, and if he doesn't, he at least knows that we're looking for him. If he thinks we're a threat, he'll do something about it. He's been studying magic for two thousand years, and I don't care if Zora really is channeling Zoroaster, she's not as powerful as he is."

"We're safe here," Sakhmet said, soothing. "Zora's put many protections over this place. We're underground, hidden—"

"Any shield can be broken with enough time and effort," I said.

"What do you know about magic?" Enkidu shot back.

"Nothing," I said, a mad grin on my lips. "But I know some great magicians."

Sakhmet gathered calm to herself, folding her hands before her, closing her eyes. "We will be watchful. I will speak with Zora about it."

"Will she listen to you?" Enkidu said.

"I'll speak *gently*." The opposite of me, in other words. Giving me a sidelong look, she bowed her head to us and left through the tunnel to find the magician.

Enkidu studied me. The attention felt like a challenge. I was tired of meeting his challenges, but I did, because what choice did I have? I glared until he lowered his gaze. As if he wasn't aware he'd been staring. He was just like that all the time.

I said, "The next time Zora works a ritual against Roman, he'll be ready. He'll strike back at us. We're waging war, there's going to be a battle."

"We have to have faith that her magic will protect us." The words came rote, without any belief behind them.

Faith. And what was that? "Because that's what you do when you're dealing with gods. Have faith. Right?"

"If her magic fails, we have our claws and teeth. We are ready."

One of the bottles of water Sakhmet had given me

sat by the wall of the antechamber. It still had water in it, and I was desperate to wash the smoke and soot off my face and out of my eyes. I could imagine that the coating of grime and smoke I felt on me was really a layer of residual magic clinging to my skin, suffocating me. All the washing in the world wouldn't get rid of it. But I'd start with my eyes, and I'd take a long, much-needed drink. Since I didn't have anywhere else to go, I sat on the tunnel's dusty floor, clutching the bottle of water. When it became clear I wasn't going to try to flee, Enkidu left me alone to another day of trying to sleep, trying to calm my Wolf, who was anticipating the growing moon and ready to burst.

Can Change, can fight our way out. Yes, we could, I reassured her—myself. But not right now. Antony had thought facing Roman was worth risking his life. I couldn't do any less.

Chapter 18

SAKHMET AND Enkidu were right, I'd mostly gotten used to the silver, like I'd gotten used to the darkness-induced headache that never really went away.

The couple must have had their own space in the tunnel system, and they could have stuck me in that holding cell, but they didn't. Sometime later, they returned to the antechamber, as if together we might feel safer. A surrogate pack or pride. Surrogate for me. Enkidu and Sakhmet already had the kind of pack Ben and I had—our pack of two, I used to call it, when we'd first hooked up, before we'd returned to Denver and taken charge of the pack there.

Sakhmet brought a small drum with her, a bowl shape on a stand that tucked under her arm. It must have been one of the drums I'd heard my first day here. The two of them sat together, and she played softly while humming a melody I couldn't make out. The drumming was slow, off-rhythm, sounding a little like water rushing in a creek. Soothing. Her gaze distant, she seemed to play for her own comfort. To dispel some of the anxiety that had settled over us. Enkidu watched her, smiling vaguely. His arm settled over her shoulders.

It was a lullaby before bedtime. A way to bring peace before trying to sleep. After maybe twenty minutes, she set the drum aside, and the two of them curled up together. Enkidu wrapped his arm around his mate, she nestled against his body, and he nuzzled her head, breathing in her scent and kissing her above her ear. Eyes closed, she smiled, an expression full of calm and pleasure. I got the feeling she didn't much care what happened, as long as she and Enkidu were together. I'd felt that expression on my own face often enough, when Ben held me like that and kissed me just to kiss me.

I had to stop thinking about it before I started crying.

Kumarbis and Zora might have been pleased as rock stars at how their rituals were going. But the three of us were fighting instincts, struggling against a tension that made us want to bare our teeth and growl, howl, or roar. Our beasts wanted to flee.

We dozed off, then sat up suddenly, looking at the tunnel leading to the ritual chamber as if we expected to see something there. Hard to sleep, when we felt like we ought to be standing guard.

My thoughts turned. Antony couldn't stop Roman. What chance did we have? I was desperate for Kumarbis and Zora to know what they were doing. How much trouble would it save, to defeat Roman, here and now? Maybe we'd still have Roman's puppet master to deal with, but the general and his army would be gone. It was what I and my friends had been fighting for these last few years.

Sakhmet pulled away from Enkidu, found a bottle of water, and sat calmly, drinking. I watched her, and she stared back with eyes that had gone golden, hypnotic. A lion's eyes. I could see the shape of her lion self in her gaze. I suddenly wanted to see her like that, a sleek tawny creature with a flicking tail and alert ears, taking in everything.

"Can't sleep, either?" she asked. I shook my head. "I have food." Plastic crinkled, as she pulled over a grocery bag. Enkidu sat up, rubbing his eyes.

The three of us ate together. Real, human food this time. Sort of. More like camp rations, the deli sandwiches and PowerBars they must have kept packed in a cooler all week. I ate because I had to, not because I was particularly hungry. The food tasted like dust, and my mind drifted to the memory of that deer haunch, rich with blood. Prey. *Run, hunt, kill.* That would make everything better.

Sleep was one of the mind's defenses against the unknown, depression, despair. Since sleep had stopped working, I turned to my other defense: talking.

"How does it feel?" I asked around a half-chewed mouthful. "Being this close. Everything you've worked for is about to happen. Must feel strange."

"It's just another day," Sakhmet said softly. She ate daintily, dabbing the corner of her lips, licking a crumb off her finger. Focused on the task at hand, unmindful of the surroundings.

She and Enkidu sat next to each other, knees touching, but otherwise closed in on themselves. Nervous, anxious. They had the air of animals who'd been caged for a long time. Were their animal sides telling them to run, like mine was? We were all ignoring our instincts, being here. Maybe that anxiety was the power Zora needed to harness.

Enkidu studied me, like he was always studying me, glaring just shy of a challenge. Trying to intimidate me or watching for when I tried to run for it—it hardly mattered. I could only fake trying to relax while he was around.

I focused on Sakhmet instead. "What are you guys going to do when this is over?" I asked. "You have a home someplace? You want to settle down, start a farm, whatever? Or are you staying with them?" I nodded to the exit tunnel, where presumably the others slept in some branching tunnel.

She looked at Enkidu, but because he was busy staring me down, she wasn't able to catch his gaze. To silently ask him the same question.

"I don't know that we've thought so far ahead," she said, her smile thin, thoughtful. Feline, even.

"Come on," I prompted. "What keeps you going? What do you two talk about when no one else is around? There has to be more to you than this." This. Hiding out in a mine, following a vampire and his magician minion. Kidnapping werewolf queens at the vampire's behest. I let the silence hang, hoping she would fill it. But they weren't radio people and didn't have the aversion to dead air that I did. I was about to say something teasing, to get a reaction from her, when she finally spoke.

"I'm not sure we expect to survive this," she said. So fatalistic and at peace with such an outcome that she hardly expressed sadness.

Funny, I'd been thinking the same thing.

I said, "Dux Bellorum, vampires like him, would make werewolves slaves. They think we were made to be soldiers in their army. You sit here, you tell me we're fighting Dux Bellorum. Then why aren't you any better than foot soldiers in Kumarbis's army? Cannon fodder, really." I turned away, huffing in disgust.

"We believe in the war," Enkidu said. "We make sacrifices."

"I want to go home," I murmured. I had allies, I had friends. If I was going to be making sacrifices, I wanted it to be for *them*.

Sakhmet's smile was sad. "You're lucky, to have a place you belong."

I'd managed a few bites, but I wasn't hungry, even though I should have been. The bits of sandwich were only making my stomach more upset. I wrapped the remainder of the meal in its cellophane and set it on the floor. Took a long drink of water because I knew I needed it, not because I felt thirsty.

"Wake me up when the party starts." I went a few steps away, curled up, and pretended to sleep.

When I tried to sleep, I thought of Ben, and had to fight tears. I pulled my knees to my chest and wrapped my arms around my head. Wished I had a tail to tuck around myself. Wished for a lot of things.

I heard the sound of wrappers crinkling, trash being gathered up and taken away. Enkidu and Sakhmet didn't speak, but I imagined them brushing hands, shoulders, exchanging glances like longtime couples did. I tried to breathe slowly, regularly, but I probably didn't fool them into thinking I slept. Still, they didn't bother me.

Eventually, the pair of them curled up again, and they did sleep. Who knew how long they'd been sleeping on stone floors, without plumbing or lighting, eating sandwiches out of plastic or hunting the odd deer. This was their normal, why shouldn't they feel safe? And they had each other. No matter what happened, they'd be all right, because they had each other.

Me, I had something I had to do.

I went into a crouch, breathed softly, waited. Glanced at the wooden slab of a door, and crept toward it. My bare feet didn't make a sound. I got all the way to the tunnel door without waking them, which encouraged me. I could keep going.

They left the door open this time. Finally, I had earned their trust. Plan B had worked after all. I waited and listened, but Sakhmet and Enkidu maintained their steady breathing. I hadn't woken them.

I explored some of the branching tunnels and side rooms I hadn't had time to see before, searching for the storeroom I hadn't found last time. Wherever they kept their water, food, and supplies. Tranquilizer gun. And, I hoped, my shoes and my phone. Wedding ring. Maybe Kumarbis kept a diary somewhere that would lay the whole story out in sensible terms. Wouldn't that be swell?

It would probably be written in Phoenician, which wouldn't help me at all. Amelia, she would know Phoenician. God, I even missed Amelia. She'd be able to talk sense into Zora, if she were here.

Focus. I needed to focus. I didn't want Amelia and Cormac here, I didn't want anyone else to get hurt.

I paced, nose working, searching for a useful trail. I still didn't know where Kumarbis's . . . crypt, for lack of a better word, was. Not that I wanted to find it, but wouldn't it be just my luck to find out he was sleeping with my phone under his pillow?

I stood quietly, listening as hard as I could, my nose flaring for the scent of my phone, my stuff, *me.* But cell phones didn't leave nice trails to follow. The four of them had been living here for a long time, weeks probably, before they'd brought me here. Their scents were pervasive, and following any trail became impossible.

But I heard a tapping. Occasional, artificial. Not animal claws on stones, nothing like a footstep. Someone was typing on a keyboard. A computer, here?

I followed the sound.

Past the cell where they'd kept me, a tunnel curved to the left and sloped gently down. The ancient rails of the old mine cars were just visible. One of the battery-operated LED lights sat on the floor of the juncture and cast a faint white light, just enough to keep people from stubbing their toes. The light caught flashes in the wall, chips of quartz or ore.

Kumarbis's chill, bloodless scent was stronger here. I'd probably find his cave farther down. Before that, though, the tunnel branched. A side chamber forked off, and at the branch, I smelled Zora. Another light marked the turn. I crept forward, as quietly as Wolf and I knew how, crouched at the rocky corner, and leaned around to look.

Zora, lit by another of the lamps, worked at a laptop. I wondered how the hell she was powering it, until I saw the stack of battery packs and a solar-powered charger piled against the wall. She'd come prepared to work without a wall to plug into.

But what was she doing on her battery-powered computer? Googling for new ritual techniques, I might have thought, but we were in the middle of nowhere, where she couldn't possibly have an Internet connection. Maybe she had a magical Internet connection.

That sounded ridiculous even to me.

She had her back to the tunnel opening, but was too far away for me to make out any details on the screen, which was turned at exactly the wrong angle.

She'd eaten something as well—a sandwich wrapper and empty bottle of water sat against one wall. An air mattress and a couple of blankets lay piled against the opposite wall. She had her own little cozy den. This was where she'd been spending her non-ritual time—with her laptop. Doing what?

Along with the laptop she had a small pad of paper and a pencil, and she scratched notes on it every now and then, drawing diagrams and symbols. She'd chew on the end of the pencil, stare at her drawings, type a few words, read what she'd typed. Back and forth, working intently on her project.

Did I even need to ask what her project was? It was all of this. She was less than a day away from the most important ritual of her life, the culmination of all her plans. She was studying. I almost felt sorry for her.

While I watched, she must have finished, or grown too frustrated and tired to continue. She put the pad and pencil into a document bag, closed programs, powered down the computer. Last thing she did was yank a USB thumb drive out of the back of the laptop and close it up in a kind of box she wore on a chain around her neck. One of the many amulets she wore. This was a little bigger than a matchbox, made of pressed tin and inset with polished stones. Like a saint's reliquary. Only instead of bones, it held the thumb drive, close at hand.

She kept her spells on that thumb drive. A twenty-first-century wizard, with her searchable, electronic spell book. Who would have thunk?

I didn't want to draw her attention, now that she wasn't focused on the laptop. Quickly, I backed out the way I'd come, slipping quietly up the passage to the main tunnel. She didn't follow, and she didn't make any more noise. She must have curled up on her little bed to get some sleep, so she'd be at her best for tonight.

Maybe I was the crazy one. They all knew exactly

what they were doing, and I was flopping like a beached fish.

Didn't matter, I still wanted to find my phone. Maybe Zora had it under *her* pillow.

I traced my way back, praying I wasn't lost, that I remembered the curving tangle of tunnels right. I headed the direction I thought was out, and was reassured when the tunnel I'd picked started sloping up. There, I took another unexplored turn, and found the stretch of tunnel where they stored their food.

A couple of coolers sat against the wall. Opening their lids, I found them packed with snow and ice from outside. They kept a few sandwiches relatively cool. One cooler was empty. A cardboard pallet of bottled water was down to the last four bottles. They were running out of supplies—their time here was coming to an end.

After the food came a few large plastic storage bins. One of them was long enough to store a tranquilizer gun and the gear that went with it. I pulled the bin out, snapped the lid off, found the gun—a compressed air-powered rifle, plastic cases with darts tucked inside. A few people around here I'd like to use it on, just on principle. Not that it would change anything. I thought about dragging it to the ritual chamber, an extra line of defense against Roman in case something went wrong. But in the end, I decided it probably wouldn't help. A mundane weapon, in a battle stretching more than five thousand miles around the world? I left it in place.

Another bin held batteries, rope, a battery-powered drill, a few extra camp lanterns. And there, tucked in among the various bits and pieces, were my sneakers. And inside my sneakers, my phone and wedding ring on its chain.

I put the chain over my neck, tucking the ring under my sweater, grabbed my phone, and ran. Would it still have a charge, would I be able to get any reception, and if it did—what would I say? When I reached the sunshine at the mouth of the mine tunnel, I stopped. Gratefully took in a lungful of sparkling mountain air. Bright, brilliant freedom.

Run, and never go back.

Wolf wanted to howl. I tipped my head back, let my nose flare. I could howl for an hour. But I didn't. Wolf had to understand about making a sacrifice, taking a chance so the pack—so Ben—could live. But I had to at least try to tell him what was happening. About what had happened to me.

"Please work," I murmured, turning on the phone, waiting, waiting—and the screen lit up. They'd turned it off when they'd taken it, and that had saved the battery. The little green battery icon was close to empty, but it still had some juice left. I was just glad it hadn't been left on all this time. More howling in my chest, tightening my gut. The screen showed missed calls

and text messages. Yeah, I just bet. I didn't have time
for that.

I scrolled through to find Ben's number, hit the text
command—hesitated. Make it quick, make it clear.
What to say? I had too much I needed to say, and I
froze. He'd never forgive me for this.

My least favorite news stories were the ones about
how someone is in a horrible situation, knows they're
about to die, but has enough time to call a loved one
and say good-bye. An expedition leader trapped in a
storm on Mount Everest. Passengers on a hijacked
airplane. What do you say in that situation? What can
you possibly say? I breezed past those stories because
they started me thinking about what I would say, and
I could never come up with anything. Is "I love you"
enough?

I wasn't going to die. I was going to get out of this.
That was what I'd say, I'd tell him I was going to get
out of this.

*Im ok. battling evil. i hope. see you soon. I love
you.*

Send, send, send. I resisted punching the button
over and over. Instead, hand trembling, I watched the
animated thingy turn, and finally text appeared: message sent.

I held the phone between my hands, clasped prayer-
like, and brought them to my forehead. Please, let the
message get through, please let him understand. I

prayed to the gods I knew: Xiwangmu, random fairy queens, and maybe even God—Rick's God, the one that had inspired him to do good for five hundred years. Not the God who would damn him for what he was. Too many gods to choose from, and I didn't know if it would do any good, but it couldn't hurt.

The sun was setting. Four, five o'clock maybe. Darkness would fall soon, and the gang would gather for the next ritual. And something would happen. One way or another, something would happen. I watched for a long time. The slanted light turned the crystalline winter sky silver. The ice in the air stung my nose, but it didn't hurt. It felt clean. I couldn't seem to breathe deep enough, to take it all in. Or maybe I thought I could store the air and continue to breathe it when I went back into the mine, into the stone. I could already smell the dense, brimstone stink of the torches.

I'd think about this clean winter air instead.

I left the phone sitting on a clear space of rock. Maybe Ben would find it. This would be the last night in the old mine. By tomorrow, this would all be over, and it would all seem worthwhile. I hoped.

Chapter 19

I HAD NEVER met a were-frog, or even heard of one existing—all the lycanthropic beings I knew about were hard-core predators. So I considered the tale of the *Frog Prince* with some skepticism. Especially because of all the different versions, the one where the princess kisses the frog to return him to his unfroggy state is new. In earlier versions, like Grimm's, she grabs him by the leg and smashes him against a wall. How this is meant to promote virtuous behavior, if that's really what it's supposed to promote, I'm not entirely sure. Maybe the message is, "If he tries to chat you up so hard he gets annoying, don't be afraid to deck the bugger." At its heart, though, the story is another iteration of *Beauty and the Beast*—one must consider a person's inner beauty before judging the outer appearance. You cannot fall in love solely with the way someone looks.

On the other hand, maybe it's all about how kissing is magic.

Sometimes in the mornings after running on full-moon nights, Ben woke me with a kiss, and I imagined in my still half-dreaming mind that his kiss was what transformed me, drawing my human self from my Wolf's body. The human touch, the human contact was my anchor. What other creature in the world had such sensitive, pliable lips as ours, and what other purpose could such lips have but kissing?

NEAR AS I could figure, I had been in the mine for four days. I couldn't imagine what Ben was thinking now. This kind of thing had happened before—me, trapped in the wilderness, unable to answer calls and in trouble. Would he figure that I'd come out of it okay like I had before? I hoped that my message would reach him, that he'd found my trail and was on his way. On the other hand, if this situation was on a track to end badly, I wanted him as far away from here as possible.

My world was collapsing into a small space filled with my breathing and my fears.

We fight to defend ourselves. When cornered.

That's the best way. Less risky than attacking. Nothing to gain here.

That was the Wolf's calculation—would the energy you'd expend hunting and killing the food exceed what you'd get from eating the food? If so, break off the hunt. Better to run than fight, when the odds were against you. But maybe sometimes the best defense is a good offense? Wolf was anxious and had every reason to be. I wanted to pace, to wear holes in the stone under my feet. It wouldn't help at all, so I didn't. I curled up tighter.

This isn't right.

I knew it wasn't. On paper, the rituals Kumarbis and Zora had concocted seemed great. Find Roman, destroy him safely from thousands of miles away. But we weren't as safe as they pretended. If Roman knew he was being hunted, he wouldn't sit back and wait for us. We were in danger.

Staying's not worth it. We're not protecting our pack, here.

But maybe we could do more. Protect more than our pack. We could protect everyone Roman wanted to hurt.

Not our concern. Must return to the pack.

We could make sure Antony's death meant something—and wasn't that bullshit? Did I think I could trade in lives, decide what would make the sacrifice of a life worthwhile?

Wolf was right. So was I. We were gnawing our own tail, going back and forth over this. But I stayed underground, and waited.

Back in the antechamber, Sakhmet and Enkidu were still asleep. I lay down near them and curled up for warmth and comfort. However tired I felt, I couldn't sleep.

I could almost smell Ben, and the memory made my eyes sting. I wondered if I would ever see him again—and that was the first time I wondered, instead of being sure. I scrubbed my face, to banish the thought. I would see him, I would I would. *I want to run.*

I STARTED awake, surprised that I'd been asleep in the first place. I was in the antechamber, curled up, arms over my head. Enkidu and Sakhmet were awake, folding sandwich wrappers, and noises were invading. Footsteps approached.

Stumbling to a crouch, my back to the wall, I blinked my way to awareness. This still felt like a dream, the wavering light of a flickering candle in a sheltered lantern causing movement all around me, shadows of the stone itself dancing and jerking. Dressed in her white tunic and all her ritual finery, Zora held a candle. Priestlike, Kumarbis followed her, his hands clasped before him, his expression serene. He was otherworldly, in a homespun white cassock draped around him and belted with a black sash. His stance was straight and proud, statuesque. His gnarled hand pressed over his chest, and he bowed his head, a stately gesture. I gaped; I couldn't help but feel awed. I saw this from his point of view: two thousand years of effort and planning come to this. He had spent centuries seeking out his avatars, his wizards and would-be gods. A million stories lay in that history, a dozen failed attempts, dozens of people identified, indoctrinated, brought into the cult—and what had happened to them? Even if I could get Kumarbis to talk to me candidly, I'd never get all the stories.

I hurried to my feet with surprising grace—that was Wolf, moving my muscles for me, keeping us upright and stable. Dominant. We didn't want to be on the ground at this man's feet. We were better than that, so we stood before them, chin up and shoulders back. Tail straight, ears pricked. Slower, Enkidu and Sakhmet joined me. The three of us—the three animals, his avatars of the wild he'd have called us—unconsciously gathered to face them.

"Welcome, my avatars," the vampire said. As if we'd ever left. As if we'd had a choice about being here. But we did, in the end. Even me. Kumarbis spoke with that confidence that sounded like arrogance to me. "Welcome to this glorious moment, for tonight we perform the ritual that will destroy Dux Bellorum. We know our purpose. We know our power. I thank you all. I am grateful for you." He was a kindly patriarch speaking with genuine emotion. He might have been misguided, but he wasn't evil. And if this worked . . . maybe he wasn't even misguided.

"We are ready," Kumarbis concluded. And maybe we actually were. He gestured to the ritual chamber, and, solemnly, Zora led the way, and we followed her through the tunnel into the ritual space for the last time.

ZORA LIT the torches from the candle she carried. I knew my place on the pentagram drawn on the chamber's stone floor. We all knew our places and went to them, standing with feet planted, solid and confident. Trying to be. My hackles were up, the muscles of my shoulders stiff to the point of pain. My heart was racing, and I took slow breaths, trying to calm myself. I touched my wedding ring, lying against my chest, under my shirt. It felt warm.

Across the circle, Sakhmet smiled at me. I settled.

Zora had added to the circle sometime over the last day, touching up the white, adding red and yellow outlines to the original markings, painting new symbols. If possible the drawings looked even more creepy, as if they had merged into one organic thing that came alive in the torchlight. The swirls and whorls became vinelike, reaching outward.

Zora's face was bright with a kind of joy made twisted in the firelight. If the curls in the drawing seemed to be reaching out, she was reaching back to them. She was as much a part of the ritual space as the symbols and patterns she'd drawn.

A new element had been added to the circle: a wooden spear, maybe four feet long, had been placed in the center of the pentagram. One end of it had been sharpened and polished to a hard point. A perfect weapon for destroying vampires. This was the weapon we'd use on Roman, then.

Sudden relief made me want to smile; seeing the spear made me think this would work when nothing else did. We were armed. We had a chance. Faith in weaponry. The thought of finally stopping Roman made me giddy. Or maybe it was the lack of food and sleep.

Focus, I had to focus. This was important. This could still go horribly wrong, and I had to be ready. I clenched my hands into fists and calmed my Wolf, who wanted to pace.

Zora moved around the circle, much like she had during the previous ritual, placing items, murmuring incantations. If the crystals and herbs she used were different this time, I couldn't keep track. No wonder she'd had to study her notes.

The mummified white dove came out again, and she placed it in the center. Gaius Albinus—the Latin word for white was Albus, and White was another of his aliases. The dove was another link. Again, Kumarbis presented the coin, the focus for targeting Roman. Fortunately, no live mice appeared.

"*Munde Deus virtuti tuae,* confirm thy power in us, oh spirit of the world, confirm thy power against our enemy . . ." And on, and on.

"The door opens, spirit of the world, give us the strength to tread on serpents, to smash the power of our enemy, that none may harm us. The window opens, spirit of the world, deliver our enemy to us, deliver the blight that we may smash it from creation. Our hearts and intentions are pure, oh spirit of the world."

A familiar pressure of anticipation settled over the cave. The smoke rose up, and the mine shaft seemed like a tower that might reach to heaven. Maybe it was a tunnel that could take us all the way to Roman, some kind of wormhole through space. There should have been drumming, the heartbeat of the world.

Zora lowered her arms and looked around the circle, noting each of us, nodding. She said, "When the time comes, when the door opens, I will give the spear to you, Enkidu. Our hunter will strike the blow against Dux Bellorum. Are you prepared?"

"I am," said Enkidu.

"Sakhmet, our warrior, you will protect the hunter from harm. Do you stand firm?"

"I do," she said. The lion in her showed through her ready stance, her glaring golden eyes.

Then Zora said, "Regina Luporum, by your authority you will name our enemy and declare our target. You will do this?"

It was like that part in the wedding ceremony when the minister says speak now or forever hold your peace. An expectant stillness, as they waited for me to give an answer—the correct answer. I'm Kitty, I thought. But no, not here. I realized, suddenly, I was the perfect person for the job they'd picked for me. I knew Roman by sight. I could identify him. What was more, I had so many things I wanted to say to Roman, most of them angry, and if this worked, I'd have my chance. Zora and the others were counting on it. Kumarbis might have known the enemy two thousand years ago, but I knew him *now*, and I would call him out. Who better than me?

I could be Regina Luporum.

"I will," I said.

"Kumarbis, it is by your faith and effort that we stand here. Do you still stand firm?"

"I do."

Zora raised her hands high and spoke.

"Powers above and below, I call on the spirit of the world, the center of all, to open the door that will allow us to reach forth and strike in order to restore balance to your universe, I call on the four quarters, the four elements, the four powers we have gathered here in universal truth . . ."

She was speaking English, but I couldn't say I understood her. The words seemed rote, ritual phrases she had repeated so many times they had the same value as the chorus of a children's song. Rhythmic, vaguely annoying, meaningless. But maybe there was power in the repetition, because I felt something. The power she was raising, that she was drawing from us, seemed to physically increase the pressure in the room, as if her spell was crowding out the air.

Her prayer continued, repeated declarations and entreaties, increasing in desperation.

My back stiffened. I wanted to curl my lips and glare a challenge, but I forced myself to calm. This was normal, just part of the show. Sakhmet had her eyes closed, her head tipped back in relaxed meditation. In the next place on the circle, Enkidu stood solid, determined, the very picture of an ancient hunter. At the star's main point, Kumarbis held his hands spread, and his smile was full of bliss.

Easy to think I had suddenly become part of something larger than myself. Zora was tapping into some kind of universal energy.

Visually, nothing happened at first. It didn't have to—she wasn't working on a visual level. The doorway she opened wasn't physical. Then, shadows formed. Or changed. Hard to tell, with the smoke writhing patterns in the air, the designs and symbols shifting in the light. I looked across the circle, and the shadows rising up around Enkidu, Sakhmet, and Zora seemed larger and more solid.

I felt a breath behind me, a light touch on my shoulder. A kind touch. And I wasn't afraid. Which seemed strange, but I couldn't deny it. My hackles flattened, Wolf stayed calm within her cage. Someone was there, right behind me, and she was a friend. I was sure of it, but I didn't dare turn to look, because if I did, she might vanish. I very much wanted her to stay. On the stone in front of me, or maybe it was in my mind's eye, I saw her shadow, her shape. Then I saw more. A small woman, but fierce, with wild dark hair tied back with a length of leather. She wore a gold torque around her arm, a simple cloth tunic, and a knife in a sheath on her belt. It was her, somehow I knew it was her: the Capitoline Wolf. The first Regina Luporum. With her behind me, I could do anything. I swore I could see her smile.

But I blinked, and she was gone. I wanted to cry out, to beg her to stay . . .

A breeze started, as if air poured through the door Zora had opened, from the place she'd opened it to. It smelled like stone and earth—underground, which meant it smelled like the tunnels we were in. Maybe there wasn't a door at all. But the air was moving. I squinted, trying to see into the circle, past the shapes and symbols. Looking for a door that might or might not be there.

The wind changed, grew stronger, a whipping vortex that lapped the ritual chamber. This was impossible— a wind couldn't rise up and beat us down inside the closed-off shelter of the mine. It was impossible, because it was magic. Zora had opened a door out of nothing, and the wind howled. I crouched, arms up to protect my face from the flying grit.

The magician stepped forward, formally, regally, and crouched down to take hold of the spear. Raising it in both hands, making an offering of it, she turned to Enkidu.

But before he could reach and take the weapon from her, another hand reached out of the wind and grabbed hold of it. Muscular, feminine, gloved in brown leather. Zora froze, staring at the interloping hand on the spear.

The torches dimmed, their light fading, and a black smoke poured into the vortex, shrouding the room in a cloud. I gagged on the smell, an acrid tang that overpowered the odor of Zora's incense and torches. The smell pinged a memory, the way smells often could, and I had a visceral feeling of being wrenched to another time and place, a similar attack, with wind and storm, and a smell of brimstone so thick it stuck in the back of my throat.

I knew what this was, I knew what came next. Zora wasn't in control here, she only thought she was. I howled a warning, but my voice was lost in the choking wind.

A second hand joined the first on the spear, and the entire figure emerged from the smoke, yanked the spear from Zora, and shoved the magician away with a swipe from her elbow. Tall, athletic, the newcomer was dressed in leather and carried an armory's worth of weapons—spears on her back, knives on her belt, a whip, a sword. She held herself ready for battle. I imagined her gaze tracking to take in the scene, the cave and its various players, but tinted goggles lay flush against her face, enclosing her eyes. She came from a place of such utter darkness, even the shadowed firelight underground was too much light for her.

I fell back, because I *knew* her, I'd seen her before. She was a hunter, a demon, and she'd tried to kill me once. Roman didn't have to fling new terrors at me. The old ones worked just fine. I had a sudden, vivid image of exactly how Antony had died. *She* had killed him, with one of those wooden spears she carried.

Now, can we run? Wolf helpfully suggested. She knew when we were out of our league. This fight had more than lost calories at stake.

The demon's searching gaze stopped when it reached Kumarbis.

Unthinking, I ran, jumped, and tackled the vampire, who continued standing with his arms out, as if this was all part of the ritual, as if he hadn't noticed that something had gone wrong. I knocked him clean over, smashing into the stone floor, rolling to put myself between him and the spear.

A stinging pain slashed across my back, and I shoved against it, pushing it away. She'd thrown the spear, and even against the wind it had flown straight; somehow, she'd forced it to go exactly where she wanted—the vampire—but I'd gotten in the way and it struck me instead, its point tearing through my sweater and into skin. It didn't stick in me, only mangled the skin before dropping away. But I could smell the tang of my own blood, and feel the burning of the wound. It was only wood—it wouldn't kill me, as it would have killed Kumarbis if it had gone through his heart.

The vampire stared at me, like he couldn't believe I'd taken a spear for him. I couldn't quite believe it myself.

I looked back at our attacker. When the demon saw me, her lips curled. *"You."*

Yeah, so she recognized me, too. Great.

"My Master will know of you," she said.

The target I felt painted on my chest seemed to get

a whole lot bigger. "Your Master—and Roman's Master?" Because I couldn't stop poking. "Roman couldn't stop me, why should I be scared of you, or your Master?"

She pulled another spear from one of several strapped to a kind of bandolier across her back, hefted it in her left hand, and drew a sword from a scabbard at her belt. It seemed molten in the firelight, and I was absolutely sure it had some amount of silver in it. The wooden weapon might not hurt me, but the sword would.

The wind tore through the space with the noise of rusty nails on steel. My hair, tangled mess that it was, whipped into my face, and I couldn't keep it pulled back, I couldn't see anything. The remaining tongues of flame from the torches seemed to be drawn into the spiraling debris that climbed up the mine shaft. It might have been beautiful, if I wasn't in the middle of it.

Zora said she'd cast some kind of protection over the place. Whatever she'd done hadn't worked against this. And me—I'd seen magic, but I didn't know the first thing about working it myself. My wounded back itched.

The last time the demon appeared had been much like this one: a ritual to open doors or lower barriers gone awry, opposing forces gathered. Cormac had stopped her—he'd been ready with one of those inexplicable spells. But he hadn't been able to finish her off; in the end, she'd just left, or been taken, or banished herself.

Zora stood staring at her, mouth open, unmoving. Disbelieving. She didn't have a clue.

Kumarbis, however, was attempting to recover some of his dignity. He climbed to his feet, clutching at his cassock, which had become twisted in the fall. "How dare you?" Kumarbis said. "How *dare* you?"

The demon laughed, openmouthed, full-lunged. Like she thought this was hysterical.

"Kumarbis, get *down!*" I hissed at him. Her spear was a length of sharpened wood, an ideal vampire-slaying weapon. He had to see that. He had to get away from her, but this cave had no damn cover. Only the door on the far end of the antechamber. We had to get out of here.

The vampire ignored me. "Who sent you?" he demanded of the thing. As if he were still in control here.

"You of all people should have some clue," she said. "Kumarbis, is that what you're calling yourself? You've been around such a long time . . . I can smell it on you." Her nostrils flared, taking in the scent. "But you are still a traitor. You are all traitors."

Kumarbis turned on the magician. "Zora, what is this, what's happening?" She could only shake her head, her mouth working wordlessly.

I grabbed the vampire and shoved him toward the

tunnel. I had to put my shoulders into it. How did such a wizened old guy get to be so *heavy*? "We have to get out of here, *right now*!"

He resisted. "No, we must finish the ceremony, we're so close!"

Not a chance. Couldn't he see the circle was already broken, the spell had already failed? Backfired, rather. Zora had successfully opened a door, but Roman wasn't on the other side of it. He'd sent a proxy, one who couldn't be killed by a shaft of wood.

The demon arced the silver-laced sword toward me, and I scrambled away, waiting for the cut to bite into me, sure the strike would land. The walls were in the way, I had no place to go, and Wolf's claws dug inside my skin.

Enkidu and Sakhmet jumped at her in a beautiful, coordinated attack, Sakhmet tackling low and Enkidu grabbing for the demon's throat. They hit at the same time, and she stumbled but didn't fall. She should have fallen, with two lycanthropes crashing into her like that. But her feet spread out, and she kept her balance.

"Watch it, her weapons are silver!" I shouted, and they both sprang away, agile enough to reverse course almost in midair. When the demon stabbed a dagger toward them—and when had she had time to draw that?—they were scrambling backward, out of range.

We were spread out around the chamber now, and

the demon circled, not willing to turn her back on anyone. Taking time to choose her next target.

"Who is she?" Enkidu called to me. "How did she get here?"

"I told you, you open a door to them, they can come through it, too," I said.

"That's not Dux Bellorum," he said.

"No. But she works for the same guy he does." The conversation was rapid, breathless. I was backing away, staying out of range of those silver-alloy blades.

"The ritual—" Kumarbis panted, trying to catch enough breath to speak. "Where is Dux Bellorum?"

"You flushed him," I said. "He's gone. You failed."

"No, we haven't, we mustn't, he's here, he must be here—"

The demon picked her target, and accompanied by another blast of inky wind lunged forward, drawing the spear back for a strike. Kumarbis was present enough to notice and managed to pull out some slick vampire moves, dodging aside too quickly for the eye to follow, shoving the demon out of his way and into the cave wall, springing into the center of the chamber, giving himself more room to maneuver. He glared at the demon like he was finally ready to fight.

He grabbed up the coin from its place in the middle of the pentagram. The mummified dove had blown away.

"I defeated Dux Bellorum once before," he called

to the demon. "I will do it again! Again and for all time!"

"I don't care," the demon muttered and hefted her wooden spear for another strike.

We needed a weapon, but what would work against an only semicorporeal demon? We needed to banish her—did Zora know how to do that? Not that she could do anything in her current state. Fallen to her knees, she clutched the box around her neck. Hard to access a computerized book of spells when you didn't have your laptop. Not that she would have had a chance to sit down and read anything at the moment anyway. She seemed catatonic, staring in awe, unmoving. She had seen the unknowable and it had broken her. So that was what that looked like.

I ran to her side and grabbed her shoulder, trying to shake her out of it. I must have looked like a monster, my teeth bared, eyes red with smoke.

"Zora, she's a demon, like in the stories, Faust and crap. You have to banish her. Do you have a spell for that? Can you banish her?"

She seemed to wake up a little. "I didn't . . . I didn't summon anything—"

"I know you didn't, but can you banish her?"

Eyes still round and shocky, she pawed at the amulets on her chest, picked one—a Maltese cross—then went to find her bag of supplies, which she'd left lying against the cave wall.

Maybe she really could do it. We just had to hold out until then. I stood guard between her and the demon, hoping I could protect her long enough for her to do something. Hoping I could keep out of the way of those blades. I was back to the problem of weapons. As in, I needed one. I swallowed; my mouth was dry.

Weapons, what weapons did we have besides rocks and bad intentions? That plastic tub with the tranquilizer gun—suddenly, I was intensely curious about whether a tranquilizer dart would work on a demon. Too bad the demon was standing between me, the doorway to the passage, and access to the gun. Shouting across to Enkidu, "Hey, why don't you go get the gun," would not do us a lick of good. The demon would only redirect her attack at him. And start guarding the doorway.

I wondered if we could wear her down with continual harassment, like a pack of wolves nipping after a deer until the animal simply couldn't run anymore. I had a feeling demons didn't really get exhausted. I could go Wolf and just rip her throat out—if it weren't for those sharp silver weapons. In addition to the sword and dagger, along with the spear tucked under her arm, she had more knives nested in sheaths on her belt. Unless we could get rid of the metal, the three of us lycanthropes were useless.

Kumarbis was holding his own against the testing

attacks she made, sparring at him, searching for a weakness. He was dodging, batting back, using vampiric strength, speed, and experience. Eventually, though, the demon would find that opening.

This was all up to Zora. I hated that our lives depended on the crazy woman.

"Zora . . ." I couldn't help but prompt. She was still rummaging.

Meanwhile, Sakhmet had grabbed a torch out of one of the sconces and swung it at the demon. The boundary of fire, a swoop of sparks falling outward from the torch, made the demon pause. Fire, of course—magical protections based on fire to keep her out had worked the last time.

Sakhmet was also speaking in what might have been Arabic, some kind of prayer or chant. Protection against demons, maybe. I couldn't tell if it was working. She seemed to be making some progress with the fire, though. She advanced, slashing, and the demon retreated. Kumarbis dashed forward and yanked the spear from her hand, tossing it out of her reach. The demon stabbed at him with a sword while grabbing another spear from her back, but the vampire lunged away. Sakhmet drove forward again, and the demon hissed in annoyance.

Enkidu took another one of the torches and joined the were-lion, so they came at the demon from two sides, harrying her while she slashed at the torches and growled at them. She succeeded in knocking the torch out of Enkidu's hands, but he rolled away from the blow and retrieved it with little trouble.

It wasn't just the flames that slowed down the demon; it was the light. The goggles. Maybe I could make this all go away. Leaving Zora, I circled, softly as I could, not attracting attention, to the demon's back. Our attacker was occupied by the fire and Kumarbis's harassment, which at this point was mostly verbal. Declarations about how dare she and so forth. He was rather less effective than the lycanthropes.

The demon's back was to me now. I planned my strike carefully, and my limbs were all but vibrating with anticipation. This was supremely dangerous, but if it worked—it had to work, we didn't have a choice.

Two steps to reach her, then I jumped on her leather-clad back, grabbing the last pair of spears bound there to help me get leverage when I reached to her head and yanked on the strap that secured the goggles. I fell back, rolling. The strap slipped easily over her spiky dark hair, and I hit the ground and ran hard until I came up against the wall.

The demon shouted in fury, curses and threats of violence. I was damned. Yes, probably. She hunched over as if she'd been injured, and she dropped her spear to hold her hand tight over her eyes. I was right— she was effectively blind without the protection.

The goggles in my hand were just goggles, made

of leather and dark glass, held together with metal rivets and buckles. I wasn't sure what I had expected. Maybe that they would turn to ash in my hand once separated from their owner.

She didn't stay incapacitated for long. Pulling another spear from her back, she was again fully armed, and when she turned to me, she had her eyes squeezed shut.

"I can hear you gasping for breath, wolf," she muttered. "I'll kill you yet."

Assured, she came toward me. She could hear my breathing, and the more I tried to keep my adrenaline-fueled breaths quiet, the louder they sounded. If I tried holding my breath entirely, I'd just end up gasping like a gulping fish. When I moved out of her way, no matter how quietly I tried to step, my feet scraped on the stone, and she tilted her head, listening.

"Hey! You!" Enkidu shouted from the other side of the cave, then threw a rock that hit the demon's thigh. From a few feet away, Sakhmet tossed another, hitting her in the back, and the demon was suddenly on the defensive. They weren't big rocks, just stones small enough to wrap a hand around and heft. They weren't going to hurt her. But they definitely caught her attention, and she flinched away from the attack, turning to growl at her attackers. Instinctively, her eyes opened—and she cried out as the faint torchlight struck them, wincing them shut again.

I only caught the briefest glimpse, but they were black as onyx all the way through, hard and gleaming.

Scowling, clearly frustrated, she pulled out a piece of cloth from under her leather armor—undershirt of some kind—ripped off a long length of it, and tied it around her eyes. Blindfolded, she was still scary as hell.

Apt phrasing, there.

"Zora . . ." I murmured.

Back on her side of the circle, the magician looked like she'd unpacked a New Age shop. Where had she been keeping all those boxes, bags, cords, candlesticks, candles, figurines, and chunks of crystal? She was going to throw everything at the demon.

"I'm trying," she murmured. She revealed a few more items: crosses, rosaries, the implements of someone preparing to perform an exorcism. Finally, with a decisive nod, she raised her hands and called out, "By the name and power of the Primeumaton, the Tetragrammaton, I curse you! I deprive you of your power, and bind you in the depth of the bottomless pit! Two times I curse you, deprive you of your power, and bind you in the depth of the bottomless pit! Thrice I curse you, deprive you of your power, and bind you in the depth of the bottomless pit!"

The demon tilted her head, listening. Were the

chants and curses affecting her? How could you tell if a wizard was doing her spells right? Zora picked up a cross in each hand, and her voice rose to a shout.

"*Munde dues virtuti tuae,* in the name of the spirit of the world, in the name of God and all His angels, I do abjure thee, I do abjure thee, I do abjure thee! In the name of Cassiel, Sachiel, Samael, Michael, Anael . . ."

Pulling out the big guns now, was she? She approached the demon, repeating the curses, as if she really could battle her back with words.

And the demon laughed, which probably wasn't a good sign. Worse, though, she was still here. Zora might have been doing everything right—and the spell just didn't work.

Now what?

I smelled blood—whose, and where did it come from? Enkidu—a slash on his thigh, skin flapped open, dripping in streaks down his leg. What had made it, the wood weapon or the silver? I glared until I caught his gaze and shrugged a question. He waved me off. Since he was still upright, maybe he was okay. Next I checked on the magician, trying to figure out how to tell her her exorcism wasn't working. But she already knew. She sat on the cave floor, her soot-streaked white robes spread around her, one hand on her frizzed blond hair, as if she had a headache.

The demon tsked, shaking her head.

We were at a standoff—the others couldn't advance because of her weapons, and as long as we didn't make noise, she couldn't find us.

Run. Wolf had been tumbling inside me for hours, ready to go as soon as I let her off her leash. I wasn't ready to do that. But she had the right idea about running. I had a plan. It wasn't a very good one, but it was the one I had. Trouble was, I couldn't communicate it to the others with the demon listening. Her hearing was too good. Which left the question: could I somehow pantomime what I was thinking to Enkidu and Sakhmet? Well, I could try.

"Hey!" I shouted. "Hey, you!" I stuck my hands on my hips and tried to act angry, and also coolheaded. Angry wasn't hard. Avoiding panic, that was tough. I asked, "Do you even have a name?"

She cocked her head, blind, listening.

"Yeah, that's right, I'm telling you where I am," I continued. "Go ahead, track me down. But hear me out first, just for a minute."

While I talked, I caught Sakhmet's gaze and gestured out the chamber and back up the tunnel. When she furrowed her brow and looked at me questioning, I gestured harder, a quick shooing motion—as softly as I could, while talking to the demon, holding her attention.

Finally, Sakhmet understood. While I was making all the noise, they could get out. They had to understand we weren't going to kill the demon, or destroy her, or whatever. We weren't going to win this hunt. But they could run. The were-lion grabbed Enkidu's arm and pulled him back. Enkidu was limping. I kept talking.

"I've got your goggles," I said, dangling them on a finger. "You want 'em back? I want some information. Where's Dux Bellorum?"

She hesitated, considering. I kept calling her a demon because she seemed so huge, taller even than Enkidu, with the strength of an army. She seemed to fill the chamber. But she was so human, appearing to be a white woman with a graceful jawline, her thin lips turned up now in a smile.

"He's safe," she said.

Evasive, devoid of information. Except that they were connected, somehow. "Is he, now. Because you were sent to defend him?"

"I was sent to destroy *you*."

"By *whom*?" I had to keep asking the question.

"I'm not going to tell you."

"Then you don't get your goggles back."

She chuckled. "You weren't going to give them back anyway."

I actually hadn't decided that. She was equally effective with or without the goggles; it didn't make a difference. I was waving frantically at Zora, and some clarity seemed to settle on her gaze—she actually saw me, and nodded. She crept around the circle, carefully, without a sound, and took the hand that I stretched out to her.

"I don't want to fight," I said, scattering meaningless words, spending them to buy time. My own ceremonial incantation. "Our ritual failed, we're all very aware of that. Just let us go."

"You'll try again unless I stop you."

I looked around at our bruised and soot-covered faces, Zora's numb look of shock, Kumarbis's stark, open-mouthed despair. "I don't think we will."

"Then I will kill you all for being traitors."

She'd said that the last time I confronted her, she'd said it to Kumarbis. Her targets were vampires and lycanthropes, because they were traitors, but she hadn't explained then, any more than she was likely to now.

My confusion showed. "Traitors—to what? How?"

"To your kind."

Which just frustrated me. She wanted to kill us because we weren't the monsters we were supposed to be? Fuck that. Time to go.

Sakhmet and Enkidu still hadn't left—what was holding them up?

Kumarbis. Enkidu was gesturing at Kumarbis, trying to get the vampire to look at him and follow him out of the cave. Kumarbis wasn't having it, instead focusing on the demon with this look of blank fatalism.

Like someone watching his longtime home burn to the ground.

Enkidu hissed in a futile attempt to keep his words from being heard. "My lord Kumarbis, we must go."

The vampire clenched his fists, flexed his arms, roared. And charged.

The demon turned at the sound and raised her spear, homing in on her target like an arrow on a bull's-eye. I ran, thinking I could tackle her, block her, take the hit like I had the last time, knock Kumarbis's head against the floor until he came to his senses, if he had any senses to come to.

The demon braced, and Kumarbis ran himself on her spear. The wooden shaft passed through his heart.

I couldn't stop her. I couldn't save him. And I wasn't even sad about it.

The round-eyed shock on his face meant he knew what had happened. How many thousands of years of life, just gone. And wasn't that the way for most people facing death? Vampires weren't any different from the rest of us. They maybe had to cope with more denial. His expression remained stark and disbelieving while his body, every bit of undead flesh, turned to ash, and the ash crumbled further and was carried off by the wind that rose up again. If he'd lain in a grave all those centuries, he could not have decayed any more thoroughly. The spear clattered to the stone.

Along with it, the coin he'd been holding fell and lay in the dust, the scant remains of the vampire. I picked it up—still on its cord of cracked, ancient leather. Another one of these things, another death, another thread to Dux Bellorum cut. With too many remaining to count, much less fight against.

Enkidu wrestled with the demon now. Inside her guard, where I hoped she couldn't turn her blades on him. Clawing, hitting, snapping at her with teeth that had grown sharp and a jaw that had grown thick and powerful, he kept her away from the rest of us, at least for the moment.

"Sakhmet, Zora, go! Enkidu! Run!"

Sakhmet was also yelling at Enkidu, pacing outside the range of the demon's weapons, waiting for an opening she could use to strike. Zora was kneeling, pawing through her bag of gear. Nobody was running. Worse than herding cats, this was.

"Zora!"

More calmly than she done or said anything since I'd met her, she said, "Get the others out. I have to close the door so nothing else gets through."

More could get through? Come after us? Oh . . .

I punched Sakhmet in the arm; she snapped at me, new catlike fangs showing, and I growled back. "Get him and *go*!"

I grabbed up the spear the demon had used to kill Kumarbis, swung it around, thrust at her back. The weapon connected, penetrated, but I couldn't tell if it actually went all the way through her leather armor. She felt *something*—she flinched, pivoting back to strike at my assault. I dodged away, looked over— and yes, Sakhmet and Enkidu had broken off and scrambled back, out of the chamber and into the tunnel. Out, away, safe.

Striking again, I shoved harder, and this time got the spear to stick in the demon's back, lodged in her flesh. My nostrils flared, searching for the scent of her blood—I didn't see any flow from the wound—but the only blood I smelled was my own, clotted on my back, and Enkidu's, dripping on the ground.

Distracted, the demon twisted back to grasp at the spear and pull it free. I'd bought us a few more seconds.

"Zora?"

She knelt at the edge of the pentagram, preparing another spell.

She looked up and held her hand out. "Kitty. Take this. Keep it safe. Use it."

Kitty, not Regina Luporum. I grabbed on to what she offered before I could think or respond, and found myself holding the tin box that held her USB spell book.

"Run," she said. "Run, don't look back."

And Zora—Zora stayed behind. She raised her arms over her head—each hand held an item, amulets tied up with stems of herbs—and shouted, words or commands, their meaning lost in the wind and chaos. The demon turned toward the sound, raised her weapon, let loose a battle cry.

That was all I saw. I might have stayed to watch, fascinated, but Wolf carried me out. *Now, it is time to run.* I ran. I did not look back.

My legs moved, loping in long strides, night vision guiding me surely through the antechamber and past the door. The bright figures of Sakhmet and Enkidu appeared ahead of me, and I followed the long, sloping tunnel that led to the surface.

An explosion rumbled through the caves behind me. A ghost of the ancient dynamite blasts that had excavated the mine in the first place. I stumbled, the ground under my feet uncertain. I put my hand on the wall for balance, then yanked it away when my skin burned. Was my skin broken? Had silver entered the wound?

Go. Wolf kept running. She gazed through my eyes, and I wouldn't have made it out without her.

The mine kept trembling, an earthquake growing in intensity rather than fading away. Debris rained, dust clogging the air, bits of stone pelting me. My steps didn't land where'd I aimed them, because the ground under me was moving. Up ahead, Sakhmet gasped as Enkidu fell and she struggled to hold him up while keeping her own balance.

It got worse, and I realized the cracks of thunder I was hearing was the sound of stone breaking and falling. The solid granite that had remained stable for a hundred years was collapsing. The ceiling of the tunnel in front of me was failing.

I put my head down and ran. And reached fresh air. The night sky opened over me like victory, and a weight came off me as I filled my lungs. I was free.

I kept running another twenty paces or so past the mine's entrance, bare feet stomping in a snowdrift, chased by a cloud of dust and debris blasting out of the tunnel. Sakhmet and Enkidu had fallen, and I skidded to the ground next to them, sheltering my head with my arms, waiting for the world to end.

The earthquake trembling through the ground stopped eventually, and the world fell still. Behind me, though, the mine entrance had fallen into a mash of rock and dust. The hillside over it had sunk, a dip in the landscape. The entire mine had collapsed. Zora had closed whatever magical portal she'd opened by bringing down the whole damn thing. I didn't care how badass the demon was, she wasn't getting out of that.

Poor Zora.

Next to me, Sakhmet was crying, her cheeks shining with tears, her breath coming in gasps. She held Enkidu on her lap, bent over him, holding him tightly while stroking his face, his hair. Enkidu wasn't moving, and my heart caught.

A cut on his arm had blackened, and poisoned streaks crawled away from it along his veins. One of those silver blades had caught him after all. He might have died on his feet while Sakhmet carried him bodily the last few steps. He might have found the strength to carry himself all the way out, to die under open sky. Either way, he'd died in her arms.

My impulse was to ask Sakhmet if she was all right, to see if she'd gotten out unharmed. That would have been the stupidest thing I could have possibly said in that moment. So I didn't say anything. Sitting quietly, I concentrated on breathing.

She was saying something, and I tilted my head to hear better, until I made out the word she was repeating.

"Mohan."

Mohan. Enkidu's real name.

I touched Mohan's hand and said my own good-bye. My own thanks for helping to save my life. I stroked back Sakhmet's hair, rested my hand on her shoulder. Trying to give some comfort.

The crunch of footsteps in snow brought me to my feet, set my blood blazing. Ready to rip flesh, I looked for the intruder, the hunter who had found us—

Cormac stood there, pointing a rifle at me. The sight was so incongruous, I could only stare. He used to make his living hunting, but I hadn't seen him hold a gun in years—as a convicted felon, he wasn't supposed to carry firearms. All I could think of was how pissed off Ben was going to be if he saw him like this.

When he saw me, Cormac dropped his aim and shouted over his shoulder, "Ben!"

And then there he was. Ben, in jeans and a T-shirt, trotting up the hill, glaring like a wolf on the hunt. He stopped next to his cousin, so I was staring at them both, the two people I most wanted to see in the world at this moment.

I stepped forward. I wanted to run, but I seemed to have used up all my run, and I just stood there, trying to catch a breath that wouldn't be caught, my eyes filling with tears, turning the world to mush.

"I got your message," Ben said, heaving the same weary breaths I was.

When my knees finally gave way, he was at my side to catch me.

Chapter 20

W E SAT for a long time just holding each other. Ben smelled even better than the pine- and snow-laden mountain air. He smelled like home and safety. Most of all, he smelled like himself, like Ben, and his thrown-together clothes and practical soap. My mate. Right now, he also smelled more tired than he should have, laced with anxiety. I'd been gone for days; he must not have slept much in that time. I squeezed him harder, my arms tight around his chest, and he wrapped me firmly in his embrace. I sighed, finally letting my guard down.

"I don't know where to start," he murmured into my hair. "What happened?"

I didn't know where to start, either. "They grabbed me. Kidnapping, I guess. It got weird. Messy." I cuddled against him, as if I could bury myself and hide from the world. "Long story," I said finally.

"But you're okay?"

"I am now," I said.

He nodded over my shoulder at Sakhmet. "Was she kidnapped, too?"

"No, she—" I was about to say she was one of the kidnappers. But that didn't make sense anymore. She'd been simultaneously captor and victim, and she had the scars to show for it. Already, the last few days were turning into a blur in my memory.

Sakhmet kept her head bowed, hiding her face as she bent protectively over Mohan's body. I couldn't bring myself to call her name and interrupt her grief.

"Kitty—what the hell happened here?" Ben said, his tone baffled rather than demanding. I couldn't imagine what this all looked like through his eyes.

I met his gaze, ran a hand across his hair, comforting myself. "It's not going to make any sense at all. Really. Oh, Tom—" I said, in a panic. "Did you find Tom, is he okay?"

"He's okay. Got knocked out by a tranquilizer dart, and when he woke up, you were gone. He felt terrible. Took us a couple of days to calm him down." Tom would have thought protecting me was his job, and that he'd failed. He was prone to turning wolf and running off when he got upset. I could picture the scene, Ben and the rest of the pack talking him off that ledge.

"It wasn't his fault," I said. I relaxed further, relieved with confirmation that he was all right.

"He'll be happy to hear you say it. I had to keep him from spending the last few days out looking for you nonstop."

"He wouldn't have found me."

"I know," he said. His sigh was revealing. "Because I was out here looking for you."

"You? Or your wolf?"

"Yeah," he said. "I kind of lost it. Kept losing it. Cormac tried talking me down the best he could. But . . . I didn't really come back until you sent your message."

Ben in a panic, furious and worried, had let loose his wolf to search for me. He couldn't not. I'd have done the same, in his place. Was it weird that I thought it was romantic?

"I'm glad the message worked."

"Me, too."

"Ben?" Cormac said, a warning in his tone.

Voices sounded from the woods downslope, along with the growling motor of an ATV. A powerful flashlight panned across the trees. The search party. Ben and Cormac had brought the cavalry.

Ben pulled away. I almost grabbed at him in a panic, not ready to let him go. But the world intruded.

"You'll be okay?" he said, smoothing back my hair, searching my eyes. I nodded, and he kissed my lips firmly, decisively, as if to convince himself that I was really here and really safe, as much as to comfort me.

He stood and joined Cormac, who handed the rifle to him. Ben took it, tucking it under his arm. When the cops arrived, they wouldn't catch the ex-con with the loaded weapon. Like they'd discussed it beforehand or something.

Sakhmet looked up, scrubbed tears from her cheeks, smearing the ashes streaked there. Her eyes were wide, golden, and she looked wild. Quickly, she got into a crouch, gently settling Mohan's body, arranging his hands at his sides, stroking his hair one more time and kissing his forehead, a lingering farewell.

Then she moved to me. "I don't have a passport or visa. I can't let them find me."

I blinked at her. "But . . . wait a minute. Ben's a lawyer, we can get help—"

She took my face in her hands and made me look into her eyes. She had decided, and I wasn't going to talk her out of it. "I'll always know how to find you, Kitty. I'll call."

She kissed my cheek, hugged me quickly; unconsciously I reached for her, to try to hug her back, but she was already slipping away from my arms.

"Sakhmet, wait a—"

"Samira," she said, then turned and ran. Barefoot, skirt trailing, hair slipping from its braid in flying strands, she was around the hill and gone in moments. Gone, leaving me with her dead lover, my only solid evidence that any of this had happened. I had so many questions, and nothing to say.

Other figures appeared, a pair of men in dark green forest service coats, a man in a blue state patrol uniform. Wow, they'd really been looking for me. My phone, the message, I'd left it outside so Ben would find it—they must have been able to track the signal. Or the sound and fury of the collapsing mine had led them here. Both, working together, probably. I'd ask Ben about it later.

Dawn was creeping into the sky. The light faded into a tinny gray, the shadows grew thin. Features of the landscape revealed themselves, but seemed washed out. The slope of the hill had changed, and the trees seemed to loom. I had a pounding headache. Eventually, about half a dozen officials and a search crew arrived on the scene and fanned out over the area, playing flashlights over the ruined mine entrance, investigating the surroundings. I squinted when they shone lights on me, but Ben intercepted them before they could actually approach me. Keeping me safe. I'd have to talk to them eventually. But not right now.

I could sit here for a while, not thinking about anything. Just sit. The sky grew brighter.

The state patrol guy called in a coroner for Mohan. At least I could tell them his real name now. The official marking and documenting of the site began, and I was asked to move out of the way. I did, finding a tree to sit against while Ben continued running interference. I hoped we could leave soon. But oddly enough, part of me didn't want to. I wanted to make sure I had my memories firmly in place first, or I'd never be able to hold on to them. I found myself clutching three items that had gotten tangled around my arm toward the end, which I'd managed to hold on to as I escaped: Kumarbis's coin, Zora's spell book case, and the demon's goggles. More evidence than I thought. Pieces to a strange puzzle.

Cormac tracked where I went and walked toward me. Strolled, almost, his steps slow, as if giving me a chance to tell him to go away. I didn't. He slouched to the ground, resting his elbows on his knees, looking out at the view, sunrise through a snowy forest. I waited for him to say something; he didn't. The movement of him coming over was his simple way of asking how I was.

I untangled my mess of artifacts, cords and straps wrapped around my arm, and handed them over to him. He held up the goggles first. "Is this what I think it is?" I nodded, and he frowned, concerned. "The demon—she was here? What happened?"

"She's buried under that mountainside, I hope."

Shaking his head, he said, "She'd have gotten out like she did last time. And what's this one?" He shifted his grip to the coin, rubbing his finger over the damaged surface. "One of Roman's? Where'd this one come from?"

"A vampire who claimed to be Roman's progenitor. Who was conspiring against Roman in a very round-about way. He said this was the first coin Roman made."

He grunted, a response with a dozen meanings. Amazement, disbelief, calm acceptance. Maybe even amusement. He wasn't going to make demands; he had the patience to wait for further explanations. "And this?" He turned the tin box back and forth in his hand.

Reaching over, I popped open the lid, revealing the thumb drive. "It's Zora's spell book, I think. She's the magician behind this mess. She worked on a laptop, and that's her backup. There might be something there you could use."

"We'll check it out." He tucked the case into a jacket pocket. "This magician—was she any good?"

I had to think about that one. Empirical evidence said no, based on the amount of damage she'd done.

Empirical evidence also said yes. She hadn't accomplished what she'd intended, but I couldn't argue against the sheer chaos she'd created. But when it counted, she'd battled the demon without flinching.

"I don't know. She was powerful, at some level. Did some really impressive stuff. But I think she was also more than a little crazy. I'm not sure she really knew what she was doing with all that power."

"Crazy and magic seem to go together an awful lot," he said.

I tilted my head, raised an inquiring brow. "What does that say about you? All this magic driving you crazy?"

His mustache curled with his smile. "Depends on what kind of crazy, I guess. You want me to hang on to this stuff, see what we can figure out about it?"

"Yeah, if you don't mind," I said, and he gave a satisfied nod. "Thanks. For coming after me."

"Always," he said, not looking at me, but off in the distance, watchful. Always watchful.

I loved my pack. I set my hand on his arm, and when he didn't move away or find an excuse to wander off, I left it there, taking in his warmth, his presence, and letting it calm me.

Ben crossed the hillside to join us, and Cormac squeezed my hand before standing and moving off to put himself in a bodyguard position, as if he expected demons to spring from the rubble. And maybe they would. Cormac I would trust to save the world if he had to.

Bemused, Ben looked after him before offering his hand to me and helping me to my feet. Time to go, then. When I was upright, he put his arms around me, and I leaned against him. I might never leave him again.

"The cops want a statement," he said. "You ready to talk?"

"Can we go home after?"

"Yes. Absolutely." Those were the only words that would have gotten me moving.

"Paramedics are on the way—"

"I don't need paramedics."

He gave me a look, half frustrated and half pleading. "Humor me. They'll check you over, and we'll get documentation. Just let them treat you like a victim for the next couple of hours. Please?"

He was in lawyer mode, and ultimately he was right. None of this was going to make sense from a legal standpoint anyway, might as well fill in as many blanks as we could. Such as an official medical exam stating that I'd gone through hell. The wound across my back was healing. Nobody would believe it had happened an hour or so ago.

We trekked back to a service road a few miles from the mine, where they'd all gathered for the search, and where an ambulance was waiting. Turned out the paramedics decided I was suffering from dehydration and wanted to give me IV fluids. My supernatural healing meant my skin kept trying to grow over the needle. I finally convinced them to just give me a bottle of Gatorade.

This was getting hilarious, and I hadn't even explained everything that had happened. The state trooper in charge stopped taking notes halfway through and then stared at me like I was crazy. He looked as if he was thinking of arresting me for something when Ben stepped in, making noises about harassing the witness. Ben in lawyer mode was a beauty to behold.

Finally, I said to the trooper, "Call Detective Jessi Hardin with the Denver Police Department. She heads up their paranatural unit. She can help."

"Help make sense of all this?" he said, brow furrowed, mouth crooked with confusion.

"Maybe not," I said. "But she knows what to put into the reports."

He scowled at his notebook and wandered off, cell phone pressed to his ear. Full morning had arrived. I was dozing, tucked under Ben's arm, when the state trooper decided he'd had enough of us and let us go. Cormac was already waiting by his Jeep.

Now, finally, I could go home.

Epilogue

She Changes before the sun sets, before the moon has fully risen, before the pack gathers, because she can't wait any longer, because she is finally free, because the fear and anger still fill her. The memory of walls closing in, of brimstone attacks and otherworldly ceremonies, writhe in her hindbrain like living things, like parasites. She runs to escape, but she can't escape, so she just runs, until her muscles feel loose, like water. She will run until dawn.

Her mate is at her flank, stride for stride. At first, she runs to escape him as well. To escape everything. Soon, though, she's glad he's followed. Grateful. Her other self, the self that thinks too much, would cry, knowing that he stays by her.

When the full, round moon has climbed overhead,

she finally slows, stops. Stands panting, exhausted. Her mate is there, licking her face, rubbing himself against her, offering what comfort he can.

When she catches a scent of something warm, fast, full of blood, her urge to hunt returns, and that simple need feels glorious. They hunt together, she chases a rabbit into his path, he grabs and twists its neck, and they feed, devouring the meat in a few bites. When they finish, they lick blood off each others' muzzles. The world feels almost normal, with a full belly and a forest full of moonlit shadows.

She ran for a long time, and they have a long journey back.

The moon is sinking when her mate blocks her path. The fur on his back has stiffened, his ears pin flat to his head, and his tail sticks straight back. Danger— her own nerves spike with a feeling of exhaustion, because such anxiety, such readiness to fight, feels too familiar.

She catches the scent that he does, that he's now circling to examine—an intruder in their territory. But not wolf. This creature is strange and musky, female, and she isn't hiding, not caring if she's found. Feline, like a mountain lion—but not. This scent is foreign—and like them. Both beast and human.

They lope, following the path until the creature appears, crouched down, flat to the ground, watching.

Stockier than a mountain lion, with a broader snout, round ears, large eyes. A long, tufted tail flicks back and forth. The stranger waits.

But not a stranger. Her smell is familiar, striking at those blazing memories. We know her.

She bumps her mate's flank, calming him, nipping his ear to tell him this is all right. She approaches the lion, head and tail low, sniffing, and finally settling to the ground in front of her. They regard each other.

The lioness stands, approaches. Rubs her cheek along Wolf's face and ruff. Stands for a moment, as if simply feeling her presence, taking in her scent. Looks over Wolf's back to eye the mate. Then, she turns and runs, loping into the woods. She's gone in seconds.

Her mate has to prod her, pushing her with his snout, nipping at her flank, to finally get her to embark on the long run home.

I REMEMBERED meeting the lion on full-moon night. I could recall her smell, and my gladness at seeing her. Worry for what was going to happen to her. I would have brought her home with me and let her into our pack, if she wanted. Back in the daylight, the human world, a week passed, and Skahmet—Samira—didn't call. Maybe she would, still, someday.

But that meeting in the forest felt like a good-bye. Or, good-bye for now. I hoped. I wanted to talk to her. If I could just find out *more*.

I had to be content with what I had.

The mine where they'd found me ended up being near Leadville. Only about a hundred miles from Denver, but high in the mountains and far from any maintained roads. The place even showed up on a USGS map. But so did a dozen other abandoned mines in the area, and Mohan and Samira had covered their tracks well when they caught me. Eventually, I had to laugh about it—I'd been that close to home, but still five thousand miles and a couple of thousand years away.

I looked up the name Kumarbis. It was the name of a Hittite god, by turns power hungry and tragic. Kumarbis, father of gods, was eventually deposed by a storm god—as many father-gods would be after him. In revenge, he decided to create a rival to the storm god, a creature who would depose him and return Kumarbis to his rightful place. But the creature, a giant made of stone, decided his true purpose was to destroy all of humanity. The other gods had to unite to stop him before he could destroy the world, and Kumarbis was no better off than he was before.

Whatever his name had originally been, the vampire Kumarbis might very well have taken the name as self-inflicted punishment. A man who kept trying

to exert his power on the world, out of the best intentions, but who instead just kept making things worse.
The father aspect of the god probably appealed to
him. The ambition to be caretaker of the world appealed to him. Not the character's utter failure to do
so. On the other hand, the vampire might not have
meant to appeal to that part of the legend. Rather, the
name might have meant something to him culturally,
from some of the stories he might have heard when
he was young and alive. If that was the case, if Kumarbis had been Hittite originally, it would have
made him well over three thousand years old. That
didn't seem outrageous to me.

I would never learn the truth. Unless I asked the
one person who must have known Kumarbis better
than anyone else: Roman. There was a thought. Since
I wasn't likely to ever have a face-to-face, civil conversation with Roman, I let the idea go. Another mystery to file away.

THE POLICE sketch artist scratched his pencil, and I
had to stop myself from leaning over to look at what
he was drawing.

"Eyebrows?" he asked, the latest in a string of questions about eyes, mouth, cheeks, earlobes, all manner
of details about someone's face I'd barely seen over
my shoulder during the ritual.

"Dark. Thick. Kind of flat."

Detective Hardin sat nearby in the conference room at the downtown police station. I'd called in a favor, asking her to help me get a picture of the woman I'd glimpsed. I didn't tell her why. Just that I'd seen a face, and I wanted a picture.

The pencil scratched a few more strokes, and then the artist turned the sketch pad around. "How is this?"

He'd drawn a square-faced woman with a crown of dark, curling hair, a slightly furrowed brow, and a hard look in her eyes. This wasn't how she looked when I saw her, but it was undoubtedly her. Somehow, my description had come through. Fierce, determined. She would defend her cubs, her pack. Regina Luporum Prima, I supposed I could call her.

"It's good," I said. "Thanks."

He tore the page from the pad and gave it to me. I studied it, awestruck. The picture made her more real, and also, somehow, more normal. Taken out of the cavern and the ritual, she was just a woman.

"What did she do?" Hardin asked. She wore a jacket over a tank top and dark trousers, and had her dark hair in a ponytail. She was overworked, tough as nails, and dogged. I'd rarely seen her smile. We'd been working together for years now, and I trusted her.

"She lived," I said simply. "Probably twenty-five hundred years ago or so. Early Roman, probably."

"So she's a vampire?" Hardin asked.

"No," I said, bemused, realizing this sounded crazy. Not caring. "She was a werewolf. I think. I thought she was just a story. But I saw her."

"Do I want to know?" Hardin said, smirking.

"Probably not. It's complicated."

"What exactly happened to you up there?" she asked. She'd been one of the first people Ben and Cormac called when I turned up missing and had been part of the search. I really did have a lot of people looking out for me.

My smile went lopsided, because I didn't know what to say. "When I figure it out, I'll let you know."

"Typical," she huffed.

"Thanks for this," I said, nodding at the sketch. She waved me off.

When I got home, I pinned the drawing next to the picture of the *Capitoline Wolf.* They seemed to match.

Ben and I talked about it. We lay in bed, all the lights out, and the darkness of the bedroom was nowhere near the absolute darkness of the mine. I understood absolute darkness now. Here, moon and ambient light from Denver seeped in around the curtains, and the bedside clock had a glow. Even without being able to identify the light source, the whole room shimmered with light. Ben glowed, with the heat and life of his body.

Our wolves didn't fully believe that all was well, and they asserted themselves in the way we curled up together at one end of the bed. We were on our sides, nestled together, his body pressed protectively across my back, my head against his shoulder, noses to skin so we could smell each other and be comforted.

"I don't even know if it was real," I said. "Or if it was some hallucination Zora cooked up. It might have been a trick. But would I have felt it so strongly if it were? Would I have been able to remember it? Remember it well enough to get a sketch out of it?"

"Kitty, I don't know." He sighed into my hair, and I snuggled more firmly in his embrace. Skin to skin. I couldn't get enough. "I know *something* happened to you. And seriously, after everything we've seen? Anything's possible. These days I'm ready to believe in Santa Claus."

St. Nicholas had been a real person, I almost said. "I want her to be real."

"I know."

"It's like if she was real, a real woman with a real face, who was really alive—then maybe we're not so different. Maybe I really can keep doing this."

"I never doubted it."

I chuckled, because of course he would say that. Turning, I brought my hand to his cheek and matched his gaze.

"Thanks. For listening," I said.

Then my own Prince Reliable kissed me.

I MISSED a show over the course of my adventure. My captivity. My . . . I wasn't sure anymore what to call it. In the end, I was there because I'd chosen to be. Didn't make it any less messed up, and I spent most of the first few days afterward at home, asleep. Sleeping meant not thinking about it.

I'd never outright missed a show. I'd had plenty of planned absences, had aired prerecorded episodes and run "best of" episodes when I needed time off, on full-moon nights for example. My engineer, Matt, was able to piece together one of these, rerunning old interviews and splicing together intros, so the show itself went on without me. The only sense of failure was my own.

Ben and Ozzie both suggested I needed to take another week off, to recover from what they sympathetically called my ordeal, but I refused. I wasn't going to miss another show, another week. The best way to get my head back on straight would be to go back to work, to do my job.

What to talk about, on that first show back? I could have told my audience about my adventure. About meeting the oldest vampire I'd yet encountered, about how practicing ceremonial magic seemed to me to be a lot like playing with dynamite and matches. I wanted to send a message to Samira, and to talk about Enkidu—Mohan—to get his story out. To memorialize him. And Zora. Kumarbis, not so much, even though he was the one people would want to hear about. But if I talked about one of them, I'd have to talk about all of them, and the demon, the rituals, the philosophies behind them, and I wasn't ready to do that.

Another consideration: I didn't flatter myself that Roman listened to my show. Then again, maybe he did, and I didn't want to tell him what exactly had happened in that abandoned mine. Let him guess, if he didn't already know.

My topic for the week: mythology. I called a couple of professors from CU Boulder to interview about historical precedents for characters like King Arthur, Robin Hood, and even Gilgamesh. I found some authors who'd written novels that combined history and mythology, and recorded interviews about their take on the likelihood that some of these old stories might have a seed of truth. Pretty good, considering how last-minute I was putting this together.

I took a few calls, and they ran the usual range from insightful to insane. That in itself was comforting. No matter what happened in the rest of the world, my callers would always be there for me, with their enthusiasm, their conspiracy theories about tunnel systems extending through the continental U.S., and rants about the Second Amendment not including silver bullets.

What conclusion, if any, could I draw from all this? Here were stories we were still telling after five hundred, a thousand, five thousand years. Maybe not a lot of time on the geologic scale, but unimaginable on the scale of human memory. That had to mean something. Stories were what lasted.

Stories, and vampires, some of whom didn't just tell the stories, but remembered when the stories were new.

I finished writing the book. Finally. Part of what motivated the last big writing push: thinking about something happening to me before I finished. Thinking about how much I would leave behind, unfinished. The book was one thing I could wrap up, so I did.

Also, I'd found my thesis, the thread that would tie the book together: stories were important. Whether they were true or not, they held their own history of the world, and we kept telling them because they meant something. Before all this happened, I had a vague notion of why I was putting this book together. Now, I *knew*. I supposed I could say I now had faith in it.

WHEN CORMAC called to ask me to meet him at New Moon, I knew he had information. After the dinner rush, Ben and I arrived at the restaurant, claimed a table in the back, ordered beers, and waited. Cormac arrived soon after and explained.

"The thumb drive you gave me—it isn't just a book of spells, it's a book of shadows."

"What's that mean?" I said.

"It's everything. Everything she learned, her journey as a magician, her plans."

"Her diary," I said, amazed.

He winced. "Sort of. But more." He cocked his head in a way I'd learned to recognize as him listening to an interior voice. Conversing with Amelia. "Something like . . . her magician's soul."

She'd given it to me there at the end because she knew she wasn't going to make it. Closing the door on the demon meant collapsing the cave on herself. She couldn't save her own life, but she'd given her soul to me. Another sacrifice. It was too much responsibility. What was I supposed to do with it?

"Did you find anything good?" Ben asked after a moment. The question seemed callous, and I almost said so, angrily. But he was only stating the obvious: what was I supposed to do with all of Zora's spells and knowledge that she'd wanted to save? Use them, of course.

Cormac said, "Her name was Amy Scanlon. She was from Monterey, California, and dropped out of college to travel the world and learn what she could.

Amelia sees a lot of herself in the kid. She had some talent as well, some natural psychic ability. Always seemed to know where to find the good stuff. The real deal."

"Like Kumarbis."

He gave an offhand shrug. "They seemed to feed into each others' obsessions. If they'd kept going they'd have either taken over the world or destroyed it."

Ben chuckled. "For real?"

"Maybe, maybe not."

I huffed. "If magic was going to destroy the world, someone would have done it by now."

Cormac gave me a look. A mustached frown, a calculating gaze. "If it hasn't happened yet, it may be because there hasn't ever been one person who's gathered enough power to be able to do it. At least not yet."

"Yet," I said, staring. "And what about Dux Bellorum? The Long Game?"

He blew out a breath, looking thoughtful. "Hard to say. Her diary, the personal stuff, she wrote out, like she was just typing it in whenever she could. The meat of the thing—the spells, the lore—she wrote in a code. There's probably a couple of hundred pages of information she learned about Roman and the Long Game, either from Kumarbis or from scrying or who the hell knows what else, but it's all coded."

"Are you kidding me?" I said, slouching back, feeling defeated all over again.

"It's a common practice," he said, although I had the feeling this was Amelia now, making the explanations like she often did. "In medieval times alchemists and mages were competitive and jealous, always trying to steal each other's secrets while protecting their own. They'd invent their own arcane systems for encrypting their work. Very effective—some old books of shadows still haven't been deciphered."

"This doesn't help us at all," I complained.

The glass door swung open then, bringing in a blast of cold air and Angelo, light hair tousled, face ruddy with recently drunk blood, wool coat flapping. He only hesitated a moment, glancing around until he found me and marched to meet me.

As usual, Cormac stayed seated and calm, but his hand had disappeared into a jacket pocket and the stake he likely kept there. Angelo didn't even notice.

He regarded me, and I raised a brow at him, prompting.

"What did you do?" he said finally.

"What do you mean, what did I do?"

"Marid called. *Marid*. He's a legend, you know, and he doesn't call *anyone*. He appears mysteriously, that's it. But he called me. Roman has fled Split in something of an uproar, I gather. Left behind hench-men, odds and ends. But apparently he found what he was looking for right before being chased off. No idea where he's gone next, but Marid is sure some-thing spooked him. So of course I assume you did something, to answer for Antony. So does Marid. He asked me, I'm asking you."

I hesitated, because my first thought was that I hadn't done anything, not really. I was the victim here, right? I tilted my head, pursed my lips. "If he calls back, can you ask him if he's ever heard of a vampire named Kumarbis?"

Angelo's brow furrowed. "I've never heard of him."

"I'm not asking if you've heard of him, but has Marid?"

"This one's old, then, I take it?"

"Oh, yes."

"And he's the one responsible for making Dux Bel-lorum bolt?"

Credit where credit was due. "I think so, yes."

"And where is this astonishing person now?"

I pressed my lips together and shook my head.

"Ah," Angelo sighed with understanding, and finally sank into one of the empty chairs at the table. "So. *What happened?*"

"I'm not sure I even know anymore."

"Is he coming here next?" Angelo said. "If Ro-man's on the move, and he thinks you had something to do with flushing him out of his last hideout, will he be coming *here*? Do I need to worry?"

"If I could predict what Roman was going to do I'd have staked him a long time ago. How many times can I say it, I don't know."

"So the answer is—maybe," he said.

Yeah, it was. Silence gave him his answer.

I expected him to whine. To wilt and moan about the unfairness of it all. To blame me for putting him this position, for driving Rick out when Rick was the one who should have been here, defending the city. But he didn't do any of that. Straightening, he set his expression, put his hands on the table as if we'd been at a formal conference.

"Right, then," he said. "Might not hurt to prepare. Call in favors and such. Kitty, Ben, I'll be in touch." He gave a decisive nod and swept out just as abruptly as he'd swept in.

We all stared after him. "Is it weird that I found that reassuring?" I said.

Ben rested his hand on my leg. A point of contact, a touch of comfort.

He said, "We need everything we can get on Roman. Cormac, do you think you can decipher the book?"

"I've got some leads. Not many, but it's a start. In her diary, she lists some of her mentors, some of the people who got her started in magic. One of them's a great-aunt who lives down in Manitou Springs. We could get in touch with her, find out if she knows Amy's code or has any ideas about cracking it."

Next of kin. I hadn't even thought about trying to find Zora's—Amy's—family to tell them what happened to her. Not something I was looking forward to, but it looked like I might have to. I rubbed my eyes, suddenly tired. "Yeah, okay."

"I can take care of that," Cormac said. "I—we—know what to ask."

"You and Amelia can talk to her, magician to magician like?" I said, trying to make light. He turned a hand in agreement. Didn't say a word. Already making plans, and I wouldn't have to worry about it.

"Are you *sure* you're okay?" Ben asked, like he had a dozen times a day since rescuing me from the mountain.

I squeezed his hand. He'd be able to feel the lingering stress, not so much about what had happened in the mine, but about what would happen next. He'd know I wasn't quite telling the truth when I said, "I'm okay." But as long as he kept asking, I would be. "I wish I could talk to Rick."

"You don't have any way of getting in touch with him?" Ben said.

I imagined trying to send a letter to Rick, of the Order of Saint Lazarus of the Shadows, care of the Vatican, but I didn't imagine him actually receiving said letter. I couldn't consult the people I most wanted to, Rick and Anastasia, who had departed on their own personal crusades. I had to be satisfied knowing that they were out there, somewhere.

Ben added, "Not even an e-mail address?"

"Nope. Though I suppose we could do something crazy like post Amy's book of shadows online with a big header saying, 'Rick, please read this,' and see what happens."

As soon as I said it, I suddenly wanted to do it. Just to see who else it pulled out of the woodwork. Because it didn't seem any less crazy than anything else we could do. Roman had his Hand of Hercules, the demon bounty hunter—he had everything, now, and we had nothing to lose.

I waited for either Cormac or Ben to tell me it was a crazy idea, and under no circumstances should we post a powerful magician's book of shadows on the Internet where everyone could see it. But they didn't. Ben donned a thoughtful look, brow furrowed and lips pursed. Probably thinking about whether posting the book would get me sued. But he didn't say anything. Cormac just raised an eyebrow. Right, if *they* weren't telling me it was a bad idea—what were we all missing?

Then I thought, this kind of knowledge had been kept secret by arcane practitioners for hundreds of years. Maybe it was time to see what crowd sourcing could do with it.

"I mean," I said, thinking out loud now. "What's the worst that could happen?"

"You really want an answer to that?" Ben said.

"It might be like reading out loud from the Necronomicon," Cormac said. "But shit, I'm game."

That should have been a warning right there.

"You might be showing your hand," Ben said. "Telling Roman how much we really know about him."

And how much did we know, really? Didn't seem like much. But if we could make him think we knew more than we really did—I'd love to see his reaction. Yeah, Kumarbis and company had poked him with a big old stick. I wanted to keep poking.

I said, "Maybe now's exactly the time to show him how much we have. Keep him nervous."

Neither one of them tried to argue against it. So we made a plan.

I TALKED to the webmaster at KNOB about what we needed, and she referred me to a friend of hers who knew more about the security aspects involved in the project. Anonymous servers, untraceable IP addresses, jargon that I sort of knew about in the abstract, but not really. We needed a level of protection between us and the big wide world of the Internet, so that it looked like the book of shadows just appeared online and couldn't be immediately traced back to me. Not foolproof, but it was something. For a while now, I'd been trying to get the word out about Roman. Telling people what I knew about him, not just so he couldn't work anonymously anymore, but also so I wouldn't feel alone. Could be, the book of shadows would languish online, one of those weird backwater websites that haven't been updated in a decade and no one ever visits except to admire the wackiness. Could be, the thing would do exactly what we wanted, and attract the attention of people who could help. Not just warn the world that Roman was out there, but raise an army to stand against him.

We edited, leaving out most of Amy's personal diary. I'd only met her at the very end of her road, when she'd been overwhelmed by her quest, a crusader with one central purpose. I hadn't met the real Amy, I decided, and reading her diary made me wish I had. She'd been a true explorer, fascinated by every culture and locale she encountered. She'd loved learning, but she'd also been searching for meaning. For a purpose for everything she was learning. Kumarbis had provided *something,* and she'd embraced his quest. That part of her journey didn't need to go on the website.

But her raw knowledge and the extensive, encrypted notes she'd made, we uploaded directly. It took a few weeks to prepare it all, but at last, the website went live.

Then we waited.